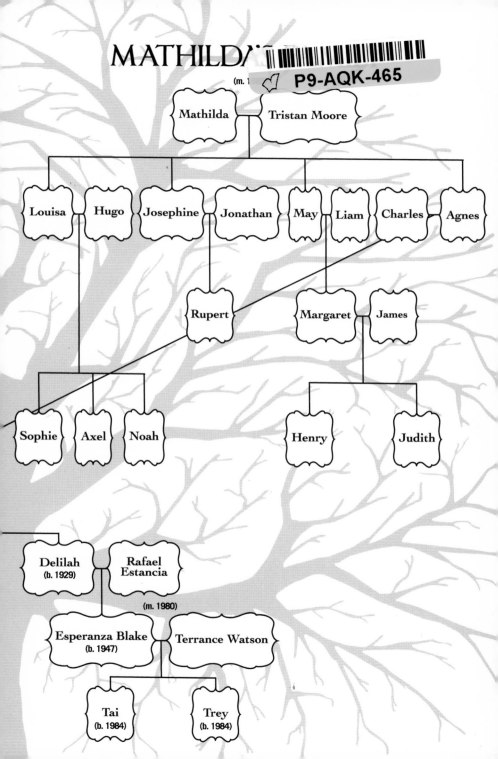

MATHILDA

P9-AQK-465

(m. 1

Mathilda — Tristan Moore

Louisa · Hugo · Josephine · Jonathan · May · Liam · Charles · Agnes

Rupert

Margaret — James

Sophie · Axel · Noah

Henry · Judith

Delilah (b. 1929) — Rafael Estancia

(m. 1980)

Esperanza Blake (b. 1947) — Terrance Watson

Tai (b. 1984) · Trey (b. 1984)

To Grandpa,
I love you, I miss you,
and I hope I've made you proud.

NEW YORK, NEW YORK—2000

T he scream didn't wake Tai, but it definitely pulled her out of bed. She threw off her blanket and raced across her semi-dark room—stubbing her foot on the desk chair along the way.

"Oh! Oh my god, ooooh." Pain shot up one leg, and the other nearly gave as a result, but she managed to stay upright and hobble over to the door.

Yanking it open, she stepped into the hall just in time to see her father emerge from his bedroom. Dad stood in his boxers, a white tank pulled over his potbelly, and shaving cream smeared on one half of his dark brown head. He blinked at his daughter in confusion they both shared.

I don't know, Tai mouthed, and shrugged. In the dim light, her attention was drawn to the closed bathroom door and the glow pouring out from under it. Nothing seemed out of place. Silence pressed in from all sides, thick and presently undisturbed. It was honestly kinda creepy. Goose bumps prickled her bare arms, and she rubbed to try and banish them. She wasn't scary or nothing like that, but screams in the early morning hours would freak anybody out, right?

If it wasn't for the fact Dad clearly heard it, too, she would've thought she imagined the whole thing. Her fault for staying up half the night reading Gundam Wing fanfic. Granted, she didn't know this vampire AU was gonna be legit horrifying, but the Heero x Duo romance was worth it.

Another handful of seconds passed before Dad hefted a sigh and strode over to knock on the door. "Trey? Son, you okay?"

Silence.

Tai joined her father. "You may as well come out and show us."

"It's prolly not even that bad," Dad offered helpfully.

For *another* few seconds there was still nothing. Then something shuffled on the other side of the door while a shadow danced beneath it. Finally the knob slowly turned, and light spilled into the hall.

Tai blinked a few times when confronted by the sudden brightness, but what she saw . . . She had to bite her lip to keep from laughing. That shit *hurt*, too.

Dad's eyes widened, and he cleared his throat before breathing a soft "Oh."

Standing in the doorway was Tai's twin brother, Trey. Twins in birth and in looks. They shared the same brown skin, wide frames, slightly round faces, and brown eyes. Even had the same thick, shoulder-length coils growing out of their heads, though Tai usually kept hers pressed and Trey wore his in cornrows.

Except his cornrows were gone, and in their place sprouted a bright red, almost orange puff of synthetic strands that was closer to doll hair than anything else. It shined and everything.

His shoulders rose and fell as he took slow, deep breaths. *"Prolly* not that bad?"

"It . . . Well . . . it could be worse." Dad's voice pitched high in that way that meant he wasn't *trying* to lie to his son's face, but that's definitely what was going on here. "It *has* been worse."

Trey's eyes flashed and his nostrils flared. *Danger! Danger, Will Robinson!* He might have seemed intimidating, if he didn't look like somebody's angry-ass Muppet Baby. The one that talks in beeps came to mind.

Tai covered a cough with a fist, then rubbed at her throat while struggling not to laugh.

*It ain't funny, it **ain't** funny.*

Dad's eyes danced over Trey, lingering on the plume on his head. "Like I said, it's been worse."

"Worse? I look like Carrot Top!"

Tai couldn't help a few giggles. "Maybe more Ronald McDonald?"

The look Trey shot her could've been a bullet to her heart with all the heat behind it. She lifted her hands and mouthed an apology, even as she half snorted, half choked on another snicker.

"What, uhm—what happened?" Dad asked in a now quiet tone that meant he wasn't sure he wanted to hear the answer, because said answer was likely "that hocus-pocus mess."

Trey's shoulders slumped. "I was in the shower telling myself today was just like every other day, and orchestra would be like every other—you know what I'm sayin'—'cept I'm lyin'. And I know I'm lyin'. And I *know* that I know, so while I'm knowingly lyin' to myself I just sorta stop and . . ."

"And what?" Dad pressed.

This time when Trey sighed, his whole body heaved with it.

"And I say, 'Trey, you sound ridiculous, you f—uh, blanking clown,' and then my hair did *this*."

"I see." Dad tilted his head and rubbed his beard. A wilting dollop of shaving cream was starting to run down the side of his face.

Another telltale quiver of humor rooted itself in Tai's chest, and she had to release a slow breath to fight it. She won this battle, but she was swiftly losing the war.

Dad nodded as if he understood what was happening. He really didn't, but he tried. "So you were in a heightened state of agitation, made a declaration—sort of—and your, uh . . . talent manifested by giving you literal clown hair."

Trey's whine started at the back of his throat, then dropped into a distraught "Whyyyyyy?"

Usually, Tai made all the distressed noises. He must really feel a way. She reached to give his shoulder a supportive squeeze and pat. As supportive as she could muster while trying not to laugh in his face. Gotta be a good big sister.

"Well, you want me to call off school for you?" Dad asked. "Unless you think you can change back in time."

Trey shook his head so quick his clown—well, they weren't exactly curls, but they still bounced around. "Not today, I can't miss orchestra."

Dad bobbed his head again. He nodded a lot when he wasn't sure what to do or say about a situation. "Right, right. Your audition thing."

"You can't just do it another time?" Tai asked while still patting Trey's shoulder. There, there.

"I can for the grade, but not for the seating arrangement. We got a competition next month, and solos need to be assigned ASAP."

Tai arched an eyebrow. "So, you tryin'a get your spotlight?"

"I'm *trying* to secure my rightful spot. Danielle Firestone graduated last year. She was the only person better than me, so now I finally got a shot at first chair." Trey talked with his hands most of the time, gesturing every which way. Now he was practically conducting his own performance. Tai had to step aside to keep from catching a stray elbow.

"Being first chair junior *and* senior year means I get the solos and the flashy arrangements," Trey continued. "Some of the judges for the competitions teach at Juilliard, Berklee, Thornton. One dude impressed them so much he ended up going to the Royal Academy of Music in London. *London*, Tai!"

Dad made an impressed *oh* face, still nodding. His eyebrows lifted and the shaving cream dipped a little lower.

Tai sniffed. "But does he have tea with the Queen?" She curled her tongue around a ridiculous accent.

There was a breath of a moment where Trey pursed his lips and looked close to tears. Or as close as he could get. He didn't really cry no more. "This ain't a joke. This is my legacy we're talking about. Ruined by some damn—"

"Language," Dad snapped as his eyes narrowed.

"Sorry. Ruined because I am, in fact, a clown."

This time Dad was the one to reach for Trey. He set both hands on his shoulders and gave him a little shake. "It'll be okay, son. You'll get through this, just like you get through Everything. Remember that time you thought you messed up at the church talent show?"

Oof. That had been bad. Poor Trey was anxious for days leading up to what would be his first public performance not tied to school. On top of that, it was his first time playing by himself. He was a mess of nerves at the start of the show, and it worsened with each passing act.

By the time his turn came around, Trey was wound so tight he couldn't breathe. Panting like a dying bull and clutching his cello until the wood creaked, he could barely move a muscle. And he certainly couldn't play a sonata.

"I think accidentally snapping your instrument in half in front of an audience is much worse than..." Dad trailed off as his eyes went to Trey's hair again.

"Instead of sounding ridiculous, I'll only look the part," Trey countered, not looking the least bit pepped by Dad's talk.

"All I'm sayin' is, when people hear you play, it's not gonna matter what's on your head."

For a moment, it didn't seem like anything Dad said was getting through. But soon Trey's fingers uncurled from fists and his shoulders slumped just a little. "I guess not."

A big grin split Dad's face, teeth showing and everything. "You're a great musician today, and you'll be one tomorrow, a year from now, ten years from now. Clown hair can't stop this train!"

Another groan escaped Trey, and he dropped his face into his hands. But he was nodding. And that meant he was calming down, at least a bit.

Funny as the situation was, Tai couldn't help feeling bad for her brother. Normally she was a little jealous. Of the two of them, Trey wound up with the more active, and thus more invasive, power. Powers? It's hard to tell whether he had multiple abilities, or it was the same one manifesting in different ways. He could knock things over, make things happen—like changing his hair—or break things, like the cello at the talent show. And it wasn't like they could ask an expert about all this, but the running theory was something to do with molecules. Whether Trey had one power or a dozen, it was still clear that—as he got a handle on them—they'd be useful in some way.

Tai's abilities were...decidedly not. Visions always sounded cool in the myths and legends. The Fates. The Oracle. The white boy from *Final Destination*. Tai didn't see anything useful like someone's destiny or their future, unless future pain counted. Her visions were often confusing and usually predicted bad things eventually happening. Or that were presently happening. If she looked directly into a reflective surface for too long, a sort of fog would push her sight sideways, revealing whatever depressing thing was waiting beneath. No lie, she would trade this "gift" for pretty much anything else.

"Now then, back to school," Dad said, drawing Tai out of her thoughts. "What if I call and tell them to let you wear your do-rag for medical reasons or something? Like it's applying pressure to a bandage." He reached to run a hand over his head in worry and too late remembered half of it was still covered in shaving cream. He snatched his fingers down to examine them, then made a face. "Damn it."

Trey sidestepped into Tai to make room in the doorway, and Dad slipped by with quiet thanks. While he hastily finished up the shave he'd started in his bathroom, she turned to face her slightly less distraught but still clearly panicked brother.

"The do-rag thing might work," she offered. "Especially if it's just for one day. And not even a whole one."

This time the look Trey gave her wasn't as hot but still equally annoyed. "In what world does that even *begin* to make sense?"

Tai cleared her throat before putting on a deep, dramatic voice. "In a world where you hit your head really hard, so you have to wear this butt-ugly bandage. To save yourself from the shame and ridicule of your peers, and to make sure the bandage stays in place, you don a do-rag to conceal the unbecoming dressing, thus allowing you to move among the masses unharassed." She waved her hands theatrically and aimed a smile Trey's way.

While he didn't fully return it, one corner of his mouth pulled upward slightly. "You're such a weirdo."

"Thank you."

"It's those cartoons you watch. They be saying dramatic shit like that."

"That was more movie-trailer guy, but they do indeed be saying dramatic shit like that."

Trey chuckled lightly, and the red-orange of his hair flickered just so before fading more to a brownish, less clownish color.

Tai pointed. "Hey! It's changing back. Kinda."

Blinking in surprise, Trey hurried to push in beside Dad, who grunted but didn't say anything more. Trey examined his hair, running his fingers through it a little before sighing softly.

"It's a start," he complained, though his words were softer, his tone gentler. He joined her in the hall again and, to her surprise, wrapped one arm around her in a quick hug. "Thanks, Tai."

Dad emerged from the bathroom, wiping at his head with a towel. He glanced back and forth between them, his gaze lingering on Trey's now brown but still very much doll-looking hair. "So, what're we doing?"

Trey dropped his head forward with a heavy breath. Still, some of the tension seeped out of his shoulders. "I guess we split the difference. Orchestra is this afternoon. I stay home and try to undo this. If I can, I just go in. If I can't, we go with the medical do-rag. Just long enough for me to land the audition."

"What about quartet practice?" Dad asked. "That's today, too, right? I remember that one."

On top of being the best cellist in the school's orchestra, Trey had to go and gang up with the best musicians from the *other* sections to form some classical music Voltron. All in the name of that legacy he was talking about earlier. Tai was suddenly glad her extracurriculars weren't so...involved.

"It is," Trey said. "But that won't be a problem. The audition is all I'm worried about."

"Then you'll be able to ride the subway home with your sister?"

"Yeah."

"Sounds like a plan. Hurry up and finish so your sister can have her turn."

With his own nod, Trey disappeared into the bathroom. The door shut behind him.

Crisis averted, Dad sighed just like Trey did a second ago, only his was a touch more resigned. Then he aimed a finger at Tai. "*You* still need to get ready. Your hair is fine. You go to school." Declaration made, he headed back down the hall, mumbling something about it being too early for a *Dungeons & Dragons* mess.

Any other day, that little, throwaway, totally-not-meant-to-be-hurtful-but-still-kinda-stung comment might've put a chink in Tai's armor, but not today. Today, she was determined to focus on doing things that *strengthened* her armor, that brought her joy. Like her plans to check out the Fall Festival after school while Trey was at practice. Or how it was her turn to pick birthday-eve dinner. Or how she definitely maybe might be finally getting a new camera for her birthday. Dad had only asked her about it "covertly" every other day for a month now.

She would focus on all the good, for now. There would be plenty of time to wallow in the negative after, especially since there was *always* negative. Two good things followed one bad. Every time.

The bathroom door swung open with a creak, and Trey stepped

out, holding his bath basket in one hand and his rolled-up pajamas in the other. He looked surprised to see her still standing there but didn't say anything as he stepped around her and headed for his room.

"I was thinking tacos," Tai called after him. "From that place around the corner from school?"

Trey paused long enough to shoot a confused glance over his shoulder. "Tacos."

"The birthday-eve dinner?"

"Oh, oh yeah." Trey nodded, then continued on his way. "Sounds good to me."

His bedroom door thunked closed behind him, and Tai was left standing in her pajamas in the hall. Man, he must be pretty worried about this audition if he didn't wanna at least put up the pretense of fighting with her about the choice. Trey *loved* tacos, too, but it was tradition for them to go back and forth a few times before the choice was made officially.

He'll feel better after he gets his first chair or whatever, she decided.

Then she made her way back to her room to start getting ready for the day. Which may or may not have included getting to the end of the current chapter in her fanfic.

Half an hour (twenty minutes of it spent reading), a quick change of clothes, and a second to make sure her hair fell right after she took it down, she met her dad at the car with her jacket on one arm, her backpack on the other, and a Toaster Strudel hanging out her mouth. She was only halfway through it when Dad started drumming his thumbs on the steering wheel and humming along to a song that wasn't playing.

That meant he wanted to talk. Great.

May as well get this over with. "Trey okayed my choice of tacos for dinner."

"He did?" Dad glanced in the rearview mirror at nothing most likely. "I'll confirm that with him when I get home."

"Figured we can get carryout from the place close to school."

"Okay. Yeah, sounds good."

She took another bite of her strudel.

Three...two...one...

"How are you and your brother doing?" Dad asked as he glanced briefly to her, then back to the street.

"We're good. Well, *I'm* good. Trey gave himself clown hair." She chuckled freely. "I think he's just nervous 'bout this audition. His legacy." She warbled her voice a little when she said it, for emphasis.

"That all he nervous about?"

Tai barely managed not to roll her eyes. "Far as I know."

"Mmm. So, there's nothing *I* need to be worried about?"

"Nope."

"No . . . situations?" He wiggled his fingers in the air when he said it, like he was waving his hand over a top hat ready to pull out a rabbit.

She did her best to ignore the slight flare of irritation. "None. We cool."

"Not even while brushing your teeth?"

"No, Dad, I'm not new at this."

"I know, I know," Dad said, like he wasn't the one pressing the issue. "And I also know you don't like talking about what you be seeing."

And you don't like listening, so what does it matter? She shut her eyes. "I promise, I didn't see anything. I haven't all week." A half-truth. A little something tried to reveal itself this past Friday. She'd just gotten out of the shower, and the mirror was all steamed up. That usually meant it was safe, at least long enough for her to wrap her head and get out.

As she stood there, tying the towel in place, a flicker of movement snatched at her attention. Before she could stop herself, she looked up. The mirror was still fogged, thankfully, so she didn't get a clear look at her reflection, but the approximation of color and shape helped her identify herself against the reflective surface. She couldn't do the same with the mass of color and light that stood beside her. Especially when she blinked and it vanished.

Tai had stood rooted to the spot by a mix of surprise, fear, and something dangerously close to curiosity. It wasn't supposed to work like that. If she didn't look directly into any reflective surfaces, then she didn't see anything. The fog should've prevented it . . . but it didn't. Did that mean her powers were getting stronger, or the visions were sick of being ignored? She didn't have the answer to that question, or any of the questions she or her brother had about their abilities. So she'd just deal with it. Like she always had.

And always will.

Dad was quiet for a while, but quiet didn't necessarily mean the previous conversation was over. And just as Tai popped the last of her breakfast into her mouth, her father clicked his tongue and ran a hand over his freshly shaved head.

"I—I'm just worried, you know? The days following y'all's birthday can be kinda rough."

Tai had a little more trouble shoving the anger down this time, but still managed. She didn't like being reminded of last year. Or any year, really. Most kids get to have their parties, open their presents, eat their cake, and go about their business. But she and Trey had to deal with the fallout from some family curse. An actual family curse, not just bouts of bad luck.

"And after last year," Dad continued, digging his finger into the invisible wound. "I just, well, I wanna make sure my babies are good, y'know? Especially you. You know you can come to me if you need to talk or something."

Dad's words took some of the heat out of her ire. What happened wasn't his fault any more than it was hers or Trey's. Their father was trying to make the best of a . . . less-than-ideal situation.

"Everything's okay, Dad. Really." Tai did her best to sound convincing, because things *were* okay. She'd been building up her armor all week so things would stay okay, no matter what the universe threw at them. She needed things to be okay this time. "The only worry is Trey and this audition. If he doesn't make it, he'll probably turn purple with green stripes or something. Or maybe blow out the pipes and flood the auditorium."

"He'll make it. I got two of the most talented, most gifted kids on the planet." Dad smirked, pride in his tone. "Situations aside."

Tai flashed a smile, then busied herself with checking through her backpack to make sure she hadn't forgotten anything in her rush. Books, pencils, binders, camera bag. No extra rolls of film, though. Crap. Maybe she could bum some off Chris until tomorrow. She could hear his teacher's-pet, ass-kissing, brown-nosing self now.

"Tai, these resources are strictly for school business, I can't just hand them out all willy-nilly. It's my responsibility as assistant yearbook adviser to make sure everyone has exactly what they need to do their jobs. Anything more would not only show favoritism but a lack of capability on my part."

Well, Mr. Adviser had one more time to try and tell her how to do her job before she told him where he could stick his responsibility. The wild part was anyone on the yearbook staff was capable of being the assistant, but he was the only one who had the time to sit with Mrs. Feeny developing pictures three days a week. That and he didn't have some literal jinx that made weird things pop up in the proofs. There's a reason she hasn't developed her own pictures in a while, and no, it's not because she doesn't care enough, Chris. God.

"Sweet sixteen," Dad said, rescuing Tai from her growing bad mood. "You excited?"

She managed a genuine smile. "Thrilled." And she was. Today and tomorrow would be great. Whatever happened after, well . . . they'd cross that bridge or whatever.

"I'm glad. And I know it's hard without your mother here to—"

"Looks like a line." Tai jerked her chin at the scene on the other side of the windshield. Under the direction of someone in a safety vest, two lanes of slow-moving traffic gradually melded into one farther up the block. Tai hurriedly gathered her things. "I can walk from here."

"O-okay, uhm, guess I better go check on your brother, then."

"Mm-hmm. Love you!" Climbing out of the car, she waved at her father before closing the door and stepping into the steadily growing stream of kids headed for the front of the building.

As she walked, some of the tension in her body loosened. She took a slow breath and gripped the straps of her backpack, quickening her steps. The September morning air was cool and crisp. It filled her lungs and prickled against her skin, just the right side of chilly. To one side, other kids laughed and chatted, conversations converging into a low roar. Out in the street, horns honked as people wove in and out of the loading lanes.

The sun was bright, already burning off the deep pinks and bold oranges of early morning, and if the clock on the dashboard was to be believed, she had just enough time to shake that film out of Chris before making it to class. Even with the potential annoyance ahead of her, a sort of warmth settled at the center of Tai's chest. Things started out shaky, but now she could feel it.

Today was gonna be a good day.

2

"This day couldn't get any worse," Trey grumbled as he toyed with the synthetic-looking brown fringe sticking out the front of his rag. He squinted to try and see if it was curling up or showing signs that his regular hair was returning. "I can't believe I let them talk me into this."

Beside him, his best friend, Marlon, examined his reflection in one of the thin, grimy bathroom mirrors. He smoothed down an eyebrow before running a brush over the top of his waves. "It's actually brilliant. Wish my pops would fake a medical emergency so I could wear mine. You really just now getting here?"

"Walked in ten minutes ago."

"Too nice." Marlon looked up as he put his brush away. "See, what *I* can't believe is the office bought it."

"They've bought weirder," Trey mumbled. Then he sighed, resigned, and shoved his clown hair out of sight. He smoothed his hands over the front of his sweatshirt and lifted his chin. Dad was right, Trey didn't have to *look* his best today, just *play* his best.

After grabbing his bag, Trey led the way out into the hall. There wasn't really anyone standing at their lockers anymore. The bell would ring in a couple minutes.

Marlon jerked his chin up. "Aight, then. Good luck, Bologna."

Trey threw a nearly empty Gatorade bottle at him, but the asshole caught it, laughing.

"It's Boulogne! Boo-lown!" Trey said around his own grin. Then he threw up a deuce and hurried on his way.

The orchestra room buzzed with enough anxious energy that some of it poured into the hall. Trey could feel it as he approached the double doors, like a sort of electricity that crawled along his skin before curling up tight in his stomach. He took a deep breath before stepping through.

A short corridor split at the end, with the left path leading out into the stage area of the theater. Across from it, a deep, tall storage space housed shelving for the smaller instruments the school rented out to students. Next to that was Mrs. Downy's office. The door stood open.

Trey didn't consider himself a nosy person, but he couldn't help peeking inside in passing. Mrs. Downy wasn't anywhere to be found, but a Black girl stood with her back to the door. She was maybe a little shorter than him, her body round. Burgundy micros hung down to her butt. That was all he could make out before continuing on.

In the rehearsal room proper, people in various stages of setup chatted with their stand partners or other folks on the risers above or below. Some rosined up their bows, playing or plucking out errant notes. The melodic chaos of practicing scales or running through parts of favorite pieces fell over Trey.

Most people simply hear music. Some of the really lucky ones can feel it, but Trey? Trey could engage it with each of his senses. He took another breath to draw in the *smell* of music, a mix of paper, bow dust, wax and wood, metal, and the faintest hint of tar. He could even taste music. Trying to describe it was wild, but it was like music was this . . . this force, more than an energy, and he understood it on a molecular level. One of the actual benefits of his gift, instead of crap like the hair he'd been "gifted" this morning.

Trey crossed the main floor, circumventing Mrs. Downy's conductor stand before climbing the risers and pushing into the cello room at the back of the rehearsal space. More than just cellos was stored back here. though. There were the basses, some extra chairs and stands, and something that looked like it *might* belong to an old-timey pipe organ?

Most everyone from the section already had their instruments out and were making their way toward the exit. He exchanged a few *hey*s and *wassup*s as he hurriedly dropped off his backpack and started working his cello out of its hard case. Good thing he followed his instincts and left it here yesterday, because trying to wrangle it would've just added to today's stress. The bell rang as he grabbed his music folder from his backpack. He made sure he had his rosin and floor stop, and turned to go when a dark lump in the corner caught his eye.

A deep red cello case sat against the wall. Hard shell, carbon fiber from the look of it. Cool, fluorescent light gleamed along the surface, giving it a sort of muted halo effect. Trey loosed a low whistle. Someone spent some mon-neh on this. An expensive case usually meant an expensive instrument. He wondered who it belonged to. It lacked the white CLAYTON HIGH PROPERTY stamped across the front.

His fingers itched to play along the sleek, semi-reflective surface. Ahh, no one was up here, so he could give it a quick swipe.

And he did, the material cool and smooth. His fingers glided over it like glass.

"One day, baby," he murmured as he closed the door behind him.

The whole orchestra was pretty much settled by the time Trey made his way back down to the floor. The empty first chair was practically calling his name, man. He'd already been sitting there for at least a month. As last year's second chair, he'd rightfully inherited the spot since the principal cellist was no longer available. But now that the orchestra had had a few weeks to warm up, it was time to audition for permanent spots. Some people would move up, some would move back. Trey was determined to stay right the hell where he was.

"Hey," he called as he took *his* seat. It wouldn't be official until after the audition but why wait? People were always talking about manifesting things.

"Hey." His stand partner, Zoraida, finished fiddling with the tuners on her own instrument, then straightened and shoved her mass of wavy black hair over her shoulder. She froze, her hand still tangled in dark strands. Her eyes pinged to the top of his head. "Uhhhhhh, what are you wearing?"

"It's just for today. Medical thing, I'm fine, though." He hated lying to her. Lying to anyone, really, even if he was good at it. Ten years of telling everyone anything but the truth had that effect.

"Better question is, who fancy-ass cello is that?" He jerked his head in the direction of the cello room. "The one in the red case?"

Zoraida blinked at him a few times—as if she wanted to say more about the rag but thankfully decided against it—then glanced over her shoulder toward the cello room. Finally, her gaze slid over the rest of their section. Everyone already had their instruments out. "No idea. Maybe a new one for the school?"

Trey snorted. "The case alone is worth two, maybe three g's. You know damn well this school ain't gonna spend that kinda money on nothing like that for us."

"Whatever you say, music nerd. How you feeling about today? Nervous?"

"Nope," Trey lied as he saw to setting up his own instrument. The pin could get fussy if he didn't tighten it just right. Man, he hoped he got a cello for his birthday this year. Especially after seeing that beauty. "And you're just as much of a music nerd as I am."

"I don't think *anyone* is as much of a music nerd as you. Least not about classical stuff."

Touché. "What about you? How you feeling?" he asked as he finally got the pin to stick.

Zoraida shrugged all nonchalant. "I'll get an A no matter where I sit, so." In truth? Z was the only person here anywhere near as good as him, but she didn't really see orchestra as her path to a better, brighter tomorrow. Zoraida Mero saw music in her future no doubt, but it was filled with more guitar riffs than études.

Trey checked the rosin on his bow. "I meant about your show." Zoraida's band was supposed to perform during the festival this afternoon. He would've liked to check it out; he'd never seen her play before, but he had quartet practice while all of that was going on.

She twisted her lips to the side. "Kinda yeah and kinda no, y'know? It's not our *first* show ever, but pretty close."

"You'll kill it. You got a really good sound. Like Linkin Park meets Selena."

A million-watt smile broke out over Zoraida's face, and she hid behind her hair a little bit. "You gonna be there? The festival, I mean."

Trey shook his head and waved the folder of music in the air a little. "Quartet practice. Next time though?"

The conversation was interrupted when Mrs. Downy emerged from wherever she'd been hiding. A wisp of a white woman, the long red braid that hung down her back swished side to side like the tail of a particularly large and agitated cat. She marched to the center of the room. The Black girl Trey had spotted in Mrs. Downy's office earlier followed.

Curious murmurs picked up beneath the sporadic waves of

musical noise that began to die down with the conductor's approach to the stand.

"Good afternoon, everyone." Mrs. Downy smiled wide and clapped her hands together beneath her chin. "Big day, big day. Auditions! But a couple of things before we get started. One, Trey."

Whenever a teacher's eyes fell on him, Trey felt his spine straighten automatically. Being singled out very rarely ended well for him.

"You know the dress code doesn't allow for head coverings. Even ones as trendy as yours." Mrs. D pursed her lips together and frowned.

Trey ignored the fresh wave of murmurs. "I know, ma'am. It's a medical thing, my dad cleared it with the office."

"Oh? Well, okay. I'll check on that in a moment. On to number two." She clapped again, her smile returning full force. "We have a new musician joining us. Everyone, this is Ayesha Davis." She threw her arm out like she was revealing the prizes in a game show or something.

The Black girl stepped forward and waved a little. "Hey, y'all." Her face was fat and cute, with dimples that showed up even as she tried to force a smile.

Mrs. D giggled and smacked her palms together in full applause now. "Don't worry, I'm not going to ask you to tell us about yourself or anything like that. But I will share that Ayesha is quite gifted, and we are fortunate that her sound will be joining and strengthening ours this year. Go ahead and get set up, Ayesha, and the rest of you pull out the Corelli piece. We're going to run through the second movement a few times to warm up." With that Mrs. D spun in place, her floor-length floral skirt slapping at her ankles, and started for the office. No doubt to confirm Trey's story.

Of all his teachers, Mrs. D was one of the cool ones. She didn't dismiss what her students had to say and really tried to listen to and understand their perspective. She could be a little airy now and then, but she didn't treat her class like a kingdom to be ruled, unlike some he could name.

As Mrs. D swept off, Ayesha wove her way through the sections and climbed the risers. Trey watched her progress all the way to the cello room before it clicked.

He latched on to Zoraida's shoulder, startling her and making her spill a little from the water bottle she held to her lips.

"Wh—" she began, eyes wide.

Trey cut her off. "Yo, I think the fancy-ass cello belongs to new girl."

Both of them turned just as Ayesha took hold of the case to open it. They stared as she emerged with what had to be the most gorgeous hunk of meticulously carved and curved wood Trey had ever laid eyes on. The deep cherry color trapped the icy light of the room's fluorescents, letting it stream along the surface before bouncing out again. This wasn't just an instrument: this was a work of art. The whole thing looked smooth as butter, and he wasn't the only one to notice. A number of people either gasped or exclaimed in quiet awe.

"I take it back," Zoraida murmured, her mesmerized tone snapping Trey out of his own semi-trance. "There is at least one person as much of a classical music nerd as you."

Trey didn't say anything to that. He was too busy fighting this unfamiliar twisty feeling that had dropped into his stomach. It wasn't the exact same as the worry about his hair or the jangled nerves from the impending audition, but it pulled at him and made him uncomfortable in very similar ways. This feeling was new, a little sour and very cold. And it grew colder the longer Trey looked at the cello. That . . . that instrument was made for a professional.

"We ready to tune?" Mrs. D had returned and now fussed with her own folder on her stand.

Everyone similarly began to ready themselves, including Trey. But the whole time he kept stealing glances over his shoulder to where Ayesha set up in the empty last chair. His gaze trailed to the cello once more, sliding over that slick finish. He studied the way Ayesha positioned herself, how she gripped her bow just so, fingers curled and effortlessly loose yet firm. He scrutinized how her hand flew over the fingerboard, and the way crisp, clear notes leapt free in a strike of swift scales. Flawless.

For nearly a decade, Trey had worked his ass off. Hundreds if not thousands of hours practicing. Going over his scales. Honing his muscle memory. Training his ear. Refining his innate understanding of the language of music. Sharpening each of those individual skills to use as anchor points while he climbed each obstacle that rose before him like mountains. Sure, music came easy because of the magic in his family, but that didn't automatically equal mastery. There were stories about ancestors who were able to harness the gift directly into their ability to play. Part of him *wished* it came that easy. He still had to bust his butt to get where he was.

It had always landed him close to the top; second chair for the past three years. Today was his chance to break the streak of almost, to finally reach the peak! He simply needed to outperform perfection.

3

Tai aimed her camera at one of the festival booths, a basic red-and-white number that looked like it belonged to a circus that let the school borrow it for a little bit. One of those water-gun games was nestled inside, the kind where you aim at the clown's mouth and the balloon fills up before popping. A group of kids cheered on a few of their number who were locked in fierce, clown-balloon competition. Truth be told, more water was getting on them, the ground, and some of the prizes hanging near the front to entice potential customers than into the intended targets. The white boy minding the booth didn't seem all that bothered.

Tai snapped a few pictures of the group, including some of the eventual winner and her prize of a large, stuffed creature that kinda looked like a frog, but could've been a fat lizard? It was hard to tell. Smiling at the girl's apparent delight, Tai tracked to the side a bit, scanning the other booths for potential shots.

As she passed over a popcorn-and-cotton-candy stand, the lens flared. She blinked through it, angling the camera downward a bit, only to freeze when the glare cleared.

A white girl stood in the middle of the lane, motionless as people milled around her, her gaze fixed toward the camera. She didn't stare *at* Tai so much as through her, with eyes that were sharp but unfocused, searching. If that wasn't weird enough, she wore some old-timey nightgown. The fabric hung loose on her body but remained just as static. The contrasting movement of the crowd lent a sort of depth to her stillness, gave her presence a weight a . . . a pull that Tai felt in the pit of her stomach.

She lowered her camera and felt a sharp stab of shock when the girl disappeared. That couldn't be right. There wasn't anywhere for her to go that fast. It was as if she vanished! Unless . . .

Tai stared for a moment before slowly, hesitantly, lifting the camera. She barely saw the girl's face before yanking the camera away and simultaneously recoiling. She nearly slammed into an old Vietnamese man in the process.

"S-sorry!" she offered, her heart in her throat, still managing to pound wildly,

"Careful there."

"I'm so sorry. I— Sorry," she offered again when he gave her an irritated look.

As the man shuffled on, seeming to accept her apology despite his scowl, she lifted her camera and stole a glance toward the snack stand. The Ren faire–looking white girl was gone. Tai aimed up and down this row of booths, but there was no sign of her.

Without another word, Tai spun around toward the far end of the festival grounds and the exit beyond. Her heart continued to thrash, equally freaked and looking for escape.

"Nope," she murmured as she dodged around a mom pushing a stroller with at least three kids stacked in it. "Nope, nope, nope. I am *not* about to be dealing with no *Sixth Sense* or *House on Haunted Hill* mess. No ma'am." Situation or no, this was too much. She could wait in the band room for Trey to finish practice.

Damn it, the festival was just getting into full swing and here she was about to leave. It wasn't as if her visions had ever caused her any physical harm besides unsettling her—and her family, when she bothered to tell them what she'd seen. But she'd also never glimpsed anything so *clear* before, and *never* through her camera lens.

The images had always appeared in purely reflective surfaces, like mirrors or windows, sometimes still water. And she saw whole scenes, not people. Well, there were people *in* the scenes, but it tended to be like watching a movie or a play, never just some random person standing in the middle of the frame. This? This was . . . She didn't know, but wasn't sticking around long enough to find out.

With a final, brief glance over her shoulder, she came around a booth and faced forward just in time to see the Black girl in front of her but not soon enough to keep from plowing into her.

They collided. Tai fought to maintain her balance. Someone's hands gripped her elbows, keeping her from tumbling over. She in turn latched on to the nearest sturdy object, which just so happened to be the same girl she'd nearly run over.

"Sorry! I'm so sorry," Tai found herself saying for the second time in so many minutes.

"Are you all right?" the girl asked.

"I'm f—" Tai glanced up into the biggest, most gorgeous brown eyes she'd ever seen, and her words shriveled on her tongue. "I—I . . . I . . ."

"You're?" the girl coaxed; her brow furrowed in concern.

Something squeezed Tai's arms, alerting her to the fact the two of them were holding one another. Well, the girl was holding Tai while she clung like used Saran Wrap.

When Tai didn't answer, the girl tilted her head to the side and a curtain of red braids fell in around her shoulders. Her brown skin practically glowed in the sunlight. She played those eyes over Tai, examining her. "You're not hurt, are you?"

"Nope!" Tai squeaked as heat filled her cheeks. A swarm of butterflies fluttered to life in her stomach. "Fine, I'm . . . I'm fine—are *you* okay? Oh my god, I'm so sorry. I didn't see you. I mean, I obviously *did* see you, we made eye contact and everything."

Stop talking.

"But it was too late, and I was going too fast, you just kinda appeared."

Stop. Talking.

"Well, you were probably standing here the whole time and I—I'm the one who just appeared!"

STOP TALKING!

"I was just . . . coming from . . ." Tai cleared her throat and finally, *finally*, managed to wrangle her mouth back under control. Mostly by pursing her lips until they quit moving. Her face felt like it was going to combust.

The girl laughed. The sound was light, airy, and pleasant in a way that made Tai a little giddy at hearing it. In that instant Tai wanted to both sink into the ground and also float away, but she was stuck there between the two as the trembly feeling in her middle intensified. "S-sorry, sorry," she mumbled quietly.

The girl shook her head and squeezed where she had hold of Tai's elbows. "We already got through the apologies, so you good. But are you *good*?"

That's when Tai realized she still had a death grip on the girl's sweatshirt and promptly forced her fingers to loosen. "I'm fine."

The girl let go as well, then arched an eyebrow as a smile played over her stunning face. "I know you fine. I asked if you was good."

It took exactly three seconds for the compliment to register. Tai's brain stopped working for that long as well, skipping over those words like a scratched CD.

She thinks you're fine. She thinks you're fine! Don't just stand there, say something back! Gah!

"Gaaaaaah, I am! Good. I am good. And fine. Good and fine. Fine and good. Both."

Kill me . . .

"Good." The girl, still smiling, held Tai's gaze a moment longer before her expression sagged slightly with a soft breath. "I'm glad."

She glanced down, and Tai followed her gaze to where a paper plate lay atop a pile of flaky but definitely ruined confectionery goodness. Powdered sugar splattered the area, looking like a chalk outline at a crime scene.

Tai's stomach plummeted. "I ruined your funnel cake!"

"Yeah, you kinda did." The girl didn't sound upset about it though.

"I'll get you another!"

"That line is hella long. Don't worry about it."

Tai groaned. "See, you say don't worry about it, but I'm gonna do nothing but that for the rest of the day, then all night when I get home. I'll probably dream about it, then wake up worrying about it, and tomorrow I'll have to hunt you down and buy another funnel cake anyway. The festival is only for today, so I got no clue where I'll get a funnel cake tomorrow, or how I'll find you to give it to you after, so can we just skip all of that and let me pay for one now, please?" Her stomach twisted in on itself more and more with each word. By the end of all that she felt like she was going to throw up all over her shoes.

Now she was thinking about the feeling of puke between her toes. They wiggled in her sandals. She shut her eyes against the mental image and took a slow breath. "Please," she repeated softly.

"I'll stand in line with you and everything. Or I'll stand by myself, just..." She gestured at nothing, the words finally drying up.

What's wild? Cute Funnel Cake Girl stood there smiling the whole time. The expression filled her round face, widening it enough so dimples popped into view. She'd never admit it out loud, but Tai wondered what it would be like to trail her fingers over them.

"Okay, okay, if you insist." Cute Funnel Cake Girl bent to take hold of the plate, then used it to scoop up most of the ruined cake. "But on one condition."

Tai knelt beside her to help clean up the mess before following her to a nearby trash can to throw it away, brushing her hands off afterward. "What's that?"

"You share the new one with me." Cute Funnel Cake Girl offered her hand. "Deal?"

For a moment Tai couldn't believe what was happening. Did she really just plow into a cute girl, ruin her snack, only for said cute girl to turn around and ask her out? It was like something out of *Sex in the City*. As the reality of the moment settled over her, the butterflies that had been tearing up her stomach settled as well. The beat of their wings was less frenzy and more a gentle quiver.

Tai felt her own smile rise as she took that warm hand. "Okay. Deal."

"Bet." They shook on it. Then Cute Funnel Cake Girl didn't let go. "Think I can get your name? Since we 'bout to share funnel cake and all."

"I—I'm Tai." It came out a little breathless.

"Hey, Tai." Those dimples deepened. "I'm Ayesha."

By the time Tai met up with Trey, she felt light enough to fly. Every step she took was like walking on a cloud even though her shoes slapped against concrete. Her face hurt a little from smiling, but she didn't care.

Trey stood with his back against the school's brick building talking to Marlon, lord knows what about. Usually, any sign of the dude was enough to annoy her. Not because Marlon was particularly annoying, but he was one of those guys who could very easily spend the entire conversation talking about himself and what's going on in his life before letting anyone else get a word in. There was a fine line between confidence and arrogance, and Marlon hadn't quite learned how to walk it just yet.

But that didn't matter. Not even the sight of him running his mouth while her brother nodded along was enough to dampen Tai's spirits.

"Hey," she said as she came up.

They paused in their conversation, and Marlon flashed the same bright smile he'd been giving her since the summer between seventh and eighth grade when she got back from spending the break in St. Louis with her aunt Geri n'em.

"Hey, Taina," Marlon said as he straightened his already perfectly fine collar.

She shot him a look. "It's just Tai, and you know that. You ready?" The question was aimed at her brother, who didn't look devastated or excited one way or the other. She wondered how the audition went but decided to wait till they were alone to ask. And to share her bit of news.

"Taina your name though, right?" Marlon asked.

"Has been my whole life. What that got to do with it?"

"So what's the problem if I call you by it?"

Trey rubbed his nose with his thumb and pretended to be interested in something happening across the street. She wasn't gonna get no help from there. So she rolled her eyes and tilted her head while looking Marlon up and down.

"Same problem as if I called you Bartholomew, I'm sure," she said smoothly.

Trey coughed to cover a laugh, then kept right on pretending to be distracted by whatever over yonder.

"Oh, snap, it's like that?" Marlon asked, still smiling, though it had dimmed a little.

"It's like that. How long you known me?" she asked.

Marlon shrugged. "Long as I've known Trey."

"Then why you not calling him Terrance?"

"Ey, yo," Trey said, finally paying attention, or at least done acting like he hadn't been this whole time. "Leave me out of this."

Marlon rubbed his hands together the way dudes be doing when they trying to spit game. "I don't mean nothing by it, just trying out something new, you know, something a little more special, maybe, you feel me?"

Tai couldn't help but stare at him for a second as a conversation she had with her dad last year came creeping up in her memory.

It had been the weekend of Thanksgiving break, and the first time their family had decided to host a group gathering over any holiday since Mom went missing. Tai and her friends, Trey and his—including Marlon—all had a good time playing *Mario Party* on the new Nintendo 64 the two of them got as a present, then making s'mores and whatnot in the firepit out back. Well, not an actual pit. Those were illegal, something Dad hated and never tired of saying so.

"If New York is so great, why can't a man burn what he want in his own backyard, huh?"

No actual fire pit meant everyone just stood around this lil' baby grill holding sticks over the red embers. It was kinda whack, but still kinda tight, and meant you had to work hard to burn your marshmallows. Trey still managed.

Their yard, if it could be called that, wasn't large, and was mostly concrete with some grass along the edges where the fence separated their space from the surrounding houses. The Queensboro Bridge was just visible over the tops of the houses facing the street behind them, the spires of the city beyond. The sun was already low enough in the sky that the thousands of lights from windows were visible even in the dying twilight.

It was kinda chilly out, but not too bad. Just the right temperature for gooey goodness and cocoa. This one dude named D'shawn kept trying to sit next to Tai and talk to her. He wasn't pushy or nothing, polite and all, but it was weird. For two years he barely said anything that wasn't hi, goodbye, or small talk. All of a sudden, he was full of random questions about things she liked, music she listened too, shows she watched, etc.

"He tryin'a holler at you," Trey had said while they were cleaning up after everyone was gone.

She sucked her teeth. "No he not."

"Oh, yes he is," Dad chimed in. "And he won't be the last. You're an amazing person, baby girl. At least half your brother's knucklehead friends are gonna realize that between now and when you graduate. Sheeeeeet, few of my boys tried to talk to your aunt Geri back in the day."

Trey made a face as he stacked chairs. "We really don't wanna hear about that."

"I ain't saying nothing 'bout nothing! I'm just saying they're gonna look up and realize Tai exists."

"They know she exists now," Trey complained, clearly bothered by this bit of breaking news.

"And some of 'em will work up the nerve to ask her out." Dad shrugged. "Them's just fax, don't shoot the messenger."

Tai had long since paused in gathering up half-empty mugs of hot chocolate, her mind working over the possibility of having to deal with that from ALL of her brother's goofy-ass friends. It gave her a headache.

"Then ... what do I do?" she asked.

Dad looked up from where he was shoving the last of the embers out of the firepit into a metal bucket to be doused. "You don't do nothing you don't want to, most importantly. But if you wanna get to know one of these young men, start with a discussion. See if you like the same things, or if you wanna learn to like new things together. Young people don't talk to each other these days."

"Here he go," Trey muttered.

Dad shot a look Trey's way. "They don't. They send them instant messages on the computers or texting them phones, driving up they parents' bills—don't y'all give no one your number, and don't be texting nobody, neither." He aimed the little shovel at Trey, then her. "Talking is free, these phones ain't."

The discussion dissolved into complaints about the lost art of conversation, but what Dad had said dug its way into Tai's brain like a thorn, the way lots of things he said did, and wound up lodged there just so the memory could prick her on days like today, with Marlon licking his lips like he LL Cool J.

"Something special," she repeated Marlon's earlier statement, then blew a sigh out her nose. "Look, Marlon, you cool people and whatnot, Trey wouldn't be friends with you if you wasn't, but I'm not trying to be nothing special to nobody right now." Except maybe Ayesha, but that was neither here nor there.

Marlon nodded, his lips pursed. "Oh, so you doing your Destiny's Child thing? On that 'Independent Women' tip, I see, I see, I feel you."

Tai resisted the urge to roll her eyes again. Instead, she simply bobbed her head. "Mm-hmm. Yup. That's what that is, yeah. Thanks for understanding."

"Fo sho, fo sho. But, uh, if you change your mind about trying, know you wouldn't have to try hard with me." The instant the words were out there, the look on his face said he probably thought that sounded better in his head.

"I will keep that in mind." It took everything in her to keep her face from acting up, which wasn't helped by the fact that Trey was over there concentrating *hella* hard on his shoes while his shoulders jumped in silent laughter.

Marlon nodded again and again, gesturing at nothing really. He wouldn't meet her gaze anymore. "Cool, cool. Aight, Trey."

"You outta here?" Trey asked as he pushed away from the wall.

"Yeah, I got stuff to do." Marlon held a hand up.

Trey grasped it and the two went in for a one-armed hug, pounding each other on the back hard enough she wasn't sure how either of them walked away without a collapsed lung.

Marlon jogged off. Tai waited until he was a good ways down the block before turning and immediately slugging Trey in the shoulder.

He danced to the side with a yelp, half laughing as he complained, "The hell was that for?"

"You just gon stand there and let that happen, huh," Tai said, her mouth twisting.

Trey lifted both of his hands. "I told him it was a bad idea!"

"A terrible idea."

"I know, but he ain't listen. You know Marlon, needs to touch the water to make sure it's wet." Trey rolled his shoulders as he hefted his backpack. "Sometimes you gotta let a man make his own mistakes before he learn."

"A man, huh."

"S'what I said."

"Mm-hmm." Tai fell into step with her brother, and the two headed off in the direction of Los Amigos. They dodged through and around other people moving on the sidewalk, somehow managing to stay side by side the entire time. It was a meticulous ballet that was equal parts muscle memory and that twin thing people think exists but doesn't really, except when it does.

The block melted gradually into squat buildings where restaurants and shops were stacked on top of each other. Sidewalk signs directed people to doors hidden down narrow flights of concrete stairs, or tucked beneath rickety-looking awnings. The smell of fried veggies and meat was cut sharply by the scent of laundry steam pouring down from above as they passed a wash and fold. Tai had no complaints; it was better than catching a nose-full of garbage or exhaust if she drifted too close to the curb.

As they crossed the street, the sound of someone blasting Bobby

Brown on a boom box drifted in from somewhere to the right. Tai bobbed her head as Bobby lamented how everybody's talking all this stuff about him. A quick glance revealed Trey mouthing the words *Why don't they just let me live?*

Tai nudged him with her elbow. "How was the audition?"

A wide smile broke over Trey's face. "In-credible. I hit that joint out the park."

Tai smiled in return. "Told you you would. You really should listen to me, I be knowin' these things."

"I will keep that in mind," he said, still grinning.

She aimed another swing that he easily dodged, snickering as he weaved away then back toward her smoothly.

"For real, though," he continued. "That was probably one of my best performances yet. I'm actually kinda bummed it was just me in an empty room with a little recorder."

"I'm glad," Tai said. "Now that your legacy is secure, let's secure some tacos."

All joking aside, she knew just how stressed Trey'd been—he turned his hair orange for heaven's sake. For it to have gone so well must have meant the world to him.

At the same time she couldn't help the slight twinge of worry wiggling insistently at the back of her mind. If he—no, *when* he— got his chair, that would be one good thing. Then celebrating their birthday would be a second. That meant whatever followed would be . . . not that great.

Don't think about that now, just celebrate your brother's win, damn.

She shook herself out of any potential impending funk. Speaking of orange hair. "How's the cap?"

He reached up to smooth his fingers over the rag. "I haven't checked since before class. Feels like we might be good." He undid the ties and tugged the rag free.

The clown hair was gone, replaced by his usual cornrows.

"Look at that!" Tai reached to pat the top of his head, swatting at his hand as she did so. "See, you was all stressed out for nothing."

Trey shoved the rag into his pocket. "Not nothing. This was important, and I turned my hair orange, Tai! Shit, this magic stuff is starting to get outta hand."

The sinking feeling she'd managed to fight off returned full force, and she struggled to keep her smile in place. "Yeah, well, we just gotta keep pushing, right? One day at a time, you and me."

"And Dad."

"Of course, of course. But . . . Dad isn't like us. He can't do what we do."

"Can't nobody do what we do."

"Mom could." The words were out of her mouth before she could stop them. She hadn't even thought to speak, they just leapt free.

Trey's expression fell slightly.

"I'm sorry, it—"

"Don't apologize," Trey said, his voice quiet and understanding. "I miss her, too."

He curled an arm around her shoulders, giving her a side hug. "Ten years. That's . . . a lot of birthdays without her."

"Mmm." Tai watched her shoes as they walked, knowing her brother would make sure she didn't run into anyone or anything while she battled the maelstrom of emotions she'd managed to hold off most of the day. "A lot of broken promises."

"And broken wishes . . ." She bit into her lower lip, hard. That sting was better than the burn of tears in her eyes. This was the part that bothered her the most. Well, what bothered her most was the fact that her mother was gone, but the brokenness left in Mom's absence made it so that wound never fully healed.

Neither of them spoke again until they reached the restaurant. The smell of griddled meat, onions, and peppers was just enough to lift her spirits. Food was one of the many loves in her life.

She put in the usual to-go order for the three of them. "And can you throw a few empanadas on top, and some churros, too, 'ppreciate it."

The front of the restaurant was blessedly empty, so Tai and her brother were able to sit their bags in one of the plastic seats lined up beneath the window. Trey stuck a quarter in a dingy bubble-toy machine near the door and twisted the crank. He fished out one of those rubber hands that was supposed to stick to a window or wall and crawl its way down. He spun it around his finger over and over again, his gaze trained on nothing in particular, just staring straight ahead. He did that sometimes, went inside his own mind.

Tilted against the pale wall near the cash register where the owner let people post flyers for neighborhood events or missing pets, with his heel kicked up above the baseboards, he looked like a tag come to life. Breathing art. And with the way the light poured through the slightly grimy windows, it cast a low glow across him, giving him a subtle, almost-pixelated look.

It was perfect.

She scrambled for her pack, eager to capture the moment before that slightly unfocused look like his eyes was gone. Lifting the camera, she aimed it at her brother, then nearly dropped it as fear seized hold of her, cold and sharp.

The ghostly white girl from the festival had followed them.

4

*T*rey stole a worried glance at his sister as they pushed through the doors to the gallery. A sonorous chime signaled their entry. The place was empty, most likely due to the sign in the window being switched to close. Dad would end the day early on special occasions, one of them being birthday-eve dinner.

By the time Trey finished locking the door, Tai had already crossed the main floor.

Dad's voice boomed from somewhere ahead of her. "That y'all?"

"Yeah," Tai called, sounding more cheerful than she'd looked just a second ago.

Matter of fact, she'd been acting weird ever since they left Los Amigos. When Trey asked what was up, she said they would talk about it at home. She'd insisted she wasn't hurt or anything, then didn't say nothing on the way to the subway station, the whole ride over, or the walk here. He figured it was because they talked about Mom, but this didn't really seem like that. Nah, something else was definitely going on.

Deciding to bug Tai about it later, Trey made his way to the back, which was part office, part living and dining room. Tai finished drying her hands on a dish towel before taking food out of bags and setting it on the table.

Dad shimmied his shoulders where he sat behind the desk off to the side, typing on his laptop. "I swear I smelled it a block away."

"Got a couple burritos as well, since you like both," Tai said, all smiles. "And some empanadas for you and Trey. The churros are *mine*."

Trey continued to pitch silent, curious peeks at his sister as she went about preparing everything. He tried to catch her eyes a couple times, but she was too occupied with the meal. That or she was purposefully ignoring him, which could also be the case.

It didn't take long to get everything laid out, and soon the three of them were smashing some of the best tacos. Dad did his traditional taco dance, which involved him MC Hammering in his seat. It honestly looked like he was trying to stand up but was glued to the chair. Ridiculous, but Trey couldn't help laughing. Tai grinned as well, finally looking at him, then tilting her head toward Dad as if to say *Can you believe this dude?*

"I see you don't got clown hair no more," Dad said, gesturing with a spoonful of rice before popping it into his mouth. "That mean the audition went okay?"

"Better than okay," Trey said around a bite of one of Dad's burritos. "I was telling Tai that I wish it was on a stage instead of in a back room, but nailing this means I'll get a chance to do it again."

Dad clapped him on the shoulder, the pat firm, jostling him a little. "My man. When do you find out officially?"

"Day after, so tomorrow it'll be legit."

"That's what's up." Dad nodded. "I take it practice was good, then, too?"

"It was chill. Went through the pieces a couple times, then decided to relax after the auditions."

"Fair. And what about you, baby girl?" Dad looked to Tai, who had been quiet this entire time. "You have a good day?"

The smile that pulled at Tai's face surprised Trey, especially after the way she'd been acting the past couple hours.

"You could say that." She set down her half-finished taco and glanced up. Her eyes moved back and forth between them, and she pursed her lips in that way that meant she was trying to hide how excited she was about something. Which was weird because acting like shit was no big was his thing.

"You gonna make us guess?" Trey asked, now genuinely curious.

"I met someone," Tai finally admitted, twirling her fork through the beans on her plate.

Dad paused with his burrito halfway to his mouth. "Oh *really*?"

Tai nodded and tucked some of her hair behind her ear. "At the festival. I sort of ran into her and made her drop her food."

"You replace it?" Dad asked.

"Yeah. I stood in line with her while she waited."

"That's my girl."

For a moment Trey wasn't sure he heard right. He sat up a bit straighter in his chair.

"What you mean met someone? Like *met* someone? Like a girl-friend someone?"

Tai was still smiling all big and goofy. "Like we might start talkin', but it's way too soon to be callin' each other pet names."

Part of him was, of course, happy for his sister. The other part was silently shouting at her, asking, *Why didn't you say something earlier?* "That why you gave Marlon a hard time?" See, he'd told Marlon it wasn't the best idea to ask his sister out. Not just 'cause he knew Tai liked dudes okay but was more into girls, but because if she was interested in Marlon at all, Trey would've known about it way back. Poor dude really didn't stand a chance. In fact, he stood less of a chance than Trey thought.

"I gave him a hard time 'cause he was being extra. Since when does he call me by my government name? Hey, *Taina*." She pitched her voice low to mock him, licking her lips and smoothing her hands over her collar.

Trey felt bad for laughing, but it was a pretty good impression.

Dad sucked his teeth and shook his head. "That's what he led with? Man, these young bloods doing things all wrong nowadays. I'm happy for you, baby girl. Hope things work out with your lil' friend."

Tai smiled and toyed with the ends of the hair she had tucked behind her ear. "I was thinking of inviting her over tomorrow."

Dad mopped at his mouth with a paper towel. "It's your day, you can invite who you like. Speaking of tomorrow, you two sure you don't wanna do anything special?" He glanced between them. "I'm fine with cake and presents here at the house. Makes things easier for me." He pressed a hand to his chest. "But it's not my celebration."

"We good, Dad. Really," Trey offered when it looked like Dad didn't really buy it. He'd been throwing them big birthday parties for forever now. Tai said it was to make up for Mom not being there. Trey agreed. "It'll be nice to just chill."

Dad planted his palms on the table while nodding slowly. "Oooookay. I just want y'all to be sure. I'm good with chill. I'm the most chill. The chillest. Like icccccccce."

Trey felt his groan rising but heard Tai's first.

"Daaaaaad," she protested.

"Heh ha!" Dad barked a laugh and winked. "Let's finish up here and head home."

"You need us to do anything?" Trey asked as they all started closing Styrofoam containers and paper bins, stacking paper plates to be tossed.

"I've got some pieces downstairs that need to come up to the main gallery. Was trying to get the peacock room together so I don't have to work on it tomorrow."

Tai finished packing up the leftovers to take home with them. "We can bring 'em up."

Dad settled himself behind the laptop again, slurping at what was once a Coke but now was just the remnants of watery ice. "That'd be a big help, y'all, thanks."

It didn't take the two of them long at all to finish cleaning up after dinner. Trey wiped down the table, then dropped back to shoot the sponge toward the sink.

"Kobe!" he called, and whooped in victory when it landed.

Tai shook her head, then shoved him laughing out into the gallery.

Dark wood floors glistened with a glossy finish, the light bouncing off of them and the high white walls that reached up into the industrial ceiling. Paintings of various sizes, subjects, and mediums were mounted in sets or spread apart, appearing as clusters or constellations of color and movement, even in their stillness. There were portraits, still lifes, abstract pieces, traditional scenes that mirrored the Renaissance masters, and more contemporary pieces that paid homage to the masters but were something completely new. The room was wide but not incredibly large, yet managed to be both imposing and cozy. Trey and his sister had grown up here as much as their actual house.

As they crossed the gallery, he counted the seconds that stretched between them and their father, waiting until Tai clicked on the light and they were partway down the rickety stairs before he cleared his throat.

"That ain't what you said we would talk about, is it?"

Tai didn't even look back. "What?" She opened the door, and a cool draft swept up around them, along with the smell of sterile air.

Trey smoothed his hands over the goose bumps rising on his arms. "At Los. Something happened, and you were all quiet the whole way home. You said we'd talk about it when we got here, but then you started going on about your girlfriend."

This time she nearly spun around fully. "She's not my girl-friend." Her cheeks puffed a little like they used to when the two of them fought as kids.

"What happened at the restaurant? And don't tell me nothing." Trey reached past his sister to feel around on the wall for another switch. When he found and flipped it, watery light poured in around Tai, revealing a windowless storage room. Metal and plastic shelves lined the walls, holding what looked like various thin packages wrapped in thick brown paper and ready to be mailed out.

Tai heaved a sigh as she moved toward one of the shelves, trail-ing her fingers over others in passing. "Nothing *happened*. I just . . . There was a situation."

That word made Trey stop dead in his tracks. He aimed an annoyed glance at his sister's back. "A situation isn't nothing."

"It is for me. I don't make stuff move or turn my hair funky colors."

She didn't mean nothing by it, Trey told himself. She's not

belittling his abilities, she's just venting. Despite the insistence, some small part of himself rankled all the same.

"Sorry," Tai said with a sigh, instantly deflating his ballooning offense. "It just ... freaked me out."

Trey set a hand on her shoulder. Squeezing when she didn't fight him, he turned her so they faced each other. She peered up at him, her lips pursed, her eyes glassy.

"Talk to me," he insisted, though gently.

For a moment Tai didn't say anything. She looked away and took slow, careful breaths.

"I saw something," she finally started, her voice small. For such a simple phrase, it could surely complicate a *lot*. "A girl."

"Not the maybe girlfriend, I take it."

She snorted and shoved weakly at him. "No. It was some random white girl. First at the festival, then at the restaurant."

Trey nodded along. "But you've seen people before."

She shook her head. "Not like this. She wasn't part of any scene or anything happening. She was just there. Standing in this old-timey nightgown."

"Okay, that's a new one. Isn't it?" He had to double-check.

Tai looked annoyed but nodded.

"Maybe it means your powers are getting stronger?" Trey said, holding up his hands placatingly.

Could she blame him for asking? It wasn't like she was all that talkative about her visions! As far as he knew, most of the time she tried to avoid them. He was honestly surprised she'd looked long enough to see something clearly.

"Maybe. But that's not the weird part."

"Glad to hear there's a 'weird' part."

His little joke didn't get a reaction. Tai just chewed at her lower lip while bunching her shoulders. "I saw her through my camera."

Let it never be said that Trey wasn't man enough to admit when something shocked him. And scared the crap out of him. A bit. "Your camera?" he parroted, which was all he was able to manage for a second.

"Y-yeah." Tai stepped away to start looking through the wrapped pieces of art. She was quiet for a few seconds, then a few more.

Which was fine because Trey's brain was only just now recovering from having tripped over the information it'd received. He pinched his finger and thumb together. "I'm gonna need a little more context."

She shrugged fully this time, still pretending to be searching for the art Dad sent them after. "I was taking pictures at the fair, candids for the paper and yearbook. I turned and there she is!" She flung her arm out at nothing. "Standing in the crowd. I lower my camera, she disappears. I thought she walked away real fast, y'know? So, I go to take more pictures and there she is again. Just in the camera, *only* in the camera! I'm like, 'Hell no,' and run and that's when I knocked over the funnel cake, and..." Tai trailed off. She finally looked at Trey, who grinned.

He understood what happened next. "And you got distracted."

She rubbed her face while groaning, "Hella distracted! This girl fine, I mean *foine*, and I knocked over her funnel cake, but she ain't mad, she's just mad flirty—"

"Gross."

"Shut up—so yeah, I was distracted. Until we got to the restaurant." The glow that had filled Tai's face dimmed considerably.

"And the white girl was there," Trey confirmed Tai *had* been aiming the camera at him when she shouted and jumped up from her chair. Then she'd stared at the empty space beside him for a second, her eyes wide, her face ashen. It rattled him, no lie. Not a whole lot but enough to make him wary.

When he'd asked what was up, she shook her head rapidly and said something about a bug. Probably for the girl working the register, who was eyeing the both of them like she intended to call the cops.

"You see her anywhere else?" Trey asked softly while at the same time doing everything in his power not to glance around. It wasn't like he would be able to *see* anything, but the thought that this mystery camera girl could just be hanging out nearby was creepy.

"No. But I haven't been looking, either."

"What about before?"

"You think if I was seeing white girls in my camera before today, I wouldn't say something?"

"Technically you didn't say nothing this time, but I get what you mean," he added hurriedly when she looked ready to throw that empty frame at him. "Okay, well . . . since you ain't say nothing at dinner, I take it you don't wanna tell Dad." He could see his sister's anger deflate. Her shoulders sagged, and her gaze dropped to the floor.

"Not yet," she said, quiet. "He's— You know how he gets about this 'hocus-pocus stuff.'" She made finger quotes and everything.

"That's because he doesn't know anything about it. Not for real, for real. He doesn't like not being able to help."

Tai shook her head and didn't say anything else, but he could tell there was something more, something she was holding back. He knew his twin, and while she hadn't said everything on her mind, picking at her about it would only make her clam up. He couldn't help feeling a way about it, though. They usually were more open with one another when it came to their powers. He couldn't remember the last time either of them had held anything back. Then again, his powers were active and affected the world around him. It was hard to miss things moving on their own or suddenly changing color.

With Tai's magic, the only one who ever knew when it manifested was her. Unless you managed to be with her when it happened. Not really lots of chances to stare in mirrors together. In reality, she could have dozens of visions in a single day and he'd never know it if she didn't say anything. But that wouldn't happen . . . right?

Pushing the thought aside Trey crossed to another set of shelves, nudging her lightly in passing. "It's cool, we don't have to tell Dad, yet. Give you time to get a handle on it."

"If I even can," she muttered, sounding a little surly and more like herself. Which was good.

Trey didn't like it when his sister sounded scared. Especially when it was about something he couldn't protect her from.

The two lapsed into silence as they started to search in earnest. Usually, Dad put sticky notes on the pieces he wanted to bring upstairs, make them easier to find, but Trey didn't see any bright orange bits of paper poking out anywhere.

"Can I ask a question?" Trey asked while continuing to carefully lift, shift, or lean the wrapped pieces in search of notes. "About camera girl."

"We are *not* calling her camera girl."

"Then what do you—"

"Just 'the girl' is fine."

"Okay. Anyway, She wasn't, like ... dead or nothing, was she?"

Tai aimed a look at him that pretty much said, *Nigga, what?*

He hiked his shoulders defensively before holding out and ticking off his fingers. "First, she's in your camera, not a mirror or something, so that's weird. Second, you've never seen the same person twice! *And* she following you? Third, she was wearing an old-timey dress!"

"Nightgown."

"Whatever! I'm just sayin', all that sounds like some *Poltergeist* or *Sixth Sense* stuff."

Tai rolled her eyes. "This isn't a movie, Trey. And I don't see ghosts. I see actual people, even if I don't know them."

A memory nagged at Trey of this one time when they were ten and Tai was brushing her teeth before school. The bathroom mirror showed her an elderly white man tumble down the stairs in their old apartment building and land with a crack that was definitely some bones. She didn't recognize the guy. After she described him, Dad didn't know him either, but a few days later they ran into their neighbor Mrs. Wilson. She was on her way to see her father, who had taken a bad fall on the stairs the day before. Broke his hip but he was recovering all right.

That's when Tai stopped looking at reflective surfaces directly. Always at an angle or a side glance. The visions still tried to take her, but she ignored them best she could. Especially since they seemed to be more about bad things than good.

Trey shook off the past and refocused on the paintings. "Okay, so you saw 'the girl,' and she wasn't dead. She at least do anything? Say anything?"

Tai flapped a hand, the other poking through packages. "No, she just stood there."

"Just stood there."

"Yeah. She was kinda looking at me, like I was gonna take her picture, but her eyes were unfocused. She looked . . . lost?

"Anything distinct about her?"

"She had long blond hair and her nightgown looked like the one Rose wore in *Titanic*."

It was Trey's turn to roll his eyes. "How is that even relev— You gotta bring that movie into everything."

"Don't act like you didn't watch the tape as many times as I did, okay?"

He smacked his lips. "Whatever, man. So . . . now what?"

"I don't know." Tai sighed. The way her body sagged with it made it seem like she carried the weight of the world and then some. Then she whirled on him, coming across the room so fast it caught him off guard. "You just better keep your mouth shut like you promised. I mean it, Trey. If Dad finds out about this, I will end you." She stabbed a finger in his face, and he had to recoil to keep the tip of her nail from catching his nose ring.

As if on cue, the door at the top of the stairs swung open.

"You two okay down there?" Dad called, his shadow splashed against the wall across from the door "You get lost or something?"

Tai bucked her eyes and shoved her finger farther into Trey's face before calling, "We're good, we just got distracted. And Trey keep teasing me."

"Boy, leave your sister be."

What?! Trey mouthed, incredulous.

Tai just put her other finger to her lips. "We'll be up in a second."

The door closed, and Trey swatted her hand aside, rubbing at his nose. "I ain't doing nothing to you."

"This is payback for the thing with the water balloon last week."

Trey paused, his rebuttal dying on his lips as he recalled exactly what she was talking about. He remembered her soaked hair and runny makeup and winced. "Okay, fair." He followed her toward the far corner where the orange sticky notes finally made an appearance.

There were only three, so he gestured for Tai to hand him the two bigger ones. They laid them out on the nearby table, pushing aside some of the tools used to restring wire for hanging. The paper crinkled as they tore wide strips of it away, revealing the pieces. One was a still life, flowers curling outward in star-like patterns, the pink-and-white petals appearing soft even when rendered in thick oils. The other was a young white guy and a Black girl dressed in something outta the twenties, standing in front of some old-ass car. Looked clean though.

His burden in hand, Trey turned to head for the stairs. He'd just started his climb when Tai gasped, followed by a thump and a clatter of metal and wood. He turned to find her fighting to keep a couple pictures from toppling over where she had backed into the shelves.

"Hold up." Trey set his pictures down, then hurried over to help push the others back into place. "I got it," he said, though Tai didn't move.

He had to nudge her slightly with his hip to get her out of the way so he could make sure things were secure. The whole time she stared at something on the table.

"You good?" he asked, pushing the last of the pictures back, then turning to face her where she slowly approached the table and the now-unwrapped picture atop it.

She trailed her fingers over the frame before her eyes lifted, wide and afraid. Trey blinked, his mind hiccupping a moment. He'd never seen his sister so scared before.

"It . . . it's her," Tai breathed, her voice flaking away.

Trey shifted to get a look at the piece. It was another portrait done in the same style of the two he'd taken over to the stairs. A white girl in an old-timey gown, her blond hair hanging around her shoulders.

ai held the wooden frame gently as she followed her brother up the stairs. Trey led the way, a picture tucked under each arm. They emerged on the gallery floor, the bright lights playing across the oils, revealing the portrait fully in contrast to the cold light downstairs.

This was definitely the same white girl she'd seen in her camera, only instead of standing in the middle of the festival, the girl stood out against a backdrop of angry gray clouds that looked ready to drop a helluva storm on top of her and the farm behind her.

"Daddy," Tai called as she set the picture down on a nearby bench.

Dad came in from the back quick enough, having obviously been waiting on them. He smiled bright and rubbed his hands together. "Wow, they look even better in this light."

Trey set his pictures down beside hers. She glanced at them briefly before looking back to the white girl. "Daddy, who is this?"

Dad stared a moment, tilting his head from one side to the other, then frowned a little. "Oh, I—I don't know, baby girl. Prolly no one." His smile returned as he took a rag and wiped down the frames. "I've got the spot ready over here."

"Tai," Trey whispered while Dad talked about perfect lighting and setting a mood. He pointed at the corner of the picture, his eyes wide. "Look."

She followed his finger, her gaze moving over the paint, and the very familiar loop and swirl that was her mother's signature.

Suddenly there wasn't enough air in the room. Her chest tightened and her head went fuzzy. "These... these were Mom's?" She barely managed the words.

Dad paused in the middle of his excited ramble. His gaze bounced between her and Trey before he nodded slowly. He didn't even look down at the paintings.

"Yeah. Yeah, they ya momma's." He smiled. "Some of her older pieces. Before the others really took off, way before."

That was a surprise. Tai thought all of Mom's older stuff was tucked away in the attic of their house. Only her more recent works made it to the gallery.

Dad continued. "They been down there this whole time, and I thought it might be nice if, for your birthday, I brought some of them up. Like maybe . . . maybe I could give you a piece of her. Part of her past I could share."

While her father spoke, Tai studied each picture. The flowers seemed like something otherworldly, plain but ethereal at the same time. Enchanting. The picture of the couple practically radiated love. Their hands clasped together, the girl folded in the boy's arms, the soft night alight around them. She looked straight ahead, as if watching the painter, but he only had eyes for her. Finally, there was the white girl, her face gentle but serious, her gaze distant yet dreary. She looked so very, very tired. She stood almost exactly the same as she had at the festival.

"That's cool, Dad," Trey said quietly, brushing at his nose with his thumb, trying to disguise a swift sniff. He was likely feeling a lot of things, but so was Tai.

She was awash in emotions, predominantly curiosity, hella confusion, and a thickness in her chest that felt like the ache of grief, but there was an undercurrent of joy that she couldn't explain. This was more than just a picture. This girl was more than just a girl. Mom has seen her, and now Tai was seeing her, too. This girl provided a connection to something Tai didn't realize she needed to be tethered to.

"Did...did she say anything about them?" Tai asked the pictures, then lifted her gaze to her father. "About her subjects?"

Dad rubbed the back of his head with one hand, the other set at his hip. "Not really. Matter of fact, she talked about these the least. Her older stuff, I mean. This was from before I met her."

"Back when she lived in California?" Tai asked.

"Y-yeah," Dad grunted before coughing into a fist. "I feel like this conversation is gonna drift into territory your momma would rather we avoid."

"Living in Cali?" Tai pressed.

"Her life from before. Her family, the things she went through. Look, I know it ain't easy, doing this without your mom." Dad gestured, his fingers drifting over the picture of the white girl.

"This?"

"Yeah. Your birthday. Turning sixteen, it's supposed to be special. And it is, I just—I mean, it's hard. And I get it. Ten years is a long time." Dad pursed his lips, doing the same faint sniff thing Trey had done before. "What I'm trying to say is I want this to be a celebration. For you, especially, but for her. She wouldn't want y'all upset tomorrow. Or at all."

"Then she should be here," Tai murmured, once again unable to keep the words from leaping free.

Twin looks of shock and hurt were aimed at her.

Dad cleared his throat. "Maybe, uhm...the pictures were a bad idea."

Tai kicked herself internally. The apology was already leaving her lips. "I didn't mean that, I'm..." She trailed off and waved a hand. "Ignore me. This... The pictures were a nice surprise, Dad. Really. I'm just in my feelings."

"And that's okay." He came around the table and scooped Tai into a hug that made her feel like she was six again. "It's okay to be in your feelings. Don't apologize for being upset." He dropped a kiss to her forehead and must have waved Trey over because soon her brother was at her side and Dad was hugging both of them.

"Grief can be ugly. Make us do and say things we don't mean. But I'm your father, and it's okay." Dad's voice cracked slightly. "You don't have to hide none of that from me. I get it. Just know that we in this together."

Tai swallowed around the lump in her throat. She didn't really want to talk about this, not right now.

"Okay, okay," Dad said as if sensing her train of thought. He squeezed them one last time, then patted his stomach and cleared his throat again. "Am I really good to put these on the floor?" he asked, gesturing at the portraits. "Just through the weekend, maybe. Then they can go back downstairs."

Trey shot Tai a look but didn't say anything. He was leaving the decision up to her, which she was grateful for but also a little annoyed. This meant whatever happened as a result could be seen as her fault. If she was upset later, she did it to herself.

"Yeah, you're good." She answered, her eyes trailing to the white girl again. "Do you know the name of this one?"

Dad shook his head, the wrinkles between his eyebrows deepening. "'Fraid not. It might be in the ledger, though."

"The ledger," Tai repeated as she turned to head for the back room immediately.

It sounded like Trey started to follow her, but Dad called for her brother to give him a hand with putting up the pictures.

The back room/office still smelled like tacos. Tai hurried over to the bookshelf behind the desk that used to be their mother's.

For the first half of Tai's life, whenever she came through that door, she would see her mother sitting here, her hair pulled back, her glasses at the edge of her nose as she worked on this or that for the gallery. Mom would sometimes pull Tai into her lap, her long arms encircling her for hugs or to reach paperwork. And Tai was content to sit there, for hours, without a clue what her mother was doing, but happy just to spend time with her.

Then Mom was gone, and the desk sat empty for a long time. One year. Two. Dad worked at the table at first, afraid to touch anything, leaving it all in place for when Mom came back.

One day, after school, Tai came in here to find her father hunched over a keyboard. He'd gotten a new computer to help him keep track of everything—Mom had a system that she was somehow able to keep straight in her head, and Dad just couldn't manage it. He spent weeks typing up all of her notes, binders and notebooks full of information on each piece and the daily running of the gallery. He used it to create his own system but kept the hard copies. He didn't fully trust computers yet. All the Y2K nonsense last year didn't help.

While most of the binders and notes were stored in the file cabinet against the wall, the ledger stayed on the shelf. Tai pulled it down and flipped it open.

Then she stared at it. Her mother's handwriting, long and crisp but looped here and there, lay before her. Words her mother had written that Tai had never read. It was almost like starting a conversation with her, in a weird way. This realization set fire behind Tai's eyes, and she couldn't swallow the hurt quick enough to keep the sting from drawing tears.

She swiped at them, sniffling around deep breaths to try and ease the ache in her chest.

Can't cry now, can't cry now, she repeated to herself over and over as she flipped through the first handful of pages. Her eyes danced over the words, and two things became clear at once.

First, her mother could definitely turn a phrase. The way she wrote about the pieces she painted, the stories behind their inspiration or behind the subjects she'd chosen—if there had been any—were beautiful. It would've been easy to get lost in each description, except Tai was on a mission. A mission that was waylaid by the second thing.

After reading only a handful of entries, there was no way to tell just how she was supposed to find the info she was looking for. The pages were covered in chunks of information scrawled in a patchwork of black and blue ink, each section clearly written at different times. Some were even squeezed in at the margins, information added once the pages were full. Despite all of this, there were no dates and no way to even begin to know what to look for. She couldn't even tell if she was looking at notes for newer pieces or older ones.

A small part of her wilted. "Am I gonna have to read this whole thing?" she murmured.

"Read what?"

Tai jumped so hard it felt like her heart punched her dead in the chin. She spun and found Trey filling the doorway, his arms braced against the jamb and supporting his forward lean.

He arched an eyebrow. "Everything cool?"

The breath that rushed out of her stole some of her strength with it. She leaned into the desk to brace herself. "Yeah, you just scared the shit outta me ..."

"You awfully jumpy."

"Gee, I wonder why."

He crossed the room to open the fridge and pull out one of the Styrofoam containers that still had tacos in it. "Dad's worried the pictures upset you."

Of course he is. "I said it was okay."

"I know. But Dad's doing that thing where he goes, 'You think she's okay? She said she's okay, but I think she just wants me to think she's okay.'"

Tai heaved a sigh. She knew exactly what he was talking about. "Okay. I'll convince him."

Trey gestured at the ledger with a half-eaten taco. "You find anything?"

"Not yet. I'm probably gonna have to look through the whole ... thing. . . ." She paused as her gaze wandered over the computer.

Struck with an idea, she hurried to power it on. It took a bit before the log in window popped up, and she typed in Dad's password.

She pulled up the ledger Dad had copied over and did a search for the word *girl*. It popped up in couple dozen places. Tai then compiled those findings and copied them over into a document, along with the page numbers listed. She would have to cross reference these findings with the information in the ledger itself, but checking twenty to thirty pages was gonna be much easier than checking a couple hundred.

Shutting down the computer, she gathered up her printout and stuck it between the pages of the ledger, then put both in her backpack.

"Dad gonna be okay with you taking that out of the office?" Trey asked.

Tai snorted and shot him a look. "*If* he finds out, I'm sure he'll be fine with it. But he doesn't use this, he won't miss it, and he won't notice unless someone opens his big mouth."

Trey shoved the last of a churro into his mouth and lifted both hands in surrender.

"Good," Tai said. "And how are you hungry? We just ate!"

"I know that, my brain knows that, my stomach gives no damns."

"Whatever." She couldn't help stealing a last glance at her backpack. After nearly a decade of nothing but questions and dead ends, she would finally have an answer. She hoped. *Happy birthday to me.* Smirking faintly, she headed out into the main gallery, intending to reassure her father once more.

The instant they made it home, Tai practically flew up the stairs.

"Uh, happy birthday eve, baby girl," Dad hollered after her.

"Thanks!" She hurried down the hall and pushed into her room, closing the door behind her.

A pair of luminous eyes peered at her from a lump of fabric on her bed. She smiled, rushing over to set the backpack against the mattress and reach to draw back the blanket.

"You'll never guess what happened today, Morpheus."

The orange cat eyed her with a mix of feline disdain and indifference as she went about cleaning off a spot on her desk. "There was this girl. Okay, there were two girls, but the first one wasn't real I don't think. Or maybe she was ... will be? Anyway." She turned to the cat who didn't look the least bit bothered by or interested in this information.

And why should he. He had been around magic all his life. Morpheus was one of the few things Mom had brought with her from Cali. That and her art.

"This time," Tai continued, fetching the journal and the printed pages from her bag, "I saw her in my camera. Not *in* my camera, but when looking through it. Once at school and again at the restaurant. Haven't seen her since." She drew the camera out and set it down as well.

"I don't know who she is, but Mom might have. This is the closest I'm gonna get to asking her...." Tai trailed her fingers over the leather-bound book before flipping it open.

Her mother's elegant but urgent handwriting was the same as it had been back at the office, but now—with so many possibilities tucked between those words—Tai felt a sudden sense of dread rise from somewhere deep down.

This girl, whoever she was, was important enough for her mother to paint. And not only that, to then keep the piece. Blake Estancia Watson was a woman who treasured art but knew when there was nothing about a piece worth keeping except the lessons learned while creating it. Which is why most of her earlier work was up in the attic, unframed and all but forgotten. And yet, this picture of this girl had been important enough to keep. *So had the other two,* a small part of her whispered, and she'd look into those later, but this... Who was this girl, and why had Mom hidden her away?

"Guess I'm gonna find out," Tai sighed.

The desk jostled slightly as Morpheus leapt onto a pile of library books stacked in the corner. A *Matrix* poster hung on the wall behind them, the character for which the cat had been named framed in a downpour of green code.

Tai reached to scratch the cat's ears. "Glad to have both of you watching over me for this." She took a deep breath and opened the ledger.

Seconds stretched into minutes stretched into hours as her fingers moved over the inked pages, switching back and forth between them and the printed ones. She took in every word, rereading sentences. The smells of aged paper and fresh ink filled her senses, old and new mingling together, past and present alive in her hands as she read first the names of pieces, then their descriptions. Like that one for a picture called *Golden Girl*, a portrait of a woman walking alone beneath a full moon across an eerily empty Golden Gate Bridge.

Title: Golden Girl

Began: 11/2/1987

Completed: 3/14/1988

The woman didn't know why she started walking, only that something in her bones knew enough that she should no longer be here. That something was so certain of the truth of this, that her feet could not remain still. And so, she went. Step by step. Mile by mile. Circles and circles through the same concrete valleys and steel mountains dressed in starlight. Pressed in on one side by the unknown waters foaming white, and on the other the unceasing truth.

SPLINTERED MAGIC

She walked. Until shoes filled red soon stained the pavement. She walked. All night long and yet for years. An eternity in an evening. She walked.

Every entry mirrored that pattern, some of the "stories" several pages long, and others no more than a sentence or two. Each one contained one or a combination of keywords she'd entered. *Girl, white, dress.*

The clock at the other corner of her desk blared 2:39 a.m. in cold blue light. Morpheus had long abandoned her for a more comfortable spot on the bed. With maybe two-thirds of the search results finished, Tai was just about ready to call it a night and join him, when her fingers brushed over the shortest entry yet.

Title: I See You

Began: 1/1/1981

Completed: 1/1/1981

Tai blinked a couple of times. This was it. She had no idea how or why she knew, just that she did. She felt the same pull in her stomach reading this entry that she had the first time she saw the girl, and again when her portrait was revealed at the gallery. But something was wrong. The dates. There was no way that portrait was started and finished on the same day. Not with the details in the shading, the brush strokes that were sometimes inverted where heads were changed out. Even for a painter of her mother's skill, it would've been impossible.

L.L. McKINNEY

Her eyes trailed back to the entry.

Title: I See You

Began: 1/1/1981

Completed: 1/1/1981

Elva

6

"Elva?" Trey made a face as he paused in spooning Cheerios into his mouth long enough to peer across the table at his sister. "What kinda white-bread-ass name is that?"

"The kind that some white girl in an old-timey nightgown would definitely have." Tai bucked her eyes.

Yeah, Trey knew what she was talking about. That didn't make him any more eager to be bothered with magical mysteries at five in the freaking morning. His brain was still half-asleep.

He waved a hand dismissively. "Okay, so, the girl's name was Elva. So what?"

"So, that gives me something to go on! To find out who she is."

"You think she was a real person?"

"She had to be, if both Mom and I are seeing her." Tai poked at her now definitely cold eggs with a fork.

"And you don't think that's weird? Even for us?" he asked.

"Happy birthday!" Dad boomed as he swept into the room.

Whatever Tai was about to say, she snapped her mouth shut and smiled as he dropped kisses to the tops of both of their heads.

"Thanks," Trey said.

"Thanks, Daddy," Tai murmured with a smile. When Dad turned to fix his plate, she aimed a look at Trey that said they'd talk about this more later.

Trey simply shrugged and focused on his breakfast. Honestly? He wasn't looking forward to that conversation. Sure, he wished his sister shared more about her powers, but if what Tai said was true, and "the girl" was a real person? She had probably been alive when they wore old-timey nightgowns and was definitely dead now. Magic or not, ghosts were ghosts, and he wanted no part of messing with any spirits. Not when he was counting on the good vibes around their birthday to help him get first chair before the bad vibes inevitably showed up to shut the party down.

Dad joined them at the table with a plate piled with eggs, bacon, and toast in one hand and a glass of orange juice in the other. "How about we do presents this morning, before you two leave the house?"

Trey nearly choked on his cereal. "Really?" Normally their dad was insistent on waiting until they'd gotten home from school to bust out the gifts. That way he could make a big deal about it, with cameras and video recorders and something filled with confetti. He made a production of things ever since their Mom left, trying to make up for her not being here. It was kinda sweet.

Dad smiled big. "Really. Y'all wait here." Shoving to stand he hurried from the room. His feet thudded up the steps and down the hall.

Trey couldn't help chuckling as they "watched" their father move across the ceiling. He probably wanted this more than they did. "You'd think it was his birthday."

Tai snorted a laugh. "He just wants food on his birthday. Granted, it's good food."

By the time Dad made it back downstairs, Trey had finished eating and put his bowl in the sink.

"Okay." Dad stood partially in the doorway, fussing with

something just out of sight. "Y'all stay right there." He fumbled before stepping in and offering a package to Tai. "Oldest first."

The wrapping paper shimmered faintly, white with rainbow balloons lined in foil.

"Favoritism," Trey said, though he was still smiling.

Tai tore into the gift, sending pieces of paper flying. "Truth."

As she fought with a matching ribbon, something furry brushed against Trey's leg. He bent to scoop Morpheus into his arms, scratching at the cat's ears. "Look who came to join the party."

Tai cooed at the cat half-heartedly while she finally shoved the last of the wrapping aside and got to work opening the box.

Dad stood beside her, a smile on his face that widened as she finally managed to get it open and tug out what was inside.

A camera, and an expensive one from the look of it, shone in the kitchen lighting. But not as bright as Dad's smile.

He puffed out his chest a little. "I asked some photographer friends and some guys at the store to make sure I got the best one. Good shutter speed, whatever that means. Long battery life. Even plugs into the computers to save the pictures, no film to develop."

Tai turned the camera over in her hands, her touch light, careful, her expression a little odd. She wasn't smiling, but she wasn't exactly frowning either. She looked like she was shocked or maybe scared. Probably a bit of both.

Dad glanced between her and the camera a few times before clearing his throat. "Is . . . it good?"

Another few seconds passed before Tai blinked out of her stare. She smiled, though it didn't reach her eyes. "It's perfect. Sorry, I just . . . I'm a little overwhelmed."

Dad chuckled, clearly believing that her reaction was completely positive. He didn't know about the freaky shit going on with her camera though.

"Good, because there's more in the box. Go ahead and help yourself while I get your brother's gift." He leaned in and pressed a kiss to her forehead before hurrying back toward the door.

"Now we're talking," Trey said, rubbing his hands together.

Tai released a slow breath and flicked a glance Trey's way before she started rooting around in the bottom of the box. She produced a couple different lenses, a tripod, and a case before Dad managed to wrangle in a cello case wrapped in a blue bow.

A wash of joy took Trey's entire body and shook him like a maraca. "Yoooooo!" He rushed around the table to meet Dad at the door, taking the instrument from his father's hands.

"I thought about wrapping it, but . . . you'd still be able to tell," Dad said.

The case was soft on the outside but still had a hard interior to protect what turned out to be a gorgeous, brightly washed, brand-new cello. The wood gleamed, a light tan color marked with darker notches in the wood here and there. The strings damn near twinkled along the black fingerboard. It was beautiful, perfect for his first day as first chair, and all his. His very own.

He had a cello.

"Oh wow," Trey murmured, trying to ignore the tightening in his throat and the way his vision went a little blurry. It got dusty in the kitchen sometimes. . . .

Dad clapped him on his shoulder. "I'm proud of you. Of both of you, what you're making of yourselves, and your art." He cleared his throat before adding, "I know your momma would be proud, too."

Trey smiled as his fingers moved over the instrument. It looked better than he ever could've imagined. "Thanks, Dad."

"Yeah, thanks," Tai said as she set the camera in the bag that had come with it.

"Okay, well . . . cake and ice cream this afternoon, and nothing else. Y'all are *sure*?" Dad glanced between the two of them, his brows lifted in question.

"We're sure," Trey offered.

"Okay, well, let's finish up so I can get y'all to school. I'll have everything ready by the time you get home."

Tai moved to take her box upstairs, saying something about putting the bag together.

Trey took another moment to look over his cello, *his* cello. Man, it was wild to be able to say something like that. Zipping up the case he moved to finish putting his dishes up so he could grab his stuff and head out to the car.

"For the fifth time, it's fine in the trunk," Dad said as he shifted lanes, hit a pothole, and a suspicious thump sounded in the trunk.

Trey whipped around so hard he felt his neck crack. "Ayo, man, that didn't sound right."

"It wasn't nothing happening to your cello, I promise."

Trey wanted to argue, but there wasn't nothing for it. He would just have to wait until they got to the school to check the damage. Oh man, there was gonna be damage. . . .

"Besides," Dad continued, "this is a good test. That case was almost as much as the cello. I paid enough money for that thing to be able to survive a ride in the back of my car. It better protect it."

"Fine, fine." Trey settled into the passenger seat and tried not to focus on every bump or dip they hit.

"You okay, baby girl?" Dad peered into the rearview mirror at Tai. "You ain't took one picture yet."

Trey chanced glance over his shoulder. Tai's camera bag sat next to her backpack, unopened.

She smiled and nodded. "Yeah, I'm fine. I'm just tired. I stayed up half the night reading fanfic—I know, I know, I need to make better choices."

Dad closed his mouth where he was likely about to start a lecture.

"But it was my birthday, so I figured I could get away with it this time."

Dad huffed faintly and dragged his tongue over his teeth. "Long as it don't mess with school, I'll let it slide."

The car settled into quiet for the rest of the ride. It was short, but long enough for Trey to think over what he wanted to say to his sister once they were out of earshot. Their earlier conversation had gotten interrupted, and yeah, he wasn't in no mood to deal with no spirits, but he didn't want his sister to think she had to deal with it all alone.

Dad dropped them off a little sooner than the usual spot, at Trey's insistence that it would just be faster this way, and they didn't mind the walk—it would give them time to soak up the *happy birthdays*. They waved as he pulled off, and the moment they started toward the school, Trey nudged his sister with his elbow.

Actually he didn't so much nudge as ram into her lightly. Trying to walk with a cello strapped to his back and his book bag hanging from his front was more than a little awkward.

"What?" Tai said in feigned irritation.

"This Elva chick, that why you ain't used your camera yet?"

Tai snorted but nodded as she fidgeted with her bag, pulling out the camera. "Yeah, *and* I wanted to wait until Dad dropped us off." She took a deep breath. "Here we go," she said, lifting the camera to her face.

Trey couldn't help glancing around the sidewalk, then back to Tai. People washed around the two of them like a river parting around stone, most of them students on the way toward the front doors.

"Anything?" he asked.

"No," she said, and heard the telltale click of the camera shutter a few times.

He smiled faintly, glad she was able to enjoy her gift. There would be time to deal with all the nonsense *after* birthday goodness. "Cool, cool. I need to drop this off before class," he said, giving the cello a jostle. "I'll see you after ... Tai?" He turned when he realized his sister had fallen behind.

A few people stepped around her, aiming irritated glances in passing, but she didn't notice any. She had stopped dead in her tracks, her eyes trained ahead, her lips tight, her brow furrowed.

Trey followed that gaze, stopping short when he caught sight of a white woman flanked by two Triple H–looking mofos exiting the school. The woman's red hair was pulled back into a tight ponytail. Both guys were bald. All of them wore matching white suits.

The redhead led the way down the stairs, the kids parting like the Red Sea to give her and her guys space. It was the same as they made their way to the sidewalk, where they finally stopped. One of the men stepped over to a big black SUV that was stopped at the front of the drop-off line, the flashers blinking. He bent his hulking form forward to talk to someone through the passenger window.

Red and the other dude stayed on the sidewalk. He glanced up and down the street casually while she stared straight ahead.

Click-click, click.

Trey glanced to where Tai was snapping photos rapidly.

"This is wild," she said as she kept clicking away, checking the digital screen every few seconds.

"Is it?" Trey glanced toward the trio and the people moving around them, shooting dirty looks that both the men and woman ignored.

"Who do you think they are?" Tai asked.

"If it wasn't for the white suits, I'd say they're the Feds." He shifted his shoulders, which were starting to ache from the added burden of his cello.

Other kids were watching as well now, stopping and pointing

instead of going into the school, their murmurs rising to join the morning roar of traffic.

Tai gasped. "Holy!" She lowered the camera, her eyes wide, her mouth open.

"What?" Trey asked, nearly giving himself whiplash as he glanced back and forth between her and the three.

She lifted the camera, then lowered it again. Then repeated the motion a couple more times.

He leaned in to try and peer over her shoulder at the screen. "You see something?"

Tai nudged him aside, then snapped a few more pictures. "Shhh."

"Ahh," Trey complained as he rubbed at his abused chest.

Right that moment, the guy bent to talk into the window straightened and moved to open the back door. As he did so, the dude that had hung back gestured for Red to continue. She took a couple of steps, paused, then her head whipped around to stare right at Trey and his sister. The woman was wearing sunglasses, but Trey felt a chill of revulsion move through his body.

Beside him, Tai gasped again, her camera dropping from her hands.

"Tai!" he shouted, wanting to reach but unable to move fast enough.

Luckily, she snapped out of it in time to fumble with the camera a bit before getting a good hold of it.

She felt it, too, Trey realized, before glancing up just in time to watch the back door of the SUV close with a *thunk*. Then the truck pulled out into traffic so fast a couple of cars had to swerve to avoid a collision, earning the blare of angry horns.

After a handful of seconds, the kids that had stopped to stare started moving again, except for Trey and Tai. They stood there, almost frozen to the spot, neither of them daring to move just yet.

That feeling that had washed through him? Through them? It was very similar to the icy sensation that often accompanied the swell of energy right before his magic leapt free and latched on to something nearby. Like his cello or his hair. But this time the energy was inverted because he hadn't been the source. No, this time, he'd been a nearby object for someone else's power to grab hold of. His heart pounded in his chest. A feeling like bees buzzed behind his eyes, filled his skull with enough pressure it left him light-headed. He swayed slightly and was only made steady again when he felt a hand in his. He knew it was Tai's without having to look.

Just like he knew, without any doubt, those people in the suits were trouble, and that woman had used magic.

7

After whatever the hell that was with those people in white out front, it was obvious Tai and her brother needed a moment to discuss what had clearly been a *situation*.

"I know a place," Trey had said before leading the way through the school and toward the band room.

According to her watch, they had about ten minutes before the final bell. Not enough time to talk about any of this, but enough to talk about talking about it.

"No one's in here this early," Trey had explained as they stepped out of the crowd and into the still dark space. He flicked the lights on and started up a wide set of risers. "The first class ain't till eleven, so we good."

They climbed to a small room tucked in the back where a bunch of other cellos and some basses waited. The cello room, as Trey called it, was quiet and cozy, if not a little musty.

The moment the door shut behind them, Tai powered on her camera and started flipping through the pictures she'd taken. She knew what she saw, and she knew she saw a hint of it on one of these. . . .

She fiddled with the settings on her camera's display while Trey worked to get his rental cello out of the cubby along the wall and get his new one set up in its place.

"Do you have any idea what the hell that was about?" Trey asked, panting slightly, his hands on his hips and the instruments now successfully swapped out.

Tai tried to keep from sounding annoyed. "It look like I do?" Did he seriously expect her to know anything about those weird people and their weird vibe?

Trey sighed and gestured at nothing. "No, I just . . . just thinking out loud, I guess. What you see? On the camera?"

"I'm . . . not sure." She shook her head, but her focus remained on the pictures as she played through them. Man, this thing was fast, it took so many. "That white woman, she— When I looked at her through the camera, she was surrounded by this red energy, like an aura."

"Aura?" Trey repeated, not exactly sounding confused but more like he was thinking hard, trying to puzzle something out. He even made his thinking face where he pressed his lips together and shut his eyes.

In all honestly, she was just glad he seemed to believe her. "Yes, aura! Energy, like in *Dragon Ball Z*?"

He opened one eye. "*DBZ*? So, what, her power level over nine thousand or something?"

"No, fool, just she was surrounded by a red aura, like they be surrounded by energy or whatever. And stop playing, this is serious."

"Sorry, sorry, just trying to break the tension. But you felt that, right? That chill in the air?"

She nodded as she flipped through a few more pictures before a flash of red caught her eye. Going back she found the one frame where the coloring around the woman looked off. But that wasn't the only thing. "I did, at the same time I saw what I saw," she said, once more fiddling with the display to try and clear up the image.

"You get a picture?" Trey asked before coming to hover behind her.

"I'm not sure." When she finished, the best she'd managed to do was get the image into a high contrast. It did the trick, sort of, illuminating a wavy bit of crimson outlining the woman's body. "Proof, I guess." She held the camera up so Trey could get a look.

"Mmm, barely. If you have to do all that to see it, no one will believe it's real. It looks like one of those *I saw bigfoot* pictures."

"I know." Heaving a frustrated sigh, she shook her head. "But it's all there is. You can't prove a feeling...."

There was a moment of silence while she messed with the settings a bit more, but nothing cleared up the image enough to give a definitive view.

"You ever feel anything like that before?" Trey asked, startling her a bit.

She hesitated. A memory wiggled at the back of her mind, distant but still distinct for . . . reasons. Reasons she wasn't exactly ready to admit to aloud, but Trey wasn't asking about those, was he? She could talk about this without going into personal detail. She hoped. "Once, a long time ago. Mom and I were sitting in the park, eating ice cream. My reward for doing so well at the dentist."

Trey snorted, sounding amused. "Ice cream after the dentist. Sounds about right."

Tai smiled too. It was a fond memory, really. "We were just

sitting there when all of a sudden I felt cold. Started at the top of my head, then moved down through me, like someone was—"

"Pouring water over you?"

She nodded, still studying the picture of the aura. "I told Mom I felt funny, and when she asked, 'Funny how?' I explained." Something twisted in Tai's chest, a faint ache that came with looking on old memories with new awareness. "She got this look on her face. I didn't recognize it, but it was like she was worried or afraid. Then she smiled and said we needed to go on a walk to work the ice cream off. We left the park and went halfway up town before doubling back—twice. Finally, we headed home."

"I think I remember that," Trey said, his voice quieting to match hers. "Everything seemed fine when y'all came home, but Mom said she had to talk to Dad about something important. That's when they let us have dessert before dinner. Second dessert for you."

Tai grinned. "Strawberry cake." She paused a moment and lowered her camera. "That was magic, what I felt, wasn't it? Back then and today?"

Trey shrugged. "I can't say for sure back then, but definitely today, yeah."

She felt her breath catch faintly with the confirmation. She had known, but now she *knew*. "That woman used magic." Even though the two of them were alone, Tai still lowered her voice when she used the m-word. So used to calling it a "situation," using the true word, the word they used to use when their mother was still with them, felt like an odd sort of betrayal. To who, she wasn't sure. "And we felt it. You think she . . . could feel ours?" It was hard to shake the mental image of the lady's head whipping around, staring right at them.

"Maybe," Trey said, his voice rough with some unnamed emotion.

Tai looked up at her brother, meeting his gaze. He tilted his head to the side, his eyes open, understanding even. *We're in this together, remember*, that look said. Just like Trey used to say. Only he hadn't in a long while.

Trey rubbed at the back of his head. "Should we tell Dad?"

Tai scoffed. "Tell him what? That there were maybe-magic people visiting the school today? What's he gonna do with that?"

"I don't know, but it's more than just a little coincidental that these reverse MIB mofos turn up on the sixteenth birthday of the only two magic niggas in this place. Unless you know someone else and been holding out."

Tai sighed. He had a point. "No, I don't."

"Okay, then, it might be nothing, it might be everything. Better safe than sorry, like Mom used to say."

"Mmm." For a moment, Tai's mind was hijacked by both a

curious ache at wanting to know what Mom would say about a situation like this, and a low, furious burn at the fact that she wasn't here to guide them through it.

And it wasn't because they had lost her, that she had been killed in an accident or taken by an illness or something. She just left one day and didn't come back. And...no! Tai didn't think Mom abandoned them, but...whatever happened she...wasn't here. That's where the hurt was rooted, no matter the cause.

"Tai?" A hand gripped her shoulder.

She sniffed and wiped at her eyes when she felt the warm run of tears against her cheek. "I'm fine, just..."

"I know." Trey blew out a breath and glanced around the room, his mind once again working.

"It's wild, right?" she started. "The idea that there are other magic people in the world. I mean, I didn't think we were the only ones, the magic had to come from somewhere, but we've never met anyone else who knows anything about it. Besides Mom."

"Well, no, but it's not like we were out there looking for people. It was very much the opposite, remember?"

She did remember. Tai glanced down at the camera in her hands as those memories filled her mind. Moments here and there when she was real little and she saw the beginnings of her burgeoning visions and exclaimed excitedly before she could help herself, or Trey got really angry about something and stuff around them acted weird. Things would randomly fall over or seem to leap off shelves on their own. Each time, Mom would pull the twins aside and patiently calm them until the situation passed.

That's when she would warn them not to share the truth of themselves with anyone that wasn't family. She had never seemed . . . afraid, but she'd always been adamant. They were to keep their abilities secret. Hidden.

Tai had never really questioned why, it was just normal in their house. Part of the way they switched between who they were at home and who they were at school or other public places. It made sense for so many other aspects of their lives, why not this one?

"I remember," Tai murmured.

Trey opened his mouth to say something else but was interrupted when the five-minute bell rang. Automatically the two of them moved to gather their things, Tai putting away her camera.

They slipped out of the cello room and made their way to the hall. The sound of kids shuffling toward their homerooms grew louder and louder. Just before reaching the door that led into the main hall, Trey caught her at the elbow.

"Wait a second."

She turned to peer up at him, her brow arched curiously.

"That woman, she didn't seem to notice us until you started taking pictures of her."

Tai felt an odd prickle of offense move through her. "You saying that was my fault?"

"What? No, there was nothing for anyone to be at fault for. Just, she didn't look our way until you were snapping photos. Maybe...if she is magic...you seeing her in your camera caught her attention."

That...shit, that was a good point.

"I'm just saying, maybe you should hold off on looking through your camera for a while? Like with the mirrors and stuff."

"Wait, stop taking pictures?"

"Just for now, until we figure out if other people actually can sense when you do. You can't control what you see, yeah? Best not to risk it."

Tai narrowed her eyes slightly. Trey sounded more like their father than she appreciated right now. So what his point was valid, that didn't mean she had to like it. "I can't. I gotta get more pictures for the yearbook."

"It can't wait till tomorrow?"

"I'm supposed to take some of the orchestra this afternoon, after you all get your little seating assignments."

Trey groaned and pinched the bridge of his nose. "I'll come up with an excuse. Say you're still getting used to your new camera. Or you broke it." He shrugged. "Mrs. D won't care. Hell, she'll probably appreciate getting the fifteen minutes back for practice. We've got a competition to prep for."

The three-minute bell went off.

"Just don't look through the camera until we get a chance to really sit and talk about this."

Rolling her eyes, Tai agreed, then followed her brother out into the nearly empty hall. He spared her a look, one that said not to do whatever it was she was thinking about doing. They hugged, brief and firm, then parted ways.

Before Tai reached her homeroom door, she already had her camera out of the bag again. And for three classes, any time she peeked through the viewfinder, she saw nothing but the natural scene before her. She supposed she should be lucky it wasn't happening, especially since there was a chance Trey's guess was right. That woman hadn't just looked their way because Tai was taking pictures. She'd looked their way the instant the red aura appeared.

Maybe she was *drawn to my magic....*

The bell rang for lunch, and Tai put her camera back around her neck to free up her hands in order to gather up her stuff. She was on second lunch period, while Trey was on first. That meant she would likely eat alone, or with Jasmine and the others. Honestly she didn't know if she was feeling super social right now.

She decided to eat alone and was almost to the cafeteria when the sound of her name drew her attention.

"Tai."

She paused. That wasn't her brother's voice, or anyone she knew, but it was definitely familiar.

"Tai!"

Spinning in place, she danced out of the way of the flow of students just as bodies parted and a familiar face emerged.

She felt a smile pull at her lips immediately. "Ayesha."

The other girl looked absolutely stunning in a jean skirt and bright pink baby tee. Her braids were pinned atop her head in a sort of messy bun.

Ayesha joined her off to the side of the hall. "Coming or going?"

"Wh-what?" Tai asked as her tongue tripped over itself a bit.

"Lunch. You coming or going?"

"Oh, I'm heading down."

Ayesha's smile widened, and her gaze played over Tai in a way that left her feeling slightly dizzy, but in a good way.

"Me too," Ayesha said. "Want some company?"

"Sure," Tai said, despite having made the decision to eat alone just five minutes ago. She turned to lead the way down the stairs and toward one of the two lines that had already formed. "Today is your second day, right?"

Ayesha grabbed a couple of trays, holding one out to Tai. "Yup."

She took it, feeling silly for simply having forgotten to grab one. "How you liking it so far?"

Ayesha shrugged. "It's a school. I don't know nobody, 'cept you and a few other people."

"Eh, you ain't missing much."

The way Ayesha chuckled made Tai's butterflies go into overdrive. Heat filled her face.

"You really into taking pictures, huh?" Ayesha asked.

Tai glanced up from where she'd been rubbing at a spot on her tray to make sure it was discoloration and not dirt. "Mmm?"

Ayesha gestured to the camera hung against Tai's chest.

"O-oh, yeah, I . . . I do some pictures. I mean photography. I do . . . photography."

Ayesha's smile only widened. "You always this articulate?"

A sudden rise of excitement made Tai feel like she just might burst. "Yoooo, no one else I talk to seems to know that movie exist!"

"Girl, *Hercules* is a whole masterpiece." Ayesha stepped into the line first, pushing her tray along the counter and picking out from the selections.

"I *know*, right!"

"The music is on point, especially the songs from the Muses, and Meg is just...can cartoon characters be hot? Because she hot."

Tai lifted her free hand, the other pushing her steadily filling tray. "*Thank* you! Someone who has some sense. It's hard out here wanting to *be* a Disney Princess *and* date one."

"I hear that." Ayesha led the way over to the cashier where she paid for both their lunches, resulting in another flush of heat in Tai's face, before she came to a stop at a row of tables. "Okay, where to?"

Tai glanced around the room and spotted where she would usually sit for a few minutes before her friends joined her, but instead decided to head for the double doors that led out into the courtyard.

She chose a table near the far end, partway in the shade. A few people called out to her in greeting, and she returned the hellos.

Ayesha set her tray down and settled in behind it. She wiggled her eyebrows. "Someone's popular."

"Not really. I know a few people, and they know me." Tai toyed with her mac and cheese. In truth, calling it that was a bit generous. It was more like a random assortment of noodles and pasteurized cheese product. She swallowed down a bite.

"So, when you say you do photography, you don't mean like paparazzi or nothing, right?" Ayesha gestured up and down with her spoon at nothing in particular. "Because I have this cousin who had this boyfriend? He was paparazzi, which got his ass beat one time by Dre, so she say."

Tai's eyes widened. "That really happen?"

Ayesha shrugged. "Just what she say."

"Whoa. No, nothing like that. I'm on the yearbook staff," Tai admitted. "It's kinda whack, but it means I have a steady supply of film and, while taking pictures for the school, I can sneak in some shorts. I'm building a portfolio."

"Portfolio, ain't we fancy," Ayesha said with a smile as she took a bite of her turkey sandwich.

Tai sort of envied her, she didn't know why she chose the meat loaf and sides, *no one* chooses the meat loaf and sides, but here she was. "Less fancy and more . . ." She trailed off as a sudden wave of nerves overtook her.

She'd never really talked about what she wanted to do with her photography out loud before. There were the conversations here and there with her dad and her brother, but no one outside of the family knew that's what she wanted to do. Sure, it was probably easy to guess, but this? Confirming it?

A hand fell over Tai's drawing her out of her thoughts. She glanced up and into Ayesha's worried face.

"Everything okay?" Ayesha asked.

"Yeah." Tai pulled on what she hoped was a believable smile.

"I'm good. Just not used to people asking me about my photography. People who aren't family, anyway."

"I get it." Ayesha squeezed her hand, then withdrew her touch, leaving Tai's skin warm. "I'm a poet. Or I wanna be. But, according to everyone, that's not a real job, so I should focus on something else. And, FYI, taking pictures for the yearbook and stuff isn't whack."

Tai felt something inside her just turn to mush. She hesitated a moment before twisting her fingers to tangle with Ayehsa's, just a little. "People suck. Poetry is an incredible art form. You should do what makes your heart happy."

Ayesha smiled, her attention trained on their fingers, now sort of woven together but mostly not. "Should I? *Anything* that makes my heart happy?"

"Y-yeah . . ." Tai's fingers twitched slightly before she withdrew her hand to reach for her camera bag.

"I'll keep that in mind." Ayesha's voice dipped a little low, and the sound threatened to get Tai's butterflies going again.

"You know what would make *my* heart happy?" Tai asked, hoping her voice didn't betray her nerves. "Let me take your picture." Okay, so it wasn't the best idea. And she'd told Trey she wouldn't, but . . . what was one picture? Besides, she wanted to test a theory.

Ayesha snorted as she took another bite of her sandwich. "What, right now?"

"Yeah!" Tai beamed. "And later. Tomorrow. Anytime, really. All the time? That . . . sounds creepy, I—I'm sorry."

When Ayesha burst into laughter, Tai wanted to drop down through the ground and vanish. Everything had been going so well! Then she couldn't stop talking, and the words just fell out of her mouth after bypassing her brain completely.

"It does," Ayesha agreed. "But I know what you mean, so it's cute. Yeah, you can take my picture." She propped her elbows on the table, rested her chin in her hands, and fluttered her eyelashes. "How's this? Too much?"

The warm, trembly feeling from before returned. So did Tai's smile. "No, that's perfect."

She lifted the camera.

8

rey smoothed his hands over his cello, *his* cello—he was never going to get tired of that—as he positioned it between his knees. Around him, his fellow musicians situated themselves similarly. The usual chatter and random snatches of notes filled the air, but there was a nervous undercurrent to the cacophony.

Usually the day after auditions, there would be a string of sheets printed out and plastered on the chalkboard to display the new seating arrangement. The board was blank, and Mrs. Downy was nowhere to be found. That in and of itself wasn't strange, since orchestra was immediately after lunch; she sometimes didn't show up until right before the bell, but for the list to be missing as well?

"This feels weird," Zoraida murmured as she twisted at the pegs on her instrument. "Why does this feel weird?"

Trey shrugged, plucking idly at a few notes from *The Swan*.

"Maybe she ran out of ink and she went to print the list in the library?"

"Maybe..." But Trey didn't think that would be the issue. Zoraida was right, something about this felt weird, but he was trying not to think too hard about it, or he might mess up his hair again. He didn't have to fight it for long, because Mrs. D came sweeping into the room in a whirl of papers and a maxi skirt.

"Sorry, everyone!" she called above the shrill shriek of the bell. "Apologies for the delay." She smoothed her hands over her flushed face, her long, thin fingers catching at some of the hairs that escaped her messy French braid.

She stumbled as she stepped up onto the conductor's stand, earning a rise of gasps from around the room. Then she barked a nervous sort of laugh and held up a hand. "I'm fine. A klutz but fine." Fumbling with the folder under her arm, she set some sheet music on her stand, murmuring "Okay" to herself over and over again, her lips thin, her face pale.

Trey and Zoraida traded glances, and so did most of the rest of the orchestra.

Finally a voice called from somewhere in the viola section, "You good, Mrs. D?"

Mrs. Downy stopped mid-shuffle and took a quick breath. She plastered on one of those smiles adults often pull out, the kind that look more annoyed than happy. A smile that said she most definitely was *not* good, but she couldn't talk about it.

"Just a bit of administrative frustration, which happens, right?" She nodded eagerly and cleared her throat. "Don't worry about it, it's nothing, really."

More glances were shared.

Then Zoraida raised her hand.

Mrs. Downy heaved a breath as she smoothed a palm over her hair. "Yes, Zoraida, what is it?"

"Uhm, are we gonna get our seat assignments?"

The way Mrs. D blinked for a second made it seem like she didn't know what Zoraida was talking about. Then she huffed a breath in realization and lifted both hands into the air. "The seats! Right, the seats. Sorry, I've got a lot on my mind. And I must apologize for this as well. Something . . . happened to the recorder part way through the playback. I was able to listen to the first half of the auditions. The other half, well, unfortunately, they're just gone."

A mix of frustrated and relieved groans rose around the room.

"Thank god, do over."

"I'm not gonna be able to repeat that! It was accidental gold!"

"What happens now?"

Trey felt his own frustration rise. That audition was probably the best he'd ever played in his life. Could he do it again? Sure, maybe, but what if it wasn't as good? He'd gone through hell to make it for that audition. Literal clown-hair hell. If he had to do that again, who knew *what* he would turn into!

A slight shiver moved through Trey, followed by a soft *plunk*.

He froze. He knew that feeling. He knew that sound. He knew it intimately, and he hoped, prayed he was wrong. But when he glanced down, sure enough, his D string was slack.

"Damn," he hissed between clenched teeth.

"What happe— Oooooh." Zoraida reached to finger what was now essentially a loose bit of wire. "You got an extra?"

"Nope. Because this is new. Brand-new, I got it *today* for my birthday!"

"Oh, wow...yeah, that sucks, man."

Sucks didn't begin to cut it. Broken cello strings weren't a bad thing on their own. More than a few had popped over time, it happens. But that shudder that moved through him just before the string snapped meant it didn't break on its own. He'd done this.

Not intentionally, just like he never intentionally changed his hair or flung a chair across the room or demolished the stage at a talent show. And while he'd managed to build enough control over his abilities that he hadn't done anything destructive in a while, he definitely just snapped his string.

Damn. It.

The beginnings of another shiver settled over his shoulders, and he shut his eyes. The anxiety from before the audition was trying to make a comeback, coupled with the anger about his string, which only fed the anxiety, which then fed the anger. *Stop it! Just . . . stop.*

He tried to focus on breathing deep and slow. If he didn't rein this in, something worse could happen. In, then out. One breath, Then another. A third. When he felt he had a handle on his soft-boiled emotions, his hand shot into the air.

Mrs. D flapped a hand at him as she heaved her own breath. "Yes, Terrance?"

"My string broke; are there any extras?"

She blinked a few times before nodding rapidly, smiling brightly, clearly happy to have a basic problem to solve. "Yes, which one?"

"D."

Her expression fell. "Oh, no, I'm sorry. I expect to get a few in by the end of the week, but none at the moment."

"Can I get the one off my rental?"

"That could work, yes, go ahead. And the rest of you, pull out the concerto. We're going to get started with practice. I'll let you know when I get a new recorder for the audition redux."

Trey set his instrument down and climbed toward the cello room.

"Ayesha, could you play the solo while Terrance gets things together?"

"Yes, ma'am."

Trey paused at the door to glance over his shoulder at the back of Ayesha's head. She shuffled through the music and drew her cello up as tuning started. This close, he could hear her instrument sing beautifully, the sound full and rich, spilling thick into the air. Still slick.

Chewing on both awe and envy, he ducked into the room and made quick work to get the other cello out. Then he started to carefully unwind the string, steeling glances over his shoulder as he worked. Through the window that peered out into the practice room proper, he could see Mrs. Downy wave up the count, and then music filled the air.

The sound of Ayesha's cello rose with the other soloists, the music bubbling up against the window of the cello room, muffled slightly by the barrier of glass, but still no less powerful. The high notes pierced the air. The low ones rumbled fully.

Trey stilled, letting the music take hold of him as it often did, but usually he was caught up in playing it. Listening was . . . a completely different experience, especially when listening to a piece he knew how to play. A piece that Ayesha could clearly play just as well. Maybe even better?

Trey's fingers tightened where they had hold of the rental cello.

Another shiver rolled down his arms.

His breath caught. "Wh— No!"

Plunk.

He stared, his brain having trouble catching up with what his eyes and heart already knew. The D string he'd been unwinding carefully came loose in his fingers, useless. He balled them into a fist, his hands shaking. Behind him the window groaned, though he doubted anyone else heard it.

Another deep breath, then another. *Keep it together. . . .*

As the song crescendoed behind him, Trey closed the case and set the cello back in its case before descending the risers in defeat. When he sat down, the pieces of string in his hand, he held them up when both Mrs. Downy, then Zoraida glanced his way curiously.

Zoraida winced but kept playing. Mrs. Downy nodded but kept conducting. And behind him, as the rest of the orchestra's sound faded, Ayesha's solo crackled in the air, alive and thriving.

For sixteen minutes, Trey listened to his orchestra play without him.

Then Mrs. Downy twisted her hand into a fist, ending the piece. She breathed a delighted sigh, all previous stress faded from her face. "Well, that was splendid indeed," she said, her eyes on Ayesha. "And I'm not at all surprised."

"Thank you," Ayesha said, beaming.

"Excellent. Take a moment to rest, then we'll do it again." Mrs. Downy cleared her throat, looking at Trey as everyone started talking, marking spots on their music, or setting their instruments down to flex their fingers.

"Terrance, could I speak to you for a moment?"

"Huh? Yeah, sure." Trey pulled himself up and shuffled after her. The two stepped into her office. She shut the door behind them.

This . . . this wasn't good. "Sorry about the strings," he started, but he paused when she shook her head and smiled somewhat sadly.

"Actually," she hedged. "I wanted to talk to you about your audition."

Trey blinked, straightening slightly. "I thought you said the recording was messed up."

"It was, but that's not what I . . . Oh, heavens, what I mean is I wanted to talk to you about being section leader. I know you've been putting in a lot of work these past couple of years. The extra practice sessions with myself and your fellow students, and I know you care about the music, and the people who play with you. You are an incredibly gifted musician. Truly a one-of-a-kind talent."

Trey felt something very close to pride swell in his chest. He fought against smiling. "Thanks."

"Of course," she said, smiling enough for them. Then she sighed. "Which is why I hope you don't take this as a judgment of your abilities."

Trey felt his nonexistent smile fall. *Wait...*

"Because I didn't come to this decision lightly."

No, oh no.

"And we'll revisit it, of course, at the start of the next quarter, but for this opening competition..."

Please...

"I'm going to put Ayesha in first chair."

Trey stood in stunned silence. Again, his brain was trying to catch up with the rest of the world. This wasn't happening. This couldn't be happening. "But... the auditions."

"Yours and Ayesha's were part of the group that I was able to listen to. In truth, they're two of the best auditions I've heard my entire time here at Clayton. But I had to make a decision, and I chose—"

"The *new* girl!?" Trey hated the way his voice cracked against the sting of betrayal that bubbled up inside him.

Mrs. Downy lifted her hands. "I know, I know she's new, but I have to do what's best for the orchestra as a whole. Ayesha knows this concerto backward and forward. She's played it at competition before, she'll be able to score high on the solos, and while I know you would as well, she's a sure thing. You'd want that, for the ensemble, right?"

Trey just stared. He couldn't speak. He couldn't move. At least, he thought he couldn't. But then he felt himself nodding.

Mrs. Downy heaved a heavy and very relieved sigh. "Good, good. Great. I apologize if I made it seem like you might be in some sort of trouble, I just wanted to tell you myself before the list went up. You deserve that."

"Y-yeah," Trey said, though he didn't say, his body on autopilot did. "Thanks." *Why are you thanking her??*

"You're welcome." She patted his shoulder lightly, then reached around him with a somewhat awkward shuffle to pull the door open. "If you wish, since you don't have an instrument to play, you can study in the cello room or go to the library for an impromptu study hall."

Trey just nodded. Then he turned and slipped out of her office without another word. She followed behind him, clapping her hands to gain the orchestra's attention while he moved to gather his things.

What's wrong? Zoraida mouthed when she managed to catch his eye.

He didn't answer, instead just took his shit and headed for the back.

"Okay, focus, everyone," Mrs. Downy called. "Let's get ready to go through it again. Ayesha. Since we've lost our Terrance to an unfortunate stringing, please move down here for the rest of practice, yes?"

"Oh, yes, ma'am." Ayesha promptly gathered her things, a wide smile on her face.

It wasn't her fault. Trey knew that. But he couldn't help the flare of anger that rose inside as he watched her settle in what should've been his chair.

He couldn't stay here. He made quick work of packing up his cello, tucking it into his cubby. Then he grabbed his bag and jacket and headed for the door. The crystalline ring of Ayesha's solo chased him down the hall.

I t was the end of the day, and Tai just knew she was trippin'.

She stared at Ayesha, not entirely sure she heard right, so she asked again. "Wait, you'd...really come?"

The two of them stood in the hallway in front of Ayesha's open locker, where she swapped out books between it and her bag.

"You invited me, it would be rude to decline a birthday girl—*on* her birthday at that."

"Oh, I invited you, huh?" Tai grinned as she arched an eyebrow.

"Okay, you said cake and I invited myself." Ayesha snorted a faint laugh. "But you ain't said no, have you?"

Tai worried at her lower lip with her teeth. She'd been working her way up to seeing if Ayesha wanted to have cake and ice cream, but the other girl beat her to the punch by asking if Tai was down to visit this nice café nearby. They had some bomb cupcakes. Any other time Tai would've loved to go, especially with the cute new girl, but she already had plans. Birthday plans, in fact, a not-party with her dad and Trey.

"Just some cake, ice cream, maybe some board games or some *Mario Kart*," Tai had said, still trying to figure out how to make the ask.

"What kinda cake?"

"Usually marble. I like vanilla, my brother likes chocolate, so it's a compromise that works weirdly."

Ayesha made this little noise at the back of her throat that was almost a whine. "Marble cake—don't play with my emotions."

"I'm not! We always get it."

"My momma *hates* marble cake," Ayesha lamented. "And my grandma is allergic to chocolate anyways. Which sucks because it's my favorite, so I get it wherever I can whenever I can. Sorry, birthday girl, I have to use you for your cake."

"Use me for my cake?" Tai said around a laugh.

"If you insist."

"Wha— Oh my god! You're too much!"

Ayesha had clicked her tongue before reaching to lightly tangle her fingers with Tai's as they walked. Fire once more filled her cheeks, and she pursed her lips to try and hide the smile that wanted to open her face.

Now they held hands once more as they made their way toward the front of the school. Tai did her best to ignore some of the looks they got as they went. She knew what those looks meant. How some people would act weird tomorrow, encounters becoming more and more awkward until they stopped happening at all. Murmurs and glances behind her back, sometimes in her face. Whispered words like coals against her soul. *Dyke. Queer. Lesbo.*

Words that had followed her for a year and a half of middle school, after she confessed to having a crush on this girl in her history class. Gabriela had been sweet about the whole thing, despite it being awkward as all hell. Looking back on it, blurting out that you *like* like someone while washing your hands in the bathroom definitely wasn't the move. But Gabby was complaining about how her dress made her look like a toddler and it was picture day so she was *real* upset.

What had started out as Tai trying to reassure the other girl that she was still very pretty despite the dress soon turned into more than either of them really bargained for. Gabby told Tai it was okay, even helped her calm down from the near panic attack at having said the words aloud.

The next day it was all over school that Tai Watson kisses girls in the bathroom stalls. Took a few fights, one two-day suspension, and an almost rabid display of her genuine love for the Backstreet Boys to get people to leave her the hell alone about it, but . . .

But she didn't want to think about any of that. Especially not with Ayesha, in a brand-new moment. A magical instance buoyed by this unidentifiable feeling swelling in Tai's chest. She'd only met Ayesha yesterday, and though they'd only spent hours together, she couldn't puzzle piece together how it already felt like weeks, maybe months. Friendship was easy, but this was more, yet not enough at the same time. Just right, for right now.

No, instead of giving any energy to the homophobes and haters, Tai focused on Ayesha and the way she shone that made everything else seem to fade. She silently hoped Trey was okay with her bringing home a . . . date? Yeah, her and Trey agreed not to have a party, it would be just family, but they never said they *didn't* want people there. In fact, she had said something about maybe inviting someone to join them, and he had seemed fine with it, so it would be okay.

She needed it to be okay.

There was no reason it wouldn't be; she was just being silly.

The two girls emerged from the building and made their way down the stairs amid a throng of other students. "My brother usually has to take care of some stuff before we head home, so he'll be another ten, fifteen minutes."

"I'm not in any rush," Ayesha said as she squeezed Tai's hand.

Tai nodded, still smiling like a fool. "Mmm, let me take a few more pictures while we wait." It would be okay, she told herself again. That first picture had proven her theory correct. Kinda. Elva had only shown up when she used the old camera and wasn't nowhere to be seen with the new one.

Ayesha smiled that big, beautiful smile of hers. "Okay, where you want me?"

The front walkway was still filled with kids, though there was some space over near the tree she usually met Trey under. The sun was a little low in the sky, but still high enough to give up some golden light. Tai gestured for Ayesha to move front to back, then left and right in order to get her centered perfectly.

"Okay, tilt your head back so the light catches your skin."

Ayesha pursed her lips as if blowing a kiss while following instructions.

"Gorgeous," Tai said as she snapped pictures.

Ayesha struck a few poses, always finding her light in each. Tai was about to tell her she was a natural model when a shadow cast itself over her. The thing was, there wasn't a cloud in the sky. Tai glanced up from the camera, and the shadow vanished.

Oh no. She hesitated as Ayesha struck another pose before lifting the camera once more. The shadow had fallen over her completely now, only it wasn't a shadow, Tai realized. At least, most shadows weren't blue. The "shadow" pulsed gently, reaching in from the left in order to swallow Ayesha, nearly strangling her. Tai turned her camera and nearly recoiled at the sight of her brother striding toward them, his face tight.

"Ooooh, he mad," Tai murmured to herself. The dark blue cloud was indeed coming from her brother, the same way that red one had come from that woman.

"Trey?" Tai asked as he got within earshot. "What's wrong?"

"What makes you think something's wrong?" he muttered.

"Besides the fact that it's written all over your face?" Tai glanced around self-consciously before lifting her camera and wiggling it. "I could see it."

He blinked, his expression loosening a bit at that. "Wait, really?" He glanced around to examine the air, as if he would be able to see for himself. His gaze drifted toward Ayesha briefly, trailed off, then snapped back. He started, as if stricken to see her. "What're *you*—"

"Oh, sup, Terrance." Ayesha's voice cut through as she stepped forward from where she'd hung back a respectable distance.

"It's Trey," he corrected flatly.

"Trey, my bad. Mrs. D called you that, I didn't mean—"

"Teachers don't do nicknames." He pointed a finger and wagged it between the two of them. "Y'all know each other?"

Tai couldn't help smiling, though she felt a stab of panic. If she said Ayesha was the girl from the festival, she'd sort of be admitting she had been talking about her. No way she was going to let that happen, she didn't wanna look sprung. Despite how she might feel.

"Yeah, we met the other day," Tai said dismissively

Out of the corner of her eye, she could see Ayesha tilt her head a little.

The panic from before bubbled over into anxious regret. Did Ayesha think Tai was rejecting her somehow? She hurried to correct herself. "And we, uhm...had lunch together, today. She been helping me break in the new camera."

Trey glanced back and forth between them before his gaze lingered on his sister. "Huh."

"Wait," Tai said as something occurred to her. She then made a similar gesture between Trey and Ayesha. "You two know each other, too?"

Ayesha stole a glance at Trey. "Yup."

"Orchestra," Trey said, tight-lipped.

Tai turned a curious but impressed look toward Ayesha. She'd heard those kids play, knew the dedication that went into it after years of watching her brother. "Really? What do you play?"

"Cello." Ayesha flicked a glance toward Trey again.

"Oh! Wow, Trey plays that! Buuuuut I guess you knew that already, heh. That's cool you both play cello."

Trey made a noise at the back of his throat. "Ayesha's the one playing right now."

Tai was about to ask what he meant by that, because the energy of the conversation was really weird, but then Trey pulled his hand out of his pocket and held up what looked like a wire.

"Broke a string right at the start of practice," he muttered, his tone dropping.

And suddenly his dour mood made sense. The first day he goes to play his new cello and this happened? She stuck her lower lip out in a sympathetic pout before leaning in to give him a hug. He stiffened in her hold.

"Dad can probably get another one easy."

"Yeah," Trey mumbled, then shoved his hands into his pockets. He looked at Ayesha, and something in his expression worried Tai. "You sounded pretty good today. You been playing long?"

"Practically my whole life," Ayesha said, and that gorgeous smile of hers appeared again. "Mom said I was born with a cello in my hand. Clearly that's not possible, but it feels like that sometimes, you know?"

"Yeah." Trey chewed at his lower lip and nodded. To anyone who didn't know him, he'd look contemplative, but Tai could read the rising tension in the lines of his face. That was the thing about being a twin, while her brother might look calm and collected on the outside, she could see the roiling beneath the surface. Trey was upset. She had an idea why, but she didn't want to somehow make it worse by asking if something more than a broken string happened.

Ayesha flapped a hand to indicate the twins. "You never said how you two know each other."

"Oh!" Tai said in realization. "Trey's my brother."

Ayesha's eyebrows lifted. "For real?" She looked them both up and down, then nodded. "Okay, yeah, I definitely see it. So being an artist runs in the family?"

Tai's smile faltered a little, but she didn't let it fall. "Yeah, it does."

"We need to get going so we can meet Dad," Trey said, adjusting his backpack.

"Okay, okay, let me pack up." She moved to gather her things where she had set them aside to start their impromptu photo shoot, thanking Ayesha when she held out the camera bag. Once that was done, and there was no reason to keep avoiding the subject, Tai cleared her throat. "So, I invited Ayesha to come have cake with us." She didn't miss the look Trey tossed her way.

"I hope that's okay," Ayesha said as she grabbed her backpack.

"I told her it would be." Tai smiled, hoping to assuage some of the tension she could feel rolling off of Trey.

He was quiet a moment before shrugging. "It's whatever."

Evidently, it wasn't. But this wasn't the time or place to get into whatever was going on. Still, her brother was hurting, and Tai didn't like that. She reached to give his arm a squeeze, though paused when a sudden chill rushed through her, like ice water being poured over her head.

At the same time, Trey straightened and his eyes widened. He'd felt it, too.

Without a word, both of them glanced down the walkway, searching for . . .

"There," Trey murmured, gaze trained toward the north end of the block.

Tai hesitated a moment so it wouldn't be obvious, then turned as if she was going to start talking to Ayesha but let her eyes sweep over the sidewalk as she did. Sure enough, she spotted the trio of white folks from this morning, their white suits almost glowing in the sun. She let her gaze keep right on going to Ayesha's face and barely managed a smile. "Cake time!"

Trey lowered his gaze to fiddle with the broken string. "They're watching us."

Tai knew the truth of it without having to look. Even at this distance, she could feel the uncomfortable heat of their gazes.

"What do we do?" he continued.

"Wait, hold up, who's watching what?" Ayesha asked, her brow furrowed.

Tai swiped at the sweat starting to bead on her forehead. Shit. She didn't wanna get Ayesha mixed up in all this, whatever "this" turned out to be, especially if it had anything remotely to do with magic. For one, magic was a *family* secret to keep; it wasn't hers alone to share.

She took a breath. "This might sound out there, but those white people were here this morning, and we kinda sorta think they might be looking for us. Maybe it's a coincidence, but I don't like it, so we wanna go."

To Ayesha's credit, she didn't do more to react other than lift an eyebrow as she looked back and forth between the twins. Tai was kinda impressed; she half expected her to think they were being a little overly sensitive.

"'Nuff said, I can give you two a ride home, if you want. That way we can see if they're actually shady."

Tai blinked, fully taken by surprise. Her mouth worked wordlessly a few times before she glanced at Trey, who looked thoughtful now instead of mildly offended. He met her gaze and shrugged, which was pretty much a go ahead.

"Y-yeah, thank you," Tai said, warmth blossoming beneath the appreciation filling her chest.

"No problem. This way." Ayesha shouldered her bag and made a brief show of glancing around in search of something before finding whatever it was and heading that direction. Trey and Tai fell in behind her.

It took everything in her not to look over her shoulder as they went. Caught between that and wanting to break into a run, she focused on the sound of their steps.

"Are they following?" Ayesha asked.

"No idea," Trey said. "Don't nobody look."

Tai's neck started to ache. Thankfully they reached the edge of the parking lot and turned to—

"No, this way," Ayesha called as she kept walking straight.

Tai blinked before following, glancing at Trey, who shrugged once more. *Where are we going?* said the look he aimed at her. She was just as lost, especially when they crossed the street at the other end of the block.

She started to voice her curiosity when Ayesha cut to the side right quick and stepped up to the back door of a dark Mercedes.

Trey stopped dead in his tracks. "Is that a Maybach?" he all but squeaked.

Ayesha tugged open the back door and waved Tai over. "Trey, you hop up front with Pete. Hey, Pete."

Then Ayesha disappeared into the car.

Tai exchanged a brief glance with her brother and was able to spot over his shoulder that the people in white were headed toward them, practically at a run. "Get in the car!" She ducked into the back seat and shut the door.

When Trey did the same, the Maybach merged into the slowly but steadily moving traffic. As they pulled off, Tai watched out the window, waiting to see what the trio did. A Tahoe pulled up just in time to block her view.

She sunk down into the seat, heaving a shaky sigh. The stab of fear that took her heart just then had been brief but sharp. It had surfed her nerves, leaving her trembling slightly. Those people had come after them.

"Everything okay, Miss Davis?" a middle-aged white man said from the driver seat. Tai could only see his profile as he kept his eyes on the road. He had a thin but friendly face from what she could make of it.

Ayesha shoved her braids over her shoulder and made herself comfortable in the large leather seat. "We're good. These are some new friends from school. Tai, Trey, this is Pete."

The white man tapped two gloved fingers to the side of his head before flicking them away in a salute.

"And, uhm...I don't wanna sound rude," Trey started.

"But you're gonna power through," Tai said.

He aimed a look at her before continuing. "Just who is Pete to you?"

The white man chuckled faintly.

Ayesha buckled her seat belt, then waved her hand. "Pete's a friend of the family."

Trey twisted in his seat to stare at her. "That drives you around in a *Maybach*? Psshhh, where you find them kinda friends at?"

"The same place you find bodyguard kinda friends, I guess," Pete said, grinning. His teeth were real white and straight, almost weirdly so. His dark hair was buzzed close to his scalp.

Trey stared at him a second before reaching back to draw his seat belt on as well.

Tai swallowed thickly as her gaze traveled over the inside of this ridiculously expensive car. Probably cost more than their whole house. At the mention of bodyguards, she whipped around to peer at Ayesha. "Why do you need a bodyguard?"

"I don't! Pete just says that to mess with people." Ayesha aimed a sneer at him. "He's just my chauffeur."

"That *just* is doing a lot of heavy lifting," Trey said. "I knew that cello had to come from money. Didn't know they was gonna be *rich* rich, though."

Ayesha rolled her eyes, then snuck a side glance at Tai. "This isn't a problem, is it?"

"That you're rich? Girl, why would that ever be a problem?" Tai laughed. It somehow managed to feel both genuine and hollow at the same time. A feeling that deepened when Ayesha's relieved laughter rose as well.

"Trey, give Pete your address so we can take you home."

"At once, Madame Moneybags."

Tai had to laugh at that one, especially when Ayesha rolled her eyes. But then Tai reached out and tapped the back of Ayesha's hand where it rested on the seat between them.

"Thanks," she murmured when Ayesha glanced up at her.

"You don't have to thank me." Ayesha turned her hand so their fingers could weave together kinda like how they did at lunch. Warmth filled Tai's face, and she quickly shot a glance at the back of her brother's head, but he was caught up in something Pete was showing him about the features on the dash.

"You didn't have to offer to take us anywhere," Tai said. "And I feel bad. A lil. Especially . . . now that those people have seen your car. What if they come after you? I should've thought about that before."

"They shouldn't be going after nobody, but if they wanna try it with me? That's what Pete is for." Ayesha grinned. "He's technically not *my* bodyguard but that don't mean he's not *a* bodyguard, so he still got it." The smile faded from her face. "Do you know what they want?"

Tai shook her head. "No." A partial truth. She had an idea, especially after *feeling* them before seeing them this time. There was no mistake, it was the same light chill that moved through her whenever she saw something, only dialed up to a hundred. Magic was involved somehow.

"You need to tell someone about them," Ayesha continued.

"We'll tell my dad, definitely. See what he says." Ayesha nodded and settled back in her seat.

They rode in silence nearly the whole way home, but at some

point Pete let Trey pick the radio station. Soon enough they were *going down, down, baby, yo' street in a Range Rover.* Pete nodded along with every song while the three of them hollered the lyrics and rocked in their seats.

When they pulled onto their street, the few people who were out walking or sitting on their porches caught sight of the car. They turned and pointed, whistled and hollered compliments, especially when Trey rolled down the window and started throwing peace signs and hollering back.

"Okay, now we see you!"

"What this boy doin', who you know like that!"

"Ayyyy! Trey! Nice ride!"

"Now how you end up in something like that?"

Trey cupped his hand to shout. "It was a birthday present!"

Pete pulled in along the curb and parked, then turned to Ayesha. "Am I waiting?"

"Probably," Ayesha said. "I'm gonna have cake and ice cream with them for their birthday. Think we'll be cool for a couple of hours?"

Pete turned in his seat to look them both over. That's when Tai noticed his left eye had gone fully white. Scar tissue pulled at a long-since-healed slice across it, his brow, and his cheek, like right out of one of those violent-ass video games Trey be playing.

"Happy birthday to you both. Nice to meet you." He offered a hand to Trey, who took it with a slight look of awe on his face.

"Thanks, man. And thanks for the ride."

"Not a problem." Pete nodded to Tai, who'd already opened her door. He was nice, but she didn't like touching strangers.

"Thanks," she said, returning his nod.

"I might go a few blocks over to get some chow," he called as Ayesha climbed out.

"That's fine. I'll page you if I need you sooner."

With that he pulled off.

More shouts and whistles followed them up the stairs. As they approached the door, Tai could hear the bump-thump of music on the other side, along with the dulcet tone of a woman singing R&B in a low voice. Sure enough, when she opened the door, Toni Braxton's "He Wasn't Man Enough" poured out onto the street around them. Dad's voice carried with it, off key but still confident as hell.

"What in the world . . . ?" Tai led the way inside and through the living room to the kitchen.

Dad stood over the stove with a towel on one shoulder. He stirred something, whipping the utensil and his head on beat as he belted about dumping somebody's husband and not thinking about him.

Trey snorted a laugh and Tai shot a look at Ayesha, who had pursed her lips paper-thin to try and hide her own amusement. Dad kept singing, lifting a spoon covered in some sort of red sauce and singing into it. He turned to grab something off the island and froze when he saw them standing there.

The barest beat passed before he threw himself back into his performance, holding his hand out toward them dramatically. "Do you know he begged to stay with me? He wasn't man enough for me!"

"Glad to hear that," Trey said as he reached to turn down the volume on the radio on the counter.

"Y'all home a little early," Dad said.

"My friend Ayesha gave us a ride." Tai gestured to her by way of introduction.

Dad glanced over his shoulder again and smiled. "Nice to meet you, Ayesha. You staying for cake and ice cream?"

She nodded. "Yes, sir. Thank you for having me."

"No problem. Y'all go wash up and get everything set up in the living room." He turned back to what could be identified now both by smell and sight to be his famous Bolognese. Other ingredients lining the counter meant they would have some lasagna tonight. Dad got the recipe from his great-grandma, who—according to him—said the secret to the best lasagna was patience, attention to detail, and gossip. But if you didn't have anyone to sit and drink with you in the kitchen, you just added a little extra wine. Never hurt anyone.

Trey hit the stairs, taking them two at a time.

Tai went slower, gesturing for Ayesha to follow.

Once in her room, she felt a little self-conscious of the *Outlaw Star* poster over her bed, and the Cardcaptor Sakura wall scroll on the back of her door when she closed it. She left a crack in it a few inches so it would feel private but not weird.

"Welcome to my room." She gestured around as she let her bag slide down her arm. "I know it's probably not much compared to what your room must look like."

Ayesha turned from where she was examining a magazine fold-out of Lil' Bow Wow that had been pulled out and taped to the wall, stapler holes be damned. "Please don't do that," she said softly, setting her bag on the floor. That's when Tai noticed it was Louis Vuitton. LOUIS. FREAKING. VUITTON.

"Do what?" Tai asked, genuinely curious.

"Start putting yourself and your space down because you think I'm used to 'better' or something. Whatever I am or am not used to has no impact on the worth of you and your things, okay?"

Tai nodded slowly. It sounded like Ayesha had given this speech before. Tai hadn't considered that's what she was doing, but ... *makes sense*.

"I get that enough from cousins and stuff." Ayesha turned to peer around the room.

"My bad," Tai apologized. "Won't happen again."

Ayesha smiled, and man, she looked so good, her dimples popping into view like that. "Can I use the bathroom?"

A couple seconds passed before Tai shook herself out of staring. "Oh! Yeah, it— Second door on the left."

"Meet you downstairs." With a wink that made Tai's throat tight, Ayesha slipped through the door. Tai stared after her like some lovesick puppy before shaking herself out of it.

"Get a grip," she hissed at herself, then hurried over to her desk in order to set her camera bag down. She checked the charge and plugged it in before hurrying for her door.

Out in the hall she nearly ran smack into Trey. He must've been waiting on them.

"When you wanna tell Dad 'bout the people in white?" he asked as he glanced toward the end of the hall.

The music was turned back up. Not as loud as before, but there was no way Dad could hear them talking.

"Over dinner, maybe? Let's not mess with the vibe during the games."

"You really think we should wait?" Trey asked. "What if those mofos follow us here?"

"I...don't think they will." Tai frowned as she turned over details in her head. "They could've done something at school, but they waited until we left. Maybe they don't want witnesses, and Dad is definitely a witness. So is Ayesha, and Pete. I think we're okay for a couple of hours."

"Okay." Trey unfolded his arms and turned to head down the hall. "But if someone bust down the door shouting, 'Magic FBI,' I'mma tell them to take *you*."

Three hours, two rounds of *Mario Kart*, at least a dozen matches in *Smash Bros*, and the loudest round of UNO that Tai could remember later, she sat on the couch with her sides sore from laughing and what felt like a permanent smile on her face.

Nearby, Ayesha spoke in hushed tones with one of her parents on the phone, letting them know she was at a birthday party and would be home later. In the kitchen, Trey helped Dad get the lasagna out of the oven. The house was bombarded with the smell of sauce, meat, spices, and garlic. Dad always made garlic bread and he liked it, what he called, extra tangy. Which meant enough garlic on it that to anyone else it was like biting into a bad dream. If you could eat bad dreams, this is what they would taste like. Thankfully there was a normal load for the rest of them.

Ayesha paced back and forth as far as the cord would let her. "Yeah, yeah, I'll come home right after cake and ice cream. We're about to eat, then that comes next.... I know, I'm sorry, it was a last-minute ask. Probably because I'm the new girl? ... Okay. Pete already knows.... Mmhm. Yes, sir. Okay, love you, bye." She moved to drop the phone onto the receiver, then heaved a sigh.

"Everything okay?" Tai asked.

"Yeah. Mostly. They a little mad I didn't call first, but happy I was able to help y'all. And that I'm already making friends." Ayesha had explained that she offered the twins a ride home when it looked like someone was wanting to start trouble with them.

"Thank you again for doing that."

"Of course."

Tai smiled softly as Ayesha wove their fingers together. This ... this was fast, but ... she didn't care. Or maybe it wasn't fast. It was just hand-holding. Babies held hands.

"Soup's on!" Dad's voice boomed jovially from the kitchen.

"Finally!" Tai called in return. "We're wasting away out here."

She led the way into the dining room where Trey was setting out the drink options and Dad approached with the steaming pan in hand. He sat it on the trivet at the center, a spatula ready to serve up the precut squares. The garlic bread was already out, smelling heavenly, except for Dad's nuclear-level slices.

"Can one of y'all grab the salad?" Dad gestured into the kitchen with an oven mitt.

"I got it." Tai gave Ayesha's hand a squeeze. "Sit wherever you want."

Dad waved his mitt at the chairs to his right from where he sat at the head of the table, his back to the windows. "Tai's gonna sit here, so you can grab the one next to it."

"Thank you, Mr. Watson," came Ayesha's polite reply.

Tai's smile widened. When she'd introduced Ayesha as a girl she'd met at the festival—still careful to keep it from sounding like she'd been talking about her—Dad had been thrilled. He was glad she could join them. Especially since it helped even out teams for the games and they didn't have to play round-robin style.

Once everyone was settled in, Dad said a quick grace, then food was spooned, dipped, and slapped onto plates in heaping piles that were passed around.

Chatter rose naturally between bites, starting with Dad explaining how they had to call their grandparents before the night was over so they could talk to them and hear their birthday wishes. And it was at moments like this that Tai felt bad for thinking about the fact that they only had one set of grandparents to hear from on birthdays, holidays, or pretty much any days, because Meemaws and Pawpaws be grandparenting all the time.

Mom's folks had passed long before she and Trey were born, and there was literally no one on that side of them family they had contact with. It wasn't like Dad was keeping them hidden or away, they just . . . didn't exist. There was probably extended family, sure, but he never met any of them and didn't know how to invite them to anything. It was a lot of feelings when you thought about being cut off from half of what went into who you were, so she tried not to dwell when reminded. Instead, she focused on the food and having her maybe girlfriend with them.

The conversation moved on to how everyone's day was. Dad insisted they share, since he just stayed home to get everything together for the lasagna.

Tai and Trey exchanged a glance. Then Tai tossed one toward Ayesha, who *mmm*ed as she took a bite of lasagna.

"Well," Trey hedged. "I, uhm . . . I didn't make first chair."

Dad's smile fell and he dropped his hand to the table with a loud thud to accompany his *"What?"*

His surprise jolted through Tai. "And why the hell not?" she demanded.

It was a testament to Dad's own shock and disbelief that he didn't correct her cursing immediately.

To think, she'd believed the broken string was the problem, but now Trey's sour mood made so much more sense! Except . . . why hadn't he said anything to her?

Trey's fingers curled into fists briefly, but he played it off by stabbing and eating a bit more salad.

While everyone waited in silence he chewed, swallowed, then took a drink of his Surge. "Someone else who's just as good as me but already memorized the solo for the competition piece we're playing this quarter got the spot."

"Oooh," Ayesha squeaked.

Tai spared her a confused glance before looking back to her brother as he continued.

"Mrs. D said we can revisit it afterward, but . . ." It was impossible to miss the look Trey shot across the table, directly at Ayesha. There was anger there, but . . . it wasn't fiery hot. It was a sort of cold smolder.

Tai frowned, her confusion worsening. She glanced back and forth between the two, not sure what was going on here. The look on Dad's face suggested he felt the same.

Tai started to ask what Trey's problem was, but Ayesha's sigh cut her off.

"I . . . I didn't know that would happen when I told her about my solo," Ayesha said, her voice soft.

Dad's frown only deepened. "Wait, what's going on here?"

Trey lowered his gaze to where he pushed his food around on his plate. "Mrs. D pulled me into her office and told me she was giving first chair to Ayesha because she knows the solo cold, that this was what was best for the ensemble. That it would be easier to place this way."

Ayesha fell silent. Or maybe she was talking and Tai couldn't hear because her heart was beating so fast and loud. What was happening right now?

Dad lifted his hand with a gentle wave. "It's okay, Ayesha, ain't nobody mad at *you*. Just . . . the situation. Right?" He focused his attention on Trey.

Who drew a slow breath, then propped his cheek on a fist and shoved his plate away. "Yeah."

"I'm sorry, I really had no idea," Ayesha continued. "Yesterday she asked if I had any competition experience, since your school does that. I told her. She sounded real happy. I didn't know *this* was why."

"Then Dad's right. It's not your fault," Tai repeated quickly, an edge of something that wasn't quite hope but still familiar lightening her tone. "It . . . it's a sucky situation." She glanced at her brother, who met her gaze with that same, calm-before-the-storm softness to his expression. "But it's no one's fault."

Dad settled back in his chair. He knew just like Tai that this was Trey's dream. This was when he would start to gain the attention of music programs at his top choice schools. This year would be when he started to build his portfolio of sorts with accomplishments and number-one-ranked scores the same way she was trying to build hers with photos. All of the awards and guest performances with this or that adult orchestra were great, a nice icing on top, but these next three years were gonna be the cake. And now . . .

"That's right, baby," Dad said softly to fill the silence. "It's no one's fault. It sounds like you're pretty good, though." He smiled with a hushed laugh.

Crack!

Tai jumped and Ayesha yelped as the porcelain bowl holding the salad shattered. They all sat staring in shock. Well, Ayesha was shocked but Tai was worried—and so was her father given the look on his face. He glanced from Trey to the bowl to Ayesha, who was still staring at the bowl, then back to Trey.

Her brother thinned his lips and closed his eyes, taking a deep breath.

"Must've sat it too close to the lasagna pan," Dad said with the confidence of coming up with stories like this off the cuff for the better part of a decade. "My bad. I'll clean that up after we're done. Hope no one else wanted any salad, he-he."

Ayesha pushed her food around on her plate, same as Trey had a moment ago. Tai curled her hands in her lap, wanting to reach to her, but also stealing glances at and wanting to comfort her brother.

Everyone sort of went back to eating, taking small, half-hearted bites of an otherwise delicious meal. Tai's appetite all but dried up, which was a shame because she loved this dish.

Dad cleared his throat as he took a swig of his beer. "How about you, baby girl? How was your day?"

Eager to move on, at least for now, Tai took the easy in. "It was... kinda weird. This morning there were these suits at the school. If they were gonna have awkward conversations, better get them all out the way."

"Suits?" Dad arched an eyebrow.

Some of the tension eased as everyone's attention was directed to the subject of a new story.

Tai did most of the telling, with Ayesha filling in toward the end. Trey stayed silent the whole time. When they were finished, Dad blinked, glancing between all of them with a look that asked why the hell didn't they lead with *this*. "And you're sure they were after *you*?"

Tai nodded. "They kinda didn't move until we did. And... there's some situational circumstances involved, I think."

Dad's eyes went wide. He lowered his fork and picked up his

napkin to dab at his mouth. "I see. We can talk more about it later. You'll give me all the details." Then he turned his attention to Ayesha. "Thank you for helping them."

"Of course. And, really, you should thank Pete."

"Pete?"

"That's her driver," Trey said, singing the last word. "He dropped us off in a Maybach."

"A *what*?"

"It's probably parked in front of your house. Pete's been back for some time." Ayesha grinned.

Dad blinked, then leaned back in his chair to tug one of the curtains over the window aside. He tilted his head this way and that, and it wasn't clear whether he saw the car or not. Scooting back up to the table he released a breath.

"He just sitting out there?" Tai asked, stealing glances at Trey, who was still just messing over his food.

"He has to do that a lot. I think he reads romance novels or something," Ayesha said.

"Pete like lasagna?" Dad asked.

Ayesha beamed. "Pete likes everything."

"Then I'll send him a plate as thanks."

Dinner was over soon after that, and it didn't take long for them to bring out the cake. That was pretty short and sweet, too, since they bypassed the candles. And the singing. And the presents, since they got those this morning.

Thinking of said presents, Tai raced up to grab her camera for a picture while Dad put together a plate for Pete and Trey got a start on cleaning up the kitchen.

Morpheus mewled from the bed, startling her.

"Where have *you* been?" Tai asked, realizing she hadn't seen the cat all night. Morpheus had never been particularly shy before. Must've been all the noise they were making earlier.

He meowed again, sounding more insistent this time.

"We're almost done, then you can have the couch back." She tugged free the camera and grabbed the tripod from the foot of her bed. Then she snagged Ayesha's backpack as well.

Racing downstairs, she set all of it up in the living room just as Dad emerged from the kitchen with a plastic bag tied off with two plates covered with other plates tucked inside.

"Here we go." He handed the bag to Ayesha.

"Thanks again. He'll appreciate it."

"Before you leave let's get a picture!" Tai gestured to the camera before aiming it at the stairs. It's where they took all their group pics, since it made positioning easy.

She did her best to ignore the scowl Trey shot at her. She'd already proven that this camera was fine, since she only saw auras or whatever, so there was nothing to be worried about. Especially here at home.

With a wave, Dad and Trey took their usual places with the latter in front and the former behind. Dad showed Ayesha where to stand behind them, on the same stair Tai would stand on. Tai set the timer on the camera, then hurried over to join them.

Everyone smiled.

And smiled.

And smiled more.

"Something wrong?" Trey asked between teeth.

When nothing happened, Tai slipped down the stairs, intending to see what was up. Right when she reached for the camera, the flash went off and nearly blinded her. "Gah!"

Dad busted into a deep belly laugh. She could hear Trey snickering as well.

Tai feigned offense as she blinked back tears. Then she noticed the problem. "Sorry, I accidentally set it to thirty." Embarrassed, she lowered it to ten. "Ready ... go!"

It took three tries—at ten rapid snaps each—before everyone agreed on a photo where people didn't have their eyes closed or looked away at the last second or any number of things that weren't literally picture perfect. Tai set the camera aside and joined Dad at the door, where he loaded Ayesha up with a second bag that contained a few extra pieces of cake for her. He thought it was a crime that she couldn't have her favorite flavor since no one else in her house liked chocolate.

"Thanks," Ayesha said, smiling wide. A smile that waned when she looked to Trey. "Listen," she sighed. "I hope this doesn't become a thing."

"No reason it should," Dad said, clearly unable to help getting his last bit of two cents in. Then he made himself scarce.

Trey folded his arms over his chest where he tilted into the wall with his shoulder. "Nah," he said, and while there was no discernable anger in his tone, there *was* a dip that sounded more like defeat there than anything. "We good. Mrs. D made the choice, not you."

Ayesha nodded. "See you at practice."

"See you," Trey said, but didn't move.

When he still didn't, Tai cleared her throat and stepped forward. "I'll walk you out." She reached around Ayesha and pushed open the screen. They descended the stairs in silence, the sounds of the block sweeping in to fill what wasn't being said.

Halfway to the street, Ayesha spun to face her. "I hope your brother isn't mad. I mean, I know he mad, just not *mad* mad."

Tai grimaced. She knew Trey was mad, too. Pissed even. But,

"He'll get over it. At least, over any part he might feel you played in it. Not like that! He don't blame you, just saying ... uhm ..."

"That I'm a reminder of what happened, even if he's not mad at me as a person. I hear you." Ayesha fidgeted with the stacked bags in her hands, picking at the knot in the topmost one. "*We* good though, right? Me and you?"

"Of course," Tai said in a rushed breath. "I mean, I'm good if you're good."

Ayesha's smile returned. "Good. And I gave your dad my number. He wanted to be able to talk to my parents since we're probably gonna be spending more time together."

"Y-yeah," Tai said, unable to shake anything else from her brain. Spending more time together. She definitely wanted that. "S-see you at school, tomorrow?"

"See you."

Tai watched as Pete popped up on the other side of the already-running Maybach. He came around to open the door for Ayesha, who gave him a quiet thanks as she slipped inside.

"Night, Pete," Tai called.

"Night." He lifted a hand as he went around to the other side of the car and climbed in. "Tell your family I said the same."

"Okay."

Soon they pulled off, and Tai was left standing in the evening light, completely unbothered by the chill in the air, as it felt like nothing compared to the warmth that filled her. In fact, she stood out there for a few minutes after those brake lights vanished around a corner, basking in this feeling. Then she took a breath, steeled herself, and headed back inside.

10

Trey wrapped up the controllers and tucked them beside the 64 under the TV. He was about to go for the UNO cards when he heard the front door close and the click of the lock. Tai must be finished with her girlfriend. Her chair-thieving girlfriend.

Yeah, he knew Ayesha wasn't at fault, and he didn't plan on giving her no grief about it. He'd control his emotions and fix his face when she was around. Other than that, he was allowed to feel how he felt. The truth was, her fault or not, it wouldn't be happening at all without her. So she was the cause, and he could be mad at that.

"Pete said tell y'all good night," came Tai's dreamy voice.

"I'mma have to go out and see that car next time," Dad said from the kitchen. He had taken over finishing the dishes.

"It's real nice," Tai said with a smile before slowly approaching the table to help gather up the last of the cards.

"Don't worry, I got it," Trey said.

"I wanna help."

"No, you wanna see if I feel a way about your girl."

Tai huffed and set a hand on her hip. "I wanna see if you feel a way about my girl *and* I wanna help."

Trey sucked his teeth, trying to ignore his returning anger. And after he worked so hard to get rid of it. Mostly. Of all the girls for Tai to have her little rom com with, it had to be that one. Here comes the bad-luck birthday train, right on time. This rule of three, two good and one bad thing, was some real bullshit.

"I feel a way, but I don't," he admitted, taking the few cards she'd gathered. He already had most of them. "Not at her but it's still *because* of her."

"It's not her fault, though."

"It's not. But she's the reason it happened." Trey tossed the box onto the table before gripping the back of the nearest chair. "You know how important it is for me to start showing I'm one of the best. The only way someone with grades like mine get anywhere is being good at something else. Bs and Cs are average, but if I'm average one way, I gotta be exceptional another."

Tai looked away. "I don't see why you both can't be exceptional."

"The program I *need* to get in this summer starts looking at us right now. They only take four kids from each school. Usually one from each section. It was supposed to be my year, so yeah, I'm mad, Tai. I can be mad."

She hiked her shoulders in that shrug of hers that meant she felt helpless. "You're not . . . mad that me and her are talking, are you?"

"I'm mad at everything, right now, especially the way you're making this about *you*." He held his hands out. "I don't care, Tai. Date who you want." He grabbed up the last few empty soda cans and headed for the kitchen.

Tai's soft voice followed him. "It sure feels like you care."

Those words stopped Trey in his tracks. The metal of the cans crinkled in his grip. Across the way, a support beam behind a wall groaned and a picture hanging on it tilted.

Dad glanced up from where he was loading the pre-scrubbed dishes into the washer. "Trey? You good?"

"Yeah," Trey ground out, moving to fling the cans in the trash, then start the process of yanking the newly full bag out.

"Don't seem like it. You wanna talk about all that?"

"Nope."

"Mmmm."

He made it to the back door and pushed it open before a hand fell on his shoulder. He turned to find his father gazing at him, that pre–heart-to-heart look in his eye.

Dad said, "Just set that down outside the door, I'll take care of it in a minute. Let me holler at you a second."

Trey barely managed to keep from complaining that he could take out the damn trash, but did as he was told. Not like he had a choice, really. He dropped the bag and shut the door, following his Dad back to the table. On the way, he glanced into the living room. Tai finished taking her camera off the tripod. She glanced up, tears glistening in the corners of her eyes, and headed upstairs with both.

Feeling a little guilty, then mad all over again for feeling bad, he flopped down into one of the dining chairs. He really wasn't in the mood for all this.

Dad lowered himself almost gingerly into his seat, a purposeful opposite to Trey's display. He cleared his throat and folded his hands together. "I know this talking things out isn't really something young men are about these days. Hell, they wasn't about it back in my day. But . . . this is one of those unfortunate times your mom and I told you about where you don't get to be like other young men."

Trey folded his arms over his chest. "What, I can't be upset about what happened?" Nah, man, he wasn't hearing that.

"Yes, you can, but you can only let it get to a point. You shattered one of my best salad bowls, boy. Could've hurt somebody if the pieces flew far enough."

The anger that had been bubbling inside Trey cooled instantly. Not because he wasn't still mad—he most definitely was—but because it was a habit by now to sort of switch himself off during a discussion about their powers: how they had to be careful, stay hidden, try to mitigate as few "situations" as possible. Easy as hell for Tai; she just had to avoid looking at her reflection for too long. Trey had to bottle all of himself up and tuck it away, deep down. He understood *why* he had to do it, but sometimes it felt like no one else gave a damn what it was doing to him, what he had to endure.

"I'm sorry about first chair, son," Dad continued, holding his hands out as if presenting the apology as an offering. "I know what it meant to you, meant to what you're trying to do."

Then why are you telling me to calm down??

"You've come too far to let something like this stop you. Take the wind out your sails a lil bit, okay. Everyone experiences setbacks, hang-ups, that sorta thing. But you push past it, right? See it through. Who knows, maybe something better will present itself."

Doubtful, Trey wanted to say. Instead he just nodded. "Maybe."

"Mmm. Go get your sister, I wanna talk to y'all about these suits you mentioned."

Trey knocked on Tai's door where it stood open. "Dad wants to talk."

She glanced up from where she sat on her bed, her face drawn tight with worry. One look and he could tell this wasn't about things with Ayesha. The weight of his anger lifted a bit.

"What's wrong?" he asked.

Tai held up the camera wordlessly, and Trey crossed the room to lean in and get a look. One of the pictures they had taken on the stairs was set in high contrast similar to the way she'd messed with the settings earlier. It was easy to see what she was freaking out about. Just over Ayesha's shoulders where she stood near the top of the steps, something shimmered in the hallway. To anyone else it might look like a trick of the light caught, but Trey recognized it. Or, he thought he did.

"Is that . . . more aura stuff?"

"I think so," Tai said. "But where's it coming from?"

Trey glanced out into the hall. It didn't look no different than when he'd come down it a second ago. "Maybe it's residual?" he suggested. "I mean, both of us have powers, and we live here. Kinda makes sense the house would be filled with it."

"Maybe," Tai murmured, though she didn't sound convinced.

In truth, he wasn't either. "You wanna tell Dad about this, too? Or you wanna wait?"

She bit into her lip as she debated, and he waited for her to feel it out. Dad loved them, wanted nothing but the best for them, even though he could act a little weirded out around them from time to time.

"He's gonna ask why we think those people are involved with magic, right?" Tai finally spoke. Then she rose to her feet, camera in hand. "This is the only way to prove we aren't imagining things. That *I'm* not."

So, this was personal. Trey had a feeling that might be the case. In the beginning, when she first started seeing things, people thought she was just a little kid making up stories. It wasn't until she had one of her visions or whatever in front of them that their parents believed her and started trying to get her used to her power instead of being terrified.

Trey could remember that night clearly. Tai in her room after crying herself asleep, terrified by what she saw. Dad had carried her up to bed, Mom right behind him. They stayed with her for the better part of an hour until she stopped fretting long enough to drift off. Trey had hung out in the hallway petting Morpheus. It was just Cat back then.

When his parents finally emerged, they hugged and kissed him and told him to go on to sleep, that his sister would be fine by morning. Trey didn't stay in bed long, emerging mere minutes after being tucked in and sneaking toward the stairs. His parent's voices rose to meet him.

"I should've considered it was her abilities manifesting," Mom said, her voice thick and trembly with the weight of her haggard emotions. "When nothing happened the first few years, I thought maybe . . . maybe they wouldn't be caught up in this. That they would be spared."

"Baby, come sit down," Dad said, his voice full of gentle understanding.

"I didn't believe her, Terrance. How could I not believe my own little girl?"

Trey had never heard his mother cry before, or since. Not like that. He felt something sharp in his own little chest, the way her sobs crackled in his hearing, his own heart falling apart.

"Hey, hey, shhhh. You didn't think anything of it, neither did I. Whenever she talked about it, it was always sort of an afterthought. Except this time . . ."

"This time," Mom repeated. "When she thought people were after her? When she saw them snatch her up. God, seeing her staring at nothing like that, not able to hear us when we called to her, only for her to burst into tears! My heart."

"I know. But she's okay, now, and we know what's going on, right?"

"Mmm."

"We'll take care of this. We'll take care of her. And we'll keep an eye on Trey, just in case."

There were more whispers and quiet murmurs then, but Trey snuck back to bed when Mom mentioned going up to check on Tai one more time.

He'd all but forgotten that conversation until now. "No one has thought you were making anything up for a long time," he said, hoping to reassure her. "Come on, let's go talk to Dad."

After a pretty crude re-explanation of the whole thing with the people in white suits, this time with the footnotes included, Tai and Trey stood behind their seated father as he examined the pictures She had taken.

He frowned as he turned the camera this way and that. "The screen is so small," he complained. "Seemed bigger at the store."

"I tried adjusting the pictures after transferring them to my laptop," Tai explained. "But the aura doesn't show up. Only on the camera."

"Mmm." Dad scrutinized the red-haired woman and one of the dudes a bit longer before putting the camera down. "And you say you felt something?"

"The same thing I feel right before I see something," Tai said.

Followed by Trey's "Or whenever I've changed something."

Dad drummed his fingers on the table, his brow furrowed. The camera sat between his arms as if awaiting his judgment. "Anything else happen at school? Any other situations?"

"Just what I saw through my camera."

"I broke a couple strings. And cracked a mirror in the bathroom."

Both Dad and Tai glanced up at him.

"What, I was mad," he said, feeling a little defensive. "We been over that."

"But nothing big. Nothing that would draw attention?" Dad asked.

Trey shrugged and shook his head. So did his sister.

"Mmmmmmmm." After another minute or so of silence, Dad handed the camera back to Tai. "Don't delete those."

She cradled the device like a baby. "What're we going to do?"

"You two are going to do your homework and get ready for bed. It's still a school night."

"We're gonna go to school tomorrow with those people looking for us?" Trey asked.

"I haven't made up my mind on what's happening tomorrow, but either way, that's what you're doing *tonight*. And, Tai, baby, let me know if you see anything else, okay?"

Tai blinked, her expression surprised at first. Then it melted into a sort of wary hesitation, her brow furrowed. "If I see . . . You . . . want me to look? *Deliberately?*"

Dad smoothed a hand over his head, looking just as uncomfortable with this as she did. "What I want is for us to be able to have a little peace round here. But if I learned anything from ya momma, it's that stuff like this doesn't start happening for no reason and trying to ignore it only makes it worse."

"It could just be more birthday bad luck," Trey offered. "Like my losing first chair. Maybe Tai's bad luck is attracting whoever they are."

She whipped around on him. "So this is *my* fault?"

"What? No, you just heard me, it's the birthday bad luck. So far everything else has been going great for you, right? You got a new camera, new girlfriend—new *rich* girlfriend."

"There's no telling *what* is going on," Dad interrupted when it looked like Tai was going to fire back. "But whatever it is, we're gonna deal with it *together*, all right? Now, go on."

Still glowering, Tai took her camera and slipped from the kitchen. Trey watched her go before turning back to their old man. He hadn't seen Dad look so run-down in a long time.

"*You* good?" Trey asked quietly.

"Mmm? Yeah, yeah, I'm good. Just...missing ya momma. I always do, on holidays, anniversaries, y'all's birthday, her birthday." He took a slow breath. "And I miss her even more right now because she'd have a better idea how to help you kids."

"Maybe," Trey murmured. The way he remembered it, Mom was still in the dark about a lot of this stuff herself. There were moments he would catch her by herself, frustrated by a lack of answers for her own abilities and theirs. So much research stolen in moments between her living their normal life. She used to spend hours at her desk at the gallery, bent over books and old pictures, pulling out maps sometimes of places he couldn't pronounce. Always searching for something else, something more, something just beyond her reach. He wondered briefly if that's what happened to her. If the reason she didn't come home on that fateful day, or any day since, was because she'd found whatever it was she'd been looking for.

He wondered, and hoped, it was worth it.

11

Tai sat back in her desk chair and stretched to try and regain some of the feeling in her arms and legs. The clock in the corner of her laptop screen read 4:31 a.m. When did it get so late? Or did this count as early now? She'd have to start getting ready for school soon. Two sleepless nights in a row. Dad was going to kill her.

Something shifted on her bed and a pair of luminous eyes peered at her from beneath the blanket, Morpheus observing from his usual perch.

"Comfy?" Tai asked the cat. "Hope so, since you're taking up the whole thing." She gestured at the bed.

Morpheus merely blinked slowly, clearly not caring about her plight.

She stuck her tongue out at the animal, then turned back to her task. Her computer cast a cold glow across the open ledger and the notes she'd printed off, both spread over her desk. Her own scribbled handwriting where she'd added to the page about Elva stuck out in stark contrast against the few typed words. Hours of research had yielded few details.

Elva was an Irish name. Or at least it had been popularized in Ireland, Google and Bing couldn't agree. There were a few famous Elva's from the silent movie era, and one woman who was apparently a huge singer overseas. Tai had made a note to try and find some of her music later. No painted white girls in nightgowns, though.

"Elva," Tai said aloud. The name felt funny in her mouth, heavy, full. "Who are you? More importantly, who were you to my mom?" she asked no one in particular. There was only Morpheus, who mewled softly.

Tai ran her finger over the ledger entry as she continued her one-sided conversation. "Were you trying to tell her something?" Her gaze trailed to where her camera sat near the edge of her desk, tucked in its still open bag. "Are ... are you trying to tell *me*?"

With a chirp, Morpheus rose, arched his back in a stretch, and leapt onto the desk, which shook with his landing, sending the camera tumbling. Tai scrambled to catch it, barely managing to snag the strap.

"NnnnnnMorpheus," she groaned, her heart in her throat. She cradled the camera against her chest before aiming a finger at the cat. "You can't be doing that."

Morpheus licked his paw then leaned in to sniff her finger, butting his head against her hand afterward. "Tch, one day you won't be able to cute your way out of trouble," she complained while scratching at his chin. She could almost see his purr vibrate in the air.

Like most cats, he soaked up the attention for about a minute before jumping to the floor and heading for the door. She smiled after him with a shake of her head, then lifted her camera to aim at his kitty butt.

"*National Geogr—*" The snatch of white fabric was enough to make her freeze.

Morpheus rubbed himself against the hem of an old-timey night-gown. A pale hand lowering to run over his back as he arched it.

With her heart trying to climb up her neck, Tai lowered the camera and stared at the now empty doorframe. Her mouth went dry. A faint buzzing picked up at the base of her skull. She should get someone, her brother, her dad, to come see. But she didn't move, except to lift the camera again.

Elva straightened from her crouch, her attention locked on Tai. No, not really. Her eyes were unfocused, as if she were somewhere else, looking at something else. Her body went still, her expression . . . sad?

"Elva," Tai whispered, her voice small, the word squeaking out past the lump where her heart was in her throat.

Elva blinked and glanced around, as if searching for something just outside her range of vision.

Tai felt her whole body go cold. Like water being poured . . .

"Elva?" she tried again.

This time Elva froze, her head tilted to the side.

Tai lifted one hand and waved it in the air.

Elva didn't react.

"Can . . . can you hear me?"

Elva nodded, slowly.

"Can you see me?"

She shook her head.

Tai took a slow breath. This . . . this was the first time she was ever able to interact with one of her visions.

"Who are you? Why are you here? Did you know my mother?"

The questions poured out of Tai despite the way fear trampled over her nerves.

Elva withstood the bombardment without moving. She remained still for several moments more before she finally withdrew a step.

Tai leapt from her chair. "No, wait!"

Elva faded from sight, but she left behind a faint blue cloud. An aura. It pulsed gently, forming a trail along the carpet.

Against her better judgment, and likely the judgment of all the ancestors and every Black person ever in a horror movie, Tai followed.

Out into the darkened hall the trail arched up one wall and crawled across the ceiling to where it outlined the attic door.

"Oh you have got to be kidding me," Tai whispered to the shadows.

When she lowered the camera again, the aura vanished, but she knew what she saw. Something was up there. For a moment she debated waking her father or her brother but decided not to. She had to do this first.

Was she being selfish? Maybe. But what if she opened that door and nothing was up there? She could imagine the look on her family's faces. They wouldn't say anything, but she would see it in their eyes. After ten years of it, she just...couldn't anymore. Not right now.

And, yes, ten years was a long time, and time was capable of many miracles when it came to healing, but there was never any forgetting. People said time helped things get easier. Well, that was a lie. You just grew more and more numb to the hurt until, for whatever reason, the sting would come alive anew. Pain was patient.

Tai was not.

So she climbed those stairs into the dark.

Then she promptly climbed back down and headed for her room with the intent to find a flashlight. Drawing one from her desk drawer, she made her way back out of the hall and up the attic stairs.

The air was thick with dust and the smell of disuse. Particles swirled in the bright beam of her light flickering almost like snowflakes. Boxes and rubber tubs lined the walls, stacked and labeled. Old furniture that Mom hadn't wanted to get rid of and Dad promised to fix were shoved into open spaces here and there. Tai hadn't been up here in a while, but it still looked like a regular attic and not some sort of chamber holding magic secrets.

"Oooookay," she said to the empty air, then tried to lift the camera with one hand and hold the flashlight in the other.

It took some doing, but soon she was able to peer through the viewfinder, find the trail of blue aura, and follow it across the floor toward one of the farthest corners from the door.

She had to pause a couple times to put her things down in order to shove a chair out of the way, or move a couple of boxes. Eventually she came across what looked to be the source of the magic.

A box damn near gift wrapped in tape. It was one of the older ones but didn't look that extraordinary. In fact, it looked a little plain. She checked the camera a couple of times to make sure this was the source of the glow, then lowered herself to her knees. Setting her camera aside, she held the flashlight with one hand and picked at the tape with the other. It was slow but steady going. The tape was mostly dried up and came away easy. Soon enough, she opened it to peer inside.

At first glance, it just looked like a box of old junk. Sitting on top were some dried flowers. As Tai lifted them, careful with the delicate blossoms, a faint floral scent tickled her senses. Usually old flowers smelled like potpourri, which was gross, but these? Still somehow smelled like they'd just been picked. As she held them, familiarity prickled across her skull. She'd seen these before, or at least something that looked like them. She couldn't figure where, though.

She set the flowers aside carefully, then shined the light into the box once again. It glinted off of a reflective surface at the bottom, nearly blinding her in the process. She blinked back tears and angled the flashlight away, only for a shock of bright red to catch her attention. Drawing open one of the box flaps, Tai did a double take before reaching in to snatch something free and hold it up in the light.

Just as she suspected, a pair of red Converse All-Stars. Her mouth dropped open. Yo, these were too tight! What the hell were they doing up here packed away like this? Tai examined first one shoe, then the other. They looked brand-new almost, which was weird considering this box clearly hadn't been opened in a while. Setting the shoes aside to puzzle over later—and to try on in her room, they looked about her size—she looked into the box to find the last item staring up at her.

A mirror, and her eyes literally met her reflection's. The light played against the glass, then up along the ornate filigree banding. This looked like one of those old-timey mirrors.

Old-timey...

Hurriedly setting the shoes and flowers in the box, along with her camera, Tai closed the flaps. She fumbled a bit in trying to hold both the box and her light as she picked her way over to the ladder.

Once in her room, she shut and locked the door, clicking on the light. Morpheus mewled and paced back and forth on the bed.

Her nerves buzzing, Tai set the box on the floor and opened it. She removed the flowers, their perfume light as she disturbed them again. Her camera and the shoes came next, and she turned the latter over in her hands again. Whew, those were nice, but not now.

There, at the bottom, she could see it clearly now. A faint layer of dust coated the glass-and-gold frame. Light caught both in the reflective surface and the metal, shining softly, warmly, beckoning almost. Tai gave in and reached to hold it up in front of her.

Then she promptly dropped it again with a shout. The mirror thudded into the box, and Tai whirled around to stare . . . at her empty bedroom. Her panting breath filled the silence, save for Morpheus's agitated meows.

No, that wasn't right. She'd seen . . .

Her gaze trailed back to the mirror, now resting lopsided against the box's edge. With shaking hands she gripped and lifted it again.

Just like last time, she saw her face. Saw her room reflected around her. Then saw the girl standing at the center, over her shoulder.

"Elva," she murmured.

The girl lifted her gaze from where she'd been staring at the floor. Her eyes widened with a start.

Again Tai glanced over her shoulder, only to find she was alone in her room. Well, not fully alone, Morpheus was there, no longer making a sound but still pacing, watching her.

Tai swallowed. "You see something I don't, huh." Elva *had* pet him earlier. And he'd arched into it.

Morpheus simply gazed at her, then stopped to sit. He mewled one more time, softer.

Another deep breath and Tai lifted the mirror again, expecting to see Elva behind her once more. She was half right.... Her room was gone, and so was her reflection. Instead, a void of gray fog surrounded Elva, who stared up at Tai from *inside* the mirror itself, her hands pressed to the glass. She pounded a fist against it. Tai almost felt the mirror rattle in her hold.

"H-how is this possible?" she whispered, her voice strained, her body tight.

Morpheus starting pacing again, mewling low, almost a growl.

Elva shouted something, but no sound escaped the mirror, her mouth moving swiftly, her eyes bright with fear and something else. She smacked at the glass, the light shivering in response. Tai shook her head slowly, partially in answer and partially in denial.

"I—I can't ... I can't hear you," she wheezed against the sudden ache in her throat. Tears poured hot across her vision. She could feel Elva's helplessness, was choked by her desperation. Tai swallowed and gasped, a soft sob working free.

Out, Elva wanted OUT!

Tai blinked back into herself, her chest heaving as she panted.

"I'm sorry," she croaked, and sniffed, wiping at her nose. "I'm sorry!" She had to get help. She had to tell someone. She set the mirror down, her hands hovering over it briefly. "I—I'll be right back, okay?!"

Then she raced from her room.

12

Trey jolted awake at the feel of hands gripping his shoulders. Darkness greeted him and he fought against his sheets.

"Trey!" a familiar voice said, though it was pitched higher than memory served. "Trey!"

He blinked, lids still heavy and vision still blurry with sleep. Somehow he was able to make out the silhouette of his sister against the dull glow of the hall light.

"Tai?" he asked, his voice sliding like sandpaper against his throat and tongue. What time was it?

"Come here, you have to come here." She gripped his arm and nearly pulled him out of bed.

He barely caught himself on his knees, calling for her to slow down, let him get up.

"You have to help her!"

"Help who?" This was too much for his sleep-addled brain, but his body stood up, moving on autopilot. Stumbling after his sister, he shuffled down the hall into her room. He blinked against the brightness of her light, glancing around. There was no one in there except them. "Who am I helping?"

Tai had flung herself down on the ground. She reached into an old-ass box and pulled out a mirror. Then she hurried over to him. As she approached, he was able to take in the state of her, and he blinked in confusion.

"Have you been crying?"

She held up the mirror, obscuring his view. "See?"

Trey blinked at his confused reflection. "Uhm ... What, what am I looking at, Tai?"

She stared at him, her eyes bucked, her mouth dropped open in shock. "Y-you ..." She turned the mirror to look into it, then faced it toward him again. "You don't see her?"

Trey let his eyes wander over his reflection. He looked tired, his lids drooping, his head angled forward as if he lacked sufficient energy to keep it upright. "I see myself. Exhausted. What—" He rubbed at his eyes. "What are you talking about? Who am I helping?"

Tai's chest heaved as she turned the mirror back toward herself. Her expression pinched, her lips pursed. She looked overwhelmed.

"You *were* crying," Trey said as realization took him, followed swiftly by concern. "What's wrong?"

"You're . . . not going to believe me," Tai said, and the way her voice squeaked went straight to his heart. They were in preschool again, and she was begging her brother to listen to her about the people in the window.

"Hey," Trey said softly, reaching to take his sister by her quivering shoulders. "It's okay. I'll believe you. Just breathe, okay?"

Tai took a hiccupping breath in, then blew it out slowly.

"Good, another."

She took a second.

"Now tell me."

She hesitated, biting into her lower lip. "Elva . . . is trapped in this mirror."

Trey blinked. "The . . . girl from Mom's painting . . ."

"Yes. Which is the same one I saw at the festival, then the

restaurant. I—I saw her again, tonight. She showed me the way to the attic. There was this box." Tai turned to point to the old-ass box she'd pulled the mirror out of. "It had those flowers, those shoes, and this mirror in it. She's in the mirror, she's *in* the mirror!" Tai whined before taking a quick breath. "She's trapped; we need to get her out."

"Okay, uhm, stay calm," Trey said, trying and failing to wrap his mind around what was happening. "If you say she's in the mirror, she's in the mirror. I just can't see her. I've never been able to see your visions before, why would I now?" He took a moment to focus on his own breathing. So, the old-timey white girl was stuck in an alternate mirror dimension. Because of course.

"Where do you think it came from?" Trey asked as he crossed the room in order to kneel next to the nearly empty box. There were some flowers inside that, when he picked them up, still smelled surprisingly pungent.

Tai mumbled something about not being sure, but she'd guess it belonged to their mother.

Trey felt a slight twist in his stomach that only sharpened when he turned one of the flaps over. In permanent marker the name *Remi* was written then crossed out to be replaced by *Blake*.

So it *was* Mom's.

Trey closed his eyes and released a slow breath, nodding to

himself. "Okay," he murmured to nothing and no one in particular. "Okay."

Something soft and warm pressed against the back of his hand. He opened his eyes to find Morpheus sitting there, one paw stretched out. If he didn't know any better, he'd say the cat was trying to comfort him.

Weirder had happened. *Was* happening.

"Okay," he repeated a third time as he scratched the cat's orange ears, then pushed to his feet. "We gotta tell Dad."

Tai looked apprehensive, clutching the mirror to her chest.

"What time is it?" Trey murmured as he glanced around. The alarm clock on her nightstand said it was almost five a.m. Damn it, there was no point in trying to go back to bed, especially since he'd just have to get back up again in twenty minutes. "You make coffee; I'll get Dad."

She nodded, then glanced down to where Morpheus wound around and between her legs, mewling softly.

"What's gotten into him?" he asked.

"Morpheus was Mom's," Tai said softly. "Maybe all of this is triggering something?"

"Wouldn't be the strangest thing to happen."

Morpheus mewled as if to agree, then followed them from the

room. They split in the hall, with Tai heading downstairs and Trey turning to press into Dad's room. Morpheus followed after her. She had the mirror, after all.

Soft snores sounded in the darkness, a plume of hall light fracturing the shadows. Trey crossed the space, dodging around shoes and over what looked to be a stack of magazines, he reached the bed and gave Dad's arm a shake.

Dad snorted before jolting slightly in bed. "Wh-what—what? Who that?" he asked, his voice groggy.

"Hey, Dad. We, uhm . . . we got a situation," Trey said quietly. He wasn't certain if his father was looking at him or not, but soon Dad grumbled and the bed groaned as he rolled out of it.

"Situation?" Dad asked as he came to sit at the edge, yawning and rubbing a hand over his face.

"Yeah, Tai found this old box of Mom's stuff in the attic? Before you ask, better if you hear why she went up there from her. Actually it's best if you hear all of it from her. We got coffee downstairs."

For a moment there was a pause in silence. Again, without being able to see his father's face, Trey wasn't sure what to make of it.

"What time is it?" Dad finally asked.

"Almost five, give or take."

Another brief pause before Dad sighed. "Okay, I'll be down in a second."

Trey left the door open, heading downstairs and into the kitchen. The bold, roasted but honeyed scent of hazelnut coffee filled the room, and his stomach gave an eager burble in response. He didn't even like coffee like that, but man, it smelled good.

Tai sat atop one of the stools that lined the island. The mirror rested on the countertop beside her.

"Dad's coming down," Trey said as he made his way over to the fridge.

She made some noise at the back of her throat.

He watched her for a moment before deciding to make breakfast. That would help, right? He loaded up his arms with a carton of eggs, a pack of bacon, and some hash browns from the freezer. "What's she doing?"

Tai glanced sidelong at the mirror. "Watching. Saying ... something, but I can't hear her."

"Is she alone in there?" he asked. "She have anything she can write with? If you can't hear her, maybe you can read a message?" He had his back to his sister as he poured oil in the pan and threw in some diced onions left over from last night.

"Nothing," Tai said. "Just ... emptiness. It must be horrible."

The onions and oil started to sizzle, the scent mingling with the smell of coffee already heady in the air. "Trapped in a mirror? That sounds like some magic-princess stuff."

Tai snorted. "You still think she's a magic princess?"

"Maybe. Or just a regular one." Trey kept busy, setting bacon to cook in another pan, then mixing up the eggs. Regular conversation, regular breakfast, on a regular morning, with a girl trapped in a mirror. Perfect. "She could be some poor maiden who crossed the wrong wicked witch."

"Y'all got it smelling good in here," Dad said as he came scritch-scratching into the kitchen, his house shoes shuffling against the floor.

"Just coffee and onions so far," Trey said as he went to work on the hash browns.

Dad went after the orange juice, pouring glasses for all three of them before joining Tai at the island. His gaze fell to the mirror, his expression pinched a little.

"This it?" he asked.

Tai nodded. "Yeah. Trey can't see her though." She pushed the mirror toward him a little, almost like she was afraid to ask, "Can you?"

Dad looked at the mirror. He took a few swallows, then set it aside. "'Fraid not," he murmured, and smoothed a hand over the top of his bald head. "Lordy."

"Did Mom ever say anything about a girl in a magic mirror?" Trey asked over the sound of the bacon finally frying.

Dad shook his head slowly, rubbing at his chin. "Can't say she did, and I'd like to think I'd remember something like that." He released a slow breath then poured and drank another glass of orange juice like it was a shot. "Right, so this girl in the mirror. Do we know anything about her?"

"Her name is Elva," Tai said. "I've seen her in my . . . They weren't exactly visions, but she was there."

Dad's brow furrowed. "Visions? You've been having visions and not telling nobody?"

"Uhm . . ."

When Tai didn't elaborate, Dad's frown deepened. Clearly he expected further explanation.

Tai didn't give it, blowing right past the weird business with her camera—Trey couldn't blame her—and moving on to, "And that portrait with white girl you had us bring up yesterday? That's her, too."

Dad slumped back in his seat, blinking rapidly. His mouth worked a couple of times before he finally managed, "Your mom's piece?"

Tai rested her hand on the mirror's frame. "Mom clearly saw her at some point."

"That don't make no sense, your momma didn't have visions or nothing. Why wouldn't she tell me . . . ?" Dad pounded the rest of the orange juice straight from the jug.

Tai continued to stare at the mirror. "I think Elva's ... important. I don't know why or how, I just have this feeling."

"Okay, okay," Dad said while waving placatingly. "One thing at a time. Let's figure out how to at least talk to this Elva, or find a clue to who she is and maybe how she wound up stuck in your momma's mirror."

"Maybe Mom's painting can help?" Trey suggested.

"Okay. Guess I'll go get the portrait from the gallery." Dad pushed up from the table and headed for the stairs. "Let me go put some clothes on."

"You want a plate?" Trey asked. Breakfast was almost ready. He'd made it mostly for something to do with his hands. A way to release some of his building anxiety, otherwise he might end up giving them *all* clown hair.

"I'll take one to go," Dad called, then trundled up the stairs.

Trey went about piling everything between two pieces of buttered toast and wrapping it in a paper towel. He set it beside the thermos of coffee Tai prepared.

"You want one, too?" he asked his sister, gesturing at the sandwich with a spatula.

"Not very hungry."

"You should try to eat something. People think better on a full stomach."

She made some noncommittal sound. Trey made two more sandwiches, anyway. He set one in front of his sister just as Dad came back in, tugging his jacket on.

"Okay, I'm outta here. Y'all gonna be all right until I get back?"

Tai nodded, already nibbling on her sandwich despite what she did or didn't say earlier.

Dad snagged the sandwich and thermos with thanks. "If you need me, page me. I'll call y'all when I get there."

As he headed out the door, the first rays of sunlight were starting to barely burst across the sky. Trey rinsed out the dishes and moved to join his sister at the island. They ate in silence, with both of them stealing glances at the mirror and then each other in between bites.

"So, what do we do with her?" Trey finally asked.

Tai glanced up at him, her brow furrowing. "What do you mean?"

"I mean, you can't take her to school in your backpack, and you clearly don't wanna leave her in your room."

She hesitated a moment before swallowing thickly. "I just ... I think she's been reaching out to me for help. Maybe in a way she reached out to Mom? That portrait didn't come out of nowhere."

"Maybe," Trey agreed. "So, what, Mom just stuck her in a box in the attic and forgot about her?"

Tai shrugged and glanced over to the mirror. Then her eyes widened.

"What?" Trey asked.

"She shook her head. I think she's answering?" Tai shoved her plate aside and pulled the mirror close. "Elva, did you know our mom? Blake Estancia Watson." There was a pause before Tai gave this high pitch squeak that bore into the base of Trey's skull. He actually winced.

"Do you know what happened to her?" Tai continued, her words coming faster now. "Where she went?"

Trey watched his sister closely for her response to the answer. When her shoulders sagged, so did his. He expected a no, but getting one . . .

Damn it, he should be past this. Letting some new bit of information get his hopes up only for them to be dashed? *No, no you're better than this. Get a grip, man.*

This needed to be the end of it, didn't it? If the girl in the magic mirror didn't know anything, who could?

Trey gathered up the dishes to put them away as Tai continued speaking.

"Yes and no answers are easy, we need a way for you to tell us more. Like how to get you out of there, maybe?"

"Or how she wound up in our attic in the first place," Trey said. "I mean besides Mom stuck her up there. But did Mom put her *in* the mirror?"

Tai glanced down before shaking her head. "She says no."

"Then that means someone else did. Should we be on the look-out for someone going around sticking people in mirrors? I don't know about you, but I don't want to end up shoved in a vanity or something."

Tai looked to the mirror once more. Her expression twisted with frustration, and she flung her hands into the air. "Ugh! I—I can't . . . I don't know what you're saying, I'm sorry. . . ."

And that's when another thought occurred to Trey. One . . . a little darker than he was proud of, he could admit. But he couldn't help it. Tai was the upbeat positive twin; he was the doomsayer.

"How do we know getting her out of there is a good thing?"

Tai's head snapped up. "Excuse me?"

"Elva. How do we know freeing her wouldn't be like unleashing some ancient magical evil on the world."

The way Tai's face went blank meant she hadn't considered that possibility. "W-well . . . I . . ."

"Hate to say it, but we don't. All we know is she was upstairs in a box. What if Mom was trying to hide the mirror until she could figure out a way to safely get rid of it? What if *it's* the reason she's missing?"

The line of Tai's shoulders lifted and her lips went tight. She stared at Trey for a moment, breathing a little harshly through her nose.

"Elva needs our help," she finally said quietly. "Don't ask me how I know, I just...do. And wasn't she a magic princess just a second ago? What happened to that mindset?"

"Nothing." Trey shrugged. "She could be a princess in need of rescuing. Or she might be an evil queen who needed trapping. I'm not trying to be difficult; I'm just trying to think up every possible angle for something like this. Mom never told Dad about a girl in a mirror? But she told him about everything else? Doesn't make sense."

"Not everyone shares every detail of their life," Tai said. "People keep secrets."

"Magical prison is one helluva secret."

"Prison?"

Trey waved a hand at the mirror. "What else would you call it?"

Knock knock knock.

Someone was at the door. They both glanced toward the front hall, then at each other.

"Dad?" Tai whispered.

Trey shook his head. "Too quick. Besides, why would he knock?"

"Who else would be here this early?"

Trey pushed up from the table and crossed the kitchen to the dining room space. Then, pulling back the edge of the curtain, he peered out toward the porch.

Ayesha stood there, her braids in a ponytail, her arms swinging back and forth at her sides. A bright blue bag hung on the left one.

Trey snorted and let the curtain fall back into place. "It's your girlfriend."

"*What?*" Tai's stool scraped the ground as she hopped up and hurried into the front room.

"You're still in your pajamas," Trey called after her as he moved to finish cleaning up the remnants of their breakfast. He noticed the mirror left on the counter but didn't say anything.

The door creaked open, and the girls greeted each other with a few words he couldn't quite make out. A few seconds later, Tai made her way back into the kitchen, Ayesha behind her. Both of them carried pastry boxes.

Trey arched an inquisitive eyebrow. "And this is?"

"Thanks," Ayesha said as she placed her box on the table, then opened it to reveal an assortment of doughnuts. "For dinner and cake yesterday. There's bagels in the other one."

"Awww, you didn't have to do that," Tai said, her voice sugary.

"Glad you did though," Trey said as he snagged a glazed, despite having eaten not ten minutes ago. Then he popped open the second box to eye the bagels. "Any cream cheese?"

"You *could* say thank you," Tai chided.

"Thank you," Trey said. "Any cream cheese? Because we're out."

"They only had plain and strawberry." Ayesha poured out a bag of little individual cream cheeses.

See, that right there was a travesty. Trey winkled his nose. "Nuh-uh, can't have these without jalapeño."

"Jalapeño cream cheese?" Ayesha arched a brow as she settled into the same chair she'd sat at last night. "That sounds disgusting."

"Strawberry on an everything is what sounds disgusting." He tugged a plate down, set his bagel on it, then stuck it in the microwave to wait for him. "I'mma run down to Jimmy's. You two want anything?"

"Jimmy's?" Ayesha asked.

"Bodega on the corner," Tai said around a mouthful of something chocolate. "Some Pixy Stix? I'm almost out."

"I'll take a green tea SoBe."

Trey pointed to each girl as he repeated her order. "Pixy Stix, lizard water. Anything else, be sure to think of it by the time I get back down." He tossed the abandoned mirror one last glance before heading upstairs to change.

Jimmy's was one of the smaller places Trey's family frequented, but it had just about everything you could ever need. Which was fortunate, because by the time he left the house, he'd been given a veritable grocery list of drinks and snacks to procure. He'd been about to protest on the grounds of brokedom when Ayesha tugged out a couple crinkly twenties and said it was her treat.

Then, Pete had offered to drop Trey off on his way to run a quick errand. He said he'd be back in time to give them a ride to school, if they wanted. Trey doubted they'd need it, but thanked him anyway. Now, handbasket full, Trey stood in the candy aisle trying to decide if he was in more of a Kit-Kat or Twix mood.

Bing-bong. The door chimed when it opened, and the dull roar of the street came through the bodega briefly.

"Hello, welcome in!" Jimmy's mom was behind the counter today. Nice lady, always giving kids on the block discounts if they brought in good grades. "Let me know if you need anything."

"We're looking for someone," a woman said, her voice low, sultry. As she spoke, a chill moved through Trey.

It started with a burning sensation at the top of his head, then poured down over the rest of his body with a familiarity that sparked fear in some deep, primal part of his mind.

"No way," he whispered, and ducked to try and get a look through the shelves. He could just make out the front counter, where a white woman with red hair stood with her back to Jimmy's mom. A buff, bald white dude loomed beside her, both of them wearing white suits.

The stab of fear sharpened to a razor's edge.

"Who?" Jimmy's mom asked.

The woman removed her glasses and let her gaze roam over the small space, her head moving back and forth slowly. She said, "A young man, African American. Answers to Terrance or Trey."

13

*A*fter realizing the time, and that she was still in her pajamas, Tai excused herself to change with the promise she'd be right back. Then she rushed out of the kitchen and took the stairs two at a time, Elva's mirror clutched to her chest.

"I gotta go for a bit," she said, peering down at the girl behind the glass. "But I promise I'll be back. We're going to help you, somehow."

Elva nodded slowly, seemingly resigned to her fate.

Tai felt a pang of sympathy for the girl. "You're not going back into the box, though," she promised, and sat the mirror on her bed.

Morpheus padded over to peer down at Elva, who smiled at the sight of the cat. It was a small, sad smile.

"Morpheus is great company," Tai said. "He can even see you, it looks like!"

The cat lay down along the edge of the mirror, its tail curled around one corner.

"Okay. Okay." Tai rushed around her room, throwing off her pj's and putting on something she could wear to school. Then she put her slowly frizzing hair back into a ponytail and moved to pull on her sneakers when she paused.

The red Converse still lay just beneath her desk where she'd set them earlier. She hesitated a moment before grabbing them. Looking them over, she checked the inside and bottom for any size indicators. There were none, nor any other markings. Were these knockoffs? Did people make Converse knockoffs? Of course they did. People made knockoff everything.

Tugging them on, she was surprised to find they fit perfectly. She tied the laces and wiggled her toes before standing to examine herself in the mirror. The red was a little much but still cute. Grabbing her backpack and camera bag, she gave the cat a quick scratch and waved at Elva one last time then slipped from her room.

Partway down the stairs, she paused and glanced down at her feet. Then she took another step. And another. A few more brought her to the bottom where she stood for a moment as her mind attempted to process what was happening. Or, in actuality, what wasn't happening.

She set her bags down on the bottom step, then turned to run back up. As she did, she focused on where her feet hit the wood. She saw it happen. Felt it happen. But heard nothing. Not a whisper of sound where there should've been loud thunks and creaks.

"What in the world..." She retraced her path at least a couple more times, and when she was coming down for a third, Ayesha stepped out of the kitchen.

"Tai! What's taking so...?" She trailed off.

Tai froze, her arms in the air, one leg lifted, caught in the middle of what had to look like some sort of interpretive dance. She quickly straightened and brushed her hands along her clothes, trying to ignore the embarrassment that burned through her. "U-uhm..."

Ayesha did her best, bless her, to try and keep from laughing, but the slight snort gave it away. "Do I wanna know?"

"Y'know?" Tai started as she came the rest of the way down the stairs. "I'm not sure you do."

"Noted," Ayesha said, still grinning wide. "Next question, does it usually take your brother this long to run to the corner? It's been half an hour."

"He probably got stuck talking with Jimmy's mom or one of

the old heads who sit outside the store. They'll hold you for a good minute if you're not caref—" She was interrupted by a knock.

"Finally." Ayesha turned and headed for the door. "We were gonna leave you," she called, her tone teasing.

Tai smiled, but it faded almost instantly when the door swung inward. It wasn't her brother standing on the other side of the screen but a hulking mass of a white man, his equally white suit practically glistening in the sun.

His head angled down toward Ayesha and in a low but still somehow booming voice demanded, "Is your father home?"

"Close it," Tai said, her voice a choked whisper, a combination of shock and fear robbing her of enough breath to get the words out. But then she drew in a sharp gasp and screamed, "Close it!"

Ayesha snatched at the door, flinging it to try and get it shut, but a meaty hand gripped the edge. Tai raced forward to throw herself against it. Ayesha yelped in surprise. The two of them pushed.

It didn't budge.

With a roar, the man shoved. Tai felt the door tear out of her grip, the force of it flinging her backward. She grabbed at Ayesha, the two of them stumbling over each other as they raced deeper into the house.

The suit's steps thudded behind them as he gave chase.

14

Hunched over to hide behind the shelves, Trey crept his way to the back of the store. He had no idea what he was going to do, just that he needed to put as much distance between himself and those people as possible. All the while he pitched glances over his shoulder, listening as Jimmy's mom spoke with her newest customers.

"We don't ask our customers their names."

"But you have regulars, I assume?" the white woman said, her voice far friendlier than it had any right to be.

"You cops?"

"Friends of the family."

Liar. Trey continued to back away, moving as slow and as quiet as he could. Hopefully these assholes would give up and leave. Or maybe he could slip out the back. Did this place have a back?

"Hmmmmmmm." Jimmy's mom sounded suspicious. "Haven't seen him for a while."

"Are you su—"

"Positive."

All right, Jimmy's mom!

The white woman chuckled, though she didn't sound at all amused. "So very kind of you. Well, we won't take up any more of your time. Just going to grab a couple of things before we go."

The white woman waved a hand, and the man at her side advanced farther into the store. People scrambled out of his way as he started searching up and down the aisles.

Crap! Trey's heart thundered in his chest. He quickly pulled his hood up and pretended to examine some chocolate bars. The plastic crinkled as his hands shook. No matter how hard he clenched his fingers, he couldn't get the trembling to stop. What's worse, he could feel . . . *something* humming just beneath his skin, making it that much harder to hold still. The icy feel of magic crawled along his limbs. His whole body buzzed.

Deep breaths. He needed to take deep breaths. Stay calm. Or else—

A large hand came down on his shoulder. "Hey, kid."

Trey jumped, startled. In that same instant, he felt his magic lash out like a frightened animal. It was like being punched in the gut, only everyone around him felt the force of it.

Cookies, candies, snacks, sodas, everything on every shelf within ten feet exploded. People screamed as sweets rained down on them. One woman gasped, doused in soda.

A half-filled carafe popped like a balloon, showering the bald guy that had hold of Trey in glass shards and hot coffee. He screamed.

Trey yanked free and ran up the aisle. His shoes slipped against the slick floor. He stumbled a couple of times, dancing around a few patrons who looked to be in various stages of shock.

The door. He needed to get to the door.

People were already spilling out onto the street, grumbling complaints as they went.

He was nearly home free when the redhead stepped into his

path. She lifted something that looked like a cross between a flashlight and a gun. The "barrel" flared a faint blue.

Without thinking, Trey threw his hands out. The cold of his powers hardened, raced down his arms and erupted from his hands...only nothing happened.

Nothing moved, nothing popped, nothing changed. It was like the magic reached his fingertips, then fizzled out.

"John!" the white woman shouted as people edged around her to rush out the door.

Someone snatched at Trey's shirt and shook him so hard his skull rattled. Fingers gripped one of his wrists and twisted, jerking his arm up toward the center of his back until pain danced up to his shoulder.

"You try anything, and I rip it off," a man snarled in Trey's ear, breath hot and smelling like old coffee and menthols. It was the bald dude, his face angry and red, his white suit stained brown down the front.

Trey's panicked brain tried to come up with a response, but all he could do was stare, his chest heaving in quick pants, his knees already wobbling.

"Bring him," the woman said. She tugged what looked like a radio from her coat pocket. "This is Jane. We have the boy. What's the status on the girl?"

The girl? came the question that wouldn't reach his mouth. But he already knew the answer.

Tai...

The bruiser gave his wrist another pull and pain made him compliant. Trey stumbled forward. It felt like he was being held captive by a brick wall, no way he could break free. And the woman still had that little...whatever it was that stole his abilities.

"L-look." He dug his heels in, but John shoved him forward like he weighed nothing. "I—I'm not who you think I am!"

The woman turned a skeptical eye on him, her lips parting in what would clearly be a denial. But she didn't get the chance before *whack!* A cane came down on her hand.

She barked in pain before whirling just in time to have the business end of a shotgun shoved into her face.

Jimmy's mom glowered from the other end of the weapon. "Let him go."

The white woman's hands went up. "We don't want any trouble."

"You come in my store, harass my customer, break my shit. Now you got trouble. I said let him go." Jimmy's mom turned the gun on John, who released Trey in order to put his hands up as well.

"You don't know what you're meddling with," John growled.

"Wanna bet?" Jimmy's mom cocked the gun. Then she turned

her gaze on Trey. "Hurry home. And take this, just in case." She set something black on the counter with a thud.

A Taser, Trey realized.

Mouthing a thank-you he couldn't quite voice, he snatched up the Taser and stumbled out the door.

15

Tai raced up the stairs, practically dragging Ayesha behind her. A mountain of a man barreled after them. It was definitely one of the people that had shown up at school yesterday, same white suit and everything.

Wood cracked and groaned as their feet pounded the planks like war drums. Just as they reached the landing, fingers gripped Tai's ankle and flung her off balance. She threw out her hands to catch herself against the stairs. Her hands, knees, and every other point of contact throbbed in pain.

The grip on her ankle tightened painfully as he pulled.

She screamed and lashed out with her other foot. She felt the satisfying give and heard the crunch of bone beneath her heel. The man howled in pain, his hands going to his face as red spurted from it.

Tai took that chance to scramble the rest of the way, waving and shouting at Ayesha to get to her room. Tai dashed in behind her and flung the door shut. She barely managed to lock it before that big asshole slammed into the other side.

Both girls jerked back as the door rattled on its hinges.

"Open the door, Tai," the man called from the other side. "There's nowhere for you to go."

She shuddered as revulsion rippled through her body. They knew her name...

"H-he's right," Ayesha whimpered, her eyes wide. "What do we do?"

The door clattered and shook like a thing possessed. Backing away from it, Tai glanced around her room, trying to come up with something, anything to get them out of this. Her wailing heart mirrored the sound of that man's fist beating the wood, threatening to break out just as he threatened to break in. Both seemed like they'd give any second.

"Call Pete for help!" Tai panted. If ever they needed a chauffeur-slash-bodyguard, it was now.

Ayesha groaned, shaking her head rapidly. "I can't, he's gone. I had him drop me off, I wanted to take the train with you guys."

And Tai wanted to scream. *Are you kidding me right now?* Her gaze bounced around her room. Out, they needed a way out!

Morpheus mewed, drawing her attention to the bed, and her messy sheets. She had an idea. Not the best, but it was an idea. "Window. We'll use the sheets and go out the window. Open it!'"

Ayesha nodded and raced to the far wall. While she fought to open the window, Tai hurried over to her bed and snatched up the sheets. The mirror tumbled free, thumping against the mattress. Crap! She forgot she'd left it here!

A startled Elva pressed to the glass, glancing around questioningly.

"Th-there's a man," Tai explained in a panicked rush. "I don't know what he wants, but we have to get out of here!"

The instant the words left her mouth, the mirror started to glow. Pale light filled the glass, washing out the image of Elva entirely. It grew brighter and brighter, swallowing the frame now. The metal warmed in Tai's hands.

"Tai?" came Ayesha's strained voice.

Tai looked up into her frightened face.

"What's happening?"

"I—I don't know," Tai whispered. "I don't— Elva?"

But Elva was gone. There was only the light, which had brightened to blinding. A sudden lurch in her stomach doubled her over. Her insides floated up around her ears. In the split second it took to realize she was falling, she felt her whole body turn to ice.

Then everything went dark.

16

Trey's arm throbbed as he put more and more distance between himself and the bodega. He gripped the Taser in his hand, his fingers tight, knuckles aching.

Nearly home... He raced up the sidewalk, reached for the front door, but paused when he noticed. The door was open. Only by a couple inches, but still.

It could be nothing. It could be everything.

Taser brandished, he slowly made his way into the house.

BANG!

BANG!

Someone was pounding on something upstairs.

BANG!

His heart in his throat, Trey crept forward, peering around the corner at the bottom of the stairs.

BANG!

"Come out. I don't want to hurt you, but you if make this any more difficult," a man growled.

BANG!

Trey adjusted his hold on the Taser and practically crawled his way up the stairs.

At first he thought maybe he heard wrong and it was two men standing shoulder to shoulder at the end of the hall, but there were only two legs and one huge head. A man-shaped wall of muscle pounded steadily on Tai's bedroom door. The girls must be in there. Trey's relief was short-lived, though. Even though his sister and Ayesha were safe, there was still this asshole between them and freedom.

Trey cranked the Taser up to full charge. If he got in one good shot, the guy would go down, then they could all run for it. Taking a careful breath, he crept closer.

The rumbling of the door as the man pounded disguised Trey's steps. Thankfully, the guy was also busy muttering into a radio, asking after someone who wasn't answering fast enough given his impatient reaction. He grunted and growled, holding the receiver in one meaty hand and banging on the door with another. Jeez, the guy was huge. His fist was as big as his skull. It was like someone had shaved a gorilla and stuck it in a suit. One good punch would definitely take Trey out. He had to play this right.

Don't turn around. Don't turn around. Please don't turn around.

Inch by inch, Trey slunk until he was within arm's reach. With the push of a button electricity jumped to life, but something was wrong. It looked weak, like its batteries were running low.

Gorilla pivoted on one heel and started to turn.

Trey held his breath and jammed the charged end into the man's thigh.

Gorilla jerked, roared, but didn't go down. Instead, the back of his hand caught Trey upside his head so hard his teeth rattled. He hit the ground only half-aware he'd fallen over, the Taser skittering down the hall. He shook away the stars in his vision just in time to see Gorilla stalk toward him.

"Providence smiles on me," Gorilla gloated as he drew near.

Trey scrambled backward, fear pulsing white hot along his nerves, eyes wide with it. He glanced around for any sign of the Taser.

But Gorilla was almost on top of him, a meaty fist drawn back.

A yowl split the air, and a flash of orange shot past Trey and latched on to the man's leg. He howled in turn, dancing backward, flailing as he tried to get at Morpheus, who had tore halfway up the man's back by now.

"This fucking thing!" the guy bellowed, bouncing back and forth between the walls, his bulk making it hard for him to get after the cat.

Trey scrambled to his feet. He made for the Taser but recoiled when Gorilla stumbled into his path. Morpheus, a furious ball of hisses and claws, tore at the man's head and hands, earning more screams. Large fingers smeared blood against Gorilla's face, and he spit a stream of curses to shame a truck driver.

This was Trey's chance. Shifting his weight on the balls of his feet, Trey kicked hard as he could at Gorilla's unprotected stomach. He felt his boot hit a wall of muscle, his leg shaking slightly. The guy dropped to his knees, then swung wild. He caught Trey in the backs of his legs with a haymaker.

Trey's feet left the floor. He landed on his back, hard. Lava shot up his arm when a steel-toed boot came down with a sharp snap.

Pain burst from his wrist. His fingers flew open, dropping the Taser. Gorilla yanked him off the ground, held him up by his shirt and slammed him into the wall. Something cracked, but Trey didn't know if it was the plaster or his skull.

His insides dipped as Gorilla lifted him, held him overhead, then bounced him off the ground like a basketball. The world spun around him.

"You heathens." Gorilla stood over him, the bottom of his shoe planted on his chest. He applied enough pressure to cut off Trey's air. "I will take it out of your hide."

Fingers twisted in Trey's hair and pulled, hauling him to his feet. Flailing he twisted, clawed at Gorilla's arm, trying to free himself. Pain tore through his wrist, making his fingertips throb.

He didn't see the blow coming, only felt it as fingers drove into his face with a punch that nearly took his head off his shoulders. Blood coated his tongue with the taste of metal slid down his throat. Heat erupted from the center of his face. Spots floated in front of him in disorienting blurs, but they didn't keep him from seeing Gorilla cock his fist for a second punch.

He closed his eyes.

Gorilla screamed. His hold slackened.

Trey blinked open his eyes to see Ayesha standing behind the man, something jabbed into his back, her face streaked with tears, but her brow furrowed in determination.

The hold on Trey loosened as 50,000 volts shot through the man's massive body. Gorilla spasmed, his eyes bulged out of his sockets, his mouth frozen in a silent scream. With one final jerk, he dropped away, flopping about on the floor like a fish.

Trey nearly went down with him, sliding against the wall, gasping wildly for breath. His chest heaved as he stared down at the unconscious man mountain.

Ayesha panted similarly as she clutched the still sparking Taser tight, aiming the electrified end at the guy. Trey stumbled over to her side, his arms wrapped around himself. He was certain that was the only thing keeping him together.

"Thanks," he panted.

Ayesha nodded but didn't say anything, her face ashen and terrified.

Trey glanced toward the end of the hall, where Morpheus paced back and forth slowly, mewling low. "Thank you, too," he said to the cat.

Then he turned and limped the rest of the way down the hall, to the now open door of his sister's bedroom. Peering inside, he spotted a number of things, including the open window where the girls likely debated going out when they were trapped. Only . . . something was wrong with this picture. Leaning heavily on the doorjamb, he glanced around, then at Ayesha. Realization straightened his posture.

"Where's Tai?" he asked in a gasp, the beginnings of fear trickling in once more.

Ayesha glanced up and her expression finally faltered. "I—I . . ." She glanced to the door, then back to Trey, then down at the dude. "I don't know," she whimpered.

"What you mean, you don't know?" Trey asked. He could feel the panic he'd been fighting off starting to take root.

"I—I mean she . . . There was this light, she disappeared! She was holding that," Ayesha said, pointing at the bed. "I think . . . I think she went inside. . . ."

"Inside," Trey repeated, his voice dropping to a whisper. He limped over to find the mirror resting against the mattress.

Yeah. This totally made sense. Or maybe it didn't, but his brain was just too preoccupied with the fact that the people in white who had showed up at the corner store, were in his *house*! He'd had his ass handed to him trying to fight the bastards off, meanwhile his sister had vanished.

"I need to call my dad," he said to no one in particular.

"Wh-what . . . what do we do about that man?" Ayesha asked.

Trey shut his eyes, trying to take a deep breath. It was more shaky and stuttering than steadying, and he was quickly losing hold of the tenuous grip he had on the fear he'd managed to swallow so far.

He bit his lower lip hard enough to break skin. "Okay. We need to tie him up. Then we need to get out of here. Get the mirror, put it in Tai's backpack. I'll take care of him."

Ayesha bobbed her head in a nod a few times, and it looked like she'd forgotten how to walk before she suddenly sprang into frantic action, her jerky, shaky movements mirroring how Trey felt on the inside.

He in turn stepped back to the hall and skirted around the unconscious guy in order to hurry downstairs. There was a nearly empty roll of duct tape in the kitchen junk drawer, which Trey found and used to bind the bald dude's arms behind his back. The task was that much harder with his everything throbbing, especially his head, and his wrist—the one this asshole had stomped on—burning every time he moved his fingers. But he could still move them, and that's what mattered.

Right as he was finishing, Ayesha emerged from Tai's room wearing a backpack—containing the mirror, he assumed—to help bind the man's feet together. Trey then pressed a strip of tape over the guy's mouth for good measure.

Once that was done, he sat back on his heels and glanced

around. He needed to call his dad. He needed to find his sister. He needed to get out of here. He needed ...

He didn't know. He had no idea what he was supposed to do next. And Ayesha was looking at him with wide, fearful eyes, clearly expecting some sort of answer.

"What ... what's going on?" she finally asked.

"I—I ... don't know. ..." That wasn't entirely true. He knew that these people were after him and his sister. He knew it was likely because of their magic. And he knew just how wild that would sound when he tried to explain it.

Then again, Ayesha was wearing a backpack holding a magic mirror that Tai had, apparently, disappeared through. Maybe it wouldn't be too hard to explain.

He settled on "I'm not sure, but we can't stay here. We ... should head for the gallery. I need to call my dad." He hopped to his feet and started toward his room. He didn't make it two steps before something thumped downstairs. The screen door, he realized.

He froze. Someone else was in the house.

17

T ai felt herself falling. Felt the sickening heave of it in her stomach. Felt the air snatch at her hair, clothes, and bare skin as she plummeted. Darkness stretched in every direction. She couldn't see anything above or below her, and she had no idea how long she'd been tumbling through the air, but one second she was flailing around in the open air, and the next she felt the ground push up under her feet. It happened so fast that her balance couldn't catch up and she toppled over.

In that same instant she blinked the world into focus and found herself kneeling in the middle of a . . . forest? How the hell did she go from her room to a forest?

At least it looked like a forest. A carpet of grass spread out beneath her hands and knees. A veritable army of trees stood tall and crowded around her. But there were no animal sounds, no wind blowing. And when she glanced up, there was no sky, only a thick mist hung in the canopy.

"Wh-what . . . ?" she whispered, her voice catching on the air in a slight echo. She pushed to stand, stumbling a moment. "Ayesha?"

There was no answer, save for the sound of her own voice thick in her ears. Where . . . was she?

"Ayesha!" she tried again. Still, no answer.

At least, she thought, until a swirl of mist stirred at her feet. The cloud thickened and swelled before sweeping over her red shoes and out along the ground, parting to reveal a sudden path of dark earth that definitely hadn't been there before.

"This is a dream," Tai said to herself as she glanced around. "I . . . passed out from the stress, and I'm dreaming." But even as the words left her mouth, she didn't believe them.

This was real. This was happening. And this place, this forest of no name, in the middle of a thick mist, should have freaked her out, but she felt a strange sense of calm.

She was . . . *supposed* to be here, and she was supposed to follow that path.

Drawing a careful breath, she started down the trail. She had no idea where it was going to take her, but she knew she was headed in the right direction.

There was no way to tell how long she walked, or how far. Nothing seemed to change, no markers for distance or location revealed themselves. Trees appeared out of the mist as she approached them, then vanished back into it when she'd gone far enough. It was the same in every direction she turned.

Until she stepped into the mist and emerged in what looked like a small clearing. The trees just stopped. The path ended, but the way opened up into a stretch of green. At the center stood a large willow tree, the vined leaves fluttering in a nonexistent wind.

She drew up short when she caught sight of someone seated under the tree. Her gaze trailed over the bright yellow hair, the pale white garment, and the sense of familiarity that had hovered just outside of the reach of her senses sharpened into a fine point.

"Elva?" She didn't mean to say it out loud, but the name leapt from her tongue.

The figure glanced up. It *was* her.

Elva started, staring for a moment, her expression shifting from a frown to wide-eyed shock, then disbelief as she shook her head.

"You . . . You're here," Elva sighed, her voice carrying the same echo that had lifted Tai's.

"And where is *here*, exactly?" Tai asked, glancing around again. She felt a pull toward the willow, and didn't fight it.

Elva pushed to her feet, her arms wrapped around herself tight, almost as if holding herself together. "Inside."

"Inside?" Tai asked as she came to a stop just in front of the other girl.

Elva nodded slowly. "The mirror."

"The mi—the *mirror*?!" Tai's breath left her in a rush. She felt light-headed with it, glancing around at the hazy trees peeking in and out of the silvery mist. That's why this place seemed so familiar. Because she'd seen glimpses of it.

"I knew it!" Elva cried, her voice trembling with the sound of tears.

Tai stiffened with the sudden weight of a body pressing into hers as Elva threw her arms around her.

"I knew it would be you! Oh god, I'm so happy you're here."

For a moment, Tai stood frozen, held, and trying to process what was going on. "Hold on a second." She wriggled free of Elva's surprisingly strong hold. "You're trapped in here, right?"

Elva nodded, swiping at tears as they spilled over her cheeks. "Yes. For more than a century now."

Shock jolted through Tai. "A centu— Wait, am *I* trapped now?!"

"No, no, Tai, no. All is well, but you must breathe," Elva cautioned, drawing her hands back to clasp against her chest. "You're not trapped."

The relief that moved through Tai left her just a little dizzy. She groaned, digging the heels of her palms into her eyes. "Then there's a way out?"

"Yes, but not in the way you're thinking." Elva pressed her hands to her mouth, shaking her head as she looked Tai over. "After all this time ... you're really here."

Tai swallowed thickly. "Here. Inside the mirror."

"Yes, but more importantly, inside the enchantment."

"Enchantment?" Tai asked. "Like a spell?"

"Precisely. A spell, a *curse*, that has haunted our family for generations. . . ."

Tai blinked rapidly as something inside her head caved in on itself. "Wait a second, *our* fam— What are you talking about?"

Elva eyed her with a look of excitement tempered by concern. "There is so much I have to tell you, to show you. About the past. My past, your ancestry. I'm your aunt, Tai."

Silence stretched between them. Silence that Tai felt herself drowning in, even though she could breathe just fine. The whole time Elva continued to smile all teary-eyed and happy. Tai almost didn't have the heart to say anything.

"There's no way to say this, other than to say it. You're white. . . ."

Elva laughed softly. "Yes. I was born in 1848 in Hanau, Germany. I'm your great-great-great-aunt. And I . . ." Her voice started to tremble with the weight of emotion, her eyes glistening. But she took a breath and appeared to steel herself. "Something happened all those years ago that has troubled us ever since. Magic runs deep in our blood, in *your* blood. Not just from our family but others drawn to us. Like seeks like. It all culminated in this moment, in you, the strongest of us. And it's you who will break the curse and set us free."

For a moment Tai didn't say anything. *Couldn't* say anything. Faced with her literal ancestor, and the truth about the root of her family's powers—of the bad luck that had followed them since the beginning it seemed—she was robbed of all words save a few.

"Say *whut*, now?"

18

Trey gestured for Ayesha to back toward Tai's room. He moved to follow, trying to be as quiet as he could. Multiple voices rose from downstairs, murmurs that sounded like questions.

"Start a sweep," said a voice he felt he recognized.

The white woman from the bodega.

"I want everything of significance tagged, bagged, and ready for transport."

Trey closed the door on the rest of the conversation and twisted the lock.

"Who are those people?" Ayesha whispered, her fingers clutching the straps of her pack with shaking hands.

"Don't know," Trey said. "They came after me at the bodega, and apparently after you two here." And now they were trapped. "We gotta get outta here."

"Tai wanted to go out the window." Ayesha pointed. "We were gonna use the sheets."

Trey made his way over to the window. Four black SUVs were parked in front of the house. People in white suits moved between the cars and the house, loading tubs that no doubt contained whatever had been "tagged." A couple of the neighbors had come out to see what was going on, but the street was mostly empty midmorning on a weekday.

Maybe, if he and Ayesha managed to get outside, they could run for help. Or someone could call the cops, if they didn't think these people were the cops.

Either way, there was no chance of them going out the window without being spotted. "They'll see us," he said, his voice dipping in frustration.

Going out the window wasn't an option. Staying in this room wasn't an option. They needed to find another way.

But before he could even try to contemplate it, the door shuddered in its frame.

"What the hell?" Ayesha squeaked, voicing the very question that had lodged itself in Trey's brain.

Next the lock shivered similarly. Trey threw himself across the room, but he wasn't fast enough. The lock clicked. The knob turned, and the door swung open.

19

Tai stumbled as she tried to keep up with Elva, who marched through the mists and between the trees with the surefooted, swift stride of someone who knew exactly where they were going.

Meanwhile Tai kept tripping every handful of steps, not really watching where she was going while trying to work through everything she had been told. These shoes were good for noise but not for stability.

"Wait, wait, wait, so you were friends with a witch. A legitimate witch," Tai said.

"I don't think she would want to be called that, but . . . yes," Elva said as she continued moving.

"And she's the one that cursed us?" Tai asked.

Elva stopped, and Tai damn near broke her neck to keep from running into her. They'd been moving so fast! She couldn't help but notice the red slippers on Elva's feet but hadn't asked about them, just yet. She was still trying to make sense of everything else, magic shoes were at the bottom of that list.

"No," Elva said, her voice softening. "Mathilda would never do such a thing." She shook herself out of whatever emotion tried to catch hold of her and started forward once more.

Tai hurried to follow. "Could she break it, then? Being magical and all?"

"Mathilda was powerful, but this? This is bigger than her now."

"Was?" Tai asked softly.

"She passed. Long ago." There was strain in Elva's voice. She clearly still grieved for her former friend, even after all this time.

Tai fell silent for a moment while they walked, out of respect. But there was one question that she hadn't asked. In truth, she was scared to ask. Because the answer could mean everything . . .

or nothing. And after so many years of nothing, to have *this* of all things lead nowhere, she didn't think she could bear it.

But she wouldn't be able to live with herself if she didn't.

"How . . . how do you know my mother?" Tai asked softly, her voice cracking under the weight of sudden emotion.

Elva didn't stop walking, though she did spare a glance over her shoulder. "I met your mother years ago. She tried to help me, looked for answers. Then, one day, she said she found something that might help break the curse *and* free me."

"S-something?"

"Yes. I am not sure what she meant. She promised to explain, but I never saw her again. I am sorry. . . ."

Silence stretched between them once more. Tai didn't know what to do with that bit of information. It was an answer, and yet it wasn't. She was no closer to solving this particular mystery, and hearing those words, than Mom had been looking into something when she went missing, something about magic, hurt far more than Tai had expected.

Tears burned her eyes, blurring the path. She swiped at her face, the sting of tears sinking down to her heart. Grief intensified into anger. Anger at herself for getting her hopes up. Anger at Elva for not providing useful information. And anger at her mother, which had always been there, but she'd never let herself rest in the emotion before. Not really.

There had always been this tiny part of Tai that blamed her mother for vanishing. It was ludicrous, and she felt constant shame and horror knowing this part of her existed, no matter how small. So she did her best to ignore it, but there were times during important moments of her life—her first kiss, the first time she had her heart broken, turning thirteen and now sixteen, hell getting her period—where she'd longed for her mother so bad she'd ache all over and cry herself to sleep for weeks straight.

It was in those moments that tiny part of her she'd buried deep down managed to claw its way to the surface and puncture her insecurities like a long, thin needle at the base of her skull pressing deeper until she bled silent fury. She'd managed to convince herself for so long that magic didn't have anything to do with her mother's disappearance. That she hadn't made the choice to leave them, she'd somehow been taken. And to now learn that Mom had been searching for something to help *someone else* was the reason Tai and Trey grew up without her in their lives?

The anger blossomed, the fire of it threatening to consume her. She tried to breathe through it, same as she had every other time, but it wasn't quelling. Not this time.

She shut her eyes and took slow, deep breaths.

Stop it, she told herself. This wasn't going to help. She needed to focus on finding a way out of here. Getting back before . . .

Her eyes snapped open. "Do you know who the men in white are?"

"Men in white?" Elva asked without stopping. In fact it seemed like she'd sped up. Or maybe Tai had slowed without meaning to.

"It's like *Men in Black*, but— Never mind. They're these people who have been following us. One of them came to my house, broke in, tried to get me, and— Ayesha! She's by herself! I have to get back to her, how much farther is the exit?"

"Exit?"

"Yes! The way out! That's . . . where you're taking me, isn't it?"

Elva chuckled faintly, though it was more sympathetic amusement than anything. "If I knew of a way to leave this place, I would have departed long ago."

"Wait, so there's no way out at all?"

"Not for me. No matter how many doors I tried, I—"

"Doors?" Tai blinked.

"Yes. Doors. It'll be easier to show you than tell you. And here we are." Elva stepped into what appeared to be another clearing though, instead of a willow tree at the center of this one, there was nothing.

At least, that's how it started. They came to a stop. Mist swirled about their feet, drifting over her jeans and Elva's skirt. Then, just when Tai was about to ask what they were doing, shapes formed themselves from the fog. Tall, thin, angular—*doors*! Tai realized. She was looking at doors bleeding into existence, a number of them, dark brown with a gold willow tree etched at the center.

"What in the world..."

"As I said"—Elva finally turned to face her—"it would be easier to show rather than tell you. These are portals into the past. Into moments of personal significance. I have not fully grasped how all of it ties together—some won't even open for me, but they may for you."

Tai glanced away from the doors and back to Elva. "What makes you say that?"

"Because this began with me and my ability. To see glimpses of the future in reflective surfaces."

Tai's breath caught. "Like...like me."

"Exactly. But you can do more, can't you? See more. You're also the first and only person who has been able to enter the mirror bodily." Elva held out her hands. As she spoke, something weird happened with her fingers. They were fading, Tai realized. Growing transparent. "I am here in spirit, but my body was buried, long ago." She took a breath, and the whole of her solidified. Then she stepped over to a door in order to draw it open.

Holy shit, she is a ghost....

When Tai didn't immediately follow, Elva waved her closer.

Tai hesitated just a second before approaching to peer through the doorway and into a forest similar to this one, only the light of day shone overhead. As much as it could, anyway. Gray clouds bloated with rain and dreariness blocked out most of it.

At the center of the forest rested a crystal coffin and inside ...

Tai drew back a step. She looked to Elva, who simply nodded sadly.

"My family believed me to be dead and gone. They didn't realize my spirit had been trapped here, so they did what they thought was best."

The image shifted to show a little white boy flung over the coffin, sobbing openly. Behind him a white man held a weeping white woman by her shoulders as he stared straight ahead, his lips tight, silent tears streaking his face.

Elva said, "My spirit is trapped in this place, but you were able to come here as your full self." She let the door close on the sad scene. She then gestured around them. "I can open some of these, but others remain locked to me or my hand passes through them entirely. This began with my magic, it *has* to end with it. Rather, with its reflection. Your abilities mirror mine, but are so much more. You're the key."

Tai studied the other girl, who looked to be about her age, now that she paused a moment to take her in. "You're not sure about that, are you?" Tai said softly.

Elva bit into her lower lip. "No. I am not certain. But after seeing all that I have, the coincidences, the portents. The fact that someone with my exact ability to see the truth in mirrors has been able to follow me here, it . . . it has to mean something."

Tai recognized the desperation threading through Elva's shoulders. The way it sharpened her tone and clipped her words. It was the same desperation Tai had felt just moments ago, before she got her non-answer.

"Okay," Tai breathed. "I'll try to get us out of here."

"No." Elva reached to take Tai's hand, holding it between hers. "You'll free us all."

A lump formed in Tai's throat. She couldn't remember the last time someone believed in her so fully, so readily. Her family was always on her side, in the end, but sometimes it took some convincing.

"I don't know about all that," Tai murmured. "You—you said this was a family curse. That it's followed us for centuries? Then I need to see where it came from. Let's start with you, at the beginning."

A look of resignation crossed Elva's face. More of a flinch, really, as she braced herself for something that was no doubt about to be painful. Then she reached out and turned the knob on the nearest door.

20

$\mathbf{T}$rey backed away from the door as it swung open. He moved to place himself between Ayesha and the tall, round, dark-skinned Black woman standing in the doorway. She wore a white suit as well, though hers was trimmed in silver.

Her dark eyes gazed at them from a serious face, her lips pursed as she glanced around the room.

Movement in the hallway behind her, as well as a low

groan—likely from the still unconscious dude—meant they were likely getting him up.

Resolved to go down fighting, Trey brandished the Taser, the nodes crackling with energy.

The Black woman arched a finely sculpted brow before smirking. "That won't be necessary, Trey."

He blinked in confusion. That voice...was the one he'd heard downstairs. The one he *thought* belonged to the white woman who tried to corner him at the bodega.

"How do you know who I am?" he asked.

"I know about you, about your sister, and a number of other... gifted individuals around the world. I promise, you're not in any danger here."

Trey snorted. "Right. The asshole in the hall and the other two down the block say otherwise."

The woman nodded slowly. "The confusion is understandable. And intentional, but it was meant to throw off the very people you just described. That man"—the woman gestured out into the hall—"and those with him? Are not with *us*. They want to hurt you."

"Clearly."

"And we want to help you." She set a hand to her chest. "My name is Marissa Coleman, and I'm part of a group that tries to protect people with magic in their bloodlines from those who would seek to snuff that magic out."

Trey lowered the Taser but not completely. "So...you're not with the people who tried to kick my ass earlier?"

"No."

"You just dress exactly like them."

"All the better to blend in and do our jobs. Once we identify their intended target, the disguises usually buy us enough time to get in and get out. Speaking of which, as you no doubt realize, it's no longer safe here for you. You should come with us."

A hand gripped Trey's elbow, and he turned to peer into Ayesha's scrunched face.

"I don't trust it," she murmured. "Sounds too easy, too good to be true."

There was a thump and a muffled shout from the hall.

Marissa glanced over her shoulder. "If you don't believe *me*, maybe you'll believe your friend here." She tilted her head in an indication for them to follow, then stepped back into the hall.

People moved in and out of his bedroom and his father's. They carried tubs that maybe held some of his possessions, but he couldn't tell. The whole thing felt like a violation, and he rolled his shoulders to be rid of the creeping sensation.

Marissa stood over the now very awake and very angry Gorilla dude, who was still gagged but glared at everyone that passed by. He saved the particularly nasty looks for the bronze-skinned South-Asian woman who knelt beside him, one hand on his shoulder, the other lifted and . . . Was that electricity crackling between her *fingers*?

"Oh wow," Ayesha whispered, having seen the lightning fingers as well.

Marissa smirked. "Rhoda."

The woman with lightning fingers gripped the edge of the tape near the man's mouth before snatching it away with a satisfying *riiiip!*

The guy shouted in pain before snarling, his face drawn up with it. "You are all abominations! You will be purged from this world, you and your filthy—"

Marissa lifted a hand, and Rhoda slapped the tape back into place, leaving the man grunting and growling impotently.

"Okay," Trey sighed. "Okay. Say we believe you. We need some answers, man. What *is* all this? What's going on? Who're you? Who're *they*?!" He threw a hand out to indicate the still-glowering man.

Marissa smiled. "I'm glad you believe me, and that's the first step to building trust, but I need to ask you to extend it just a little more. It's not safe here. We need to be gone before the rest of his people—no, not the ones you left back at the bodega, nice work, by the way—get here. Come with us."

Trey hesitated. He definitely didn't want to run into any more of *those* people in white suits, but he wasn't exactly sure he was fully ready to throw his lot in with *these* people in white suits.

"You have powers," Ayesha said, stepping up beside him. "Magic." Her voice was steady, but the look in her eye reminded Trey of those frightened animals in those documentaries he and Tai used to watch obsessively on the Discovery Channel. Like, she knew something was up, and danger was in the air, but she didn't know which direction it was coming from, so she was on high alert.

"Yes," Marissa said, her voice calm, soothing, as if she could tell Ayesha was more than a little freaked out.

Ayesha stared at her for a few more seconds, then turned to Trey. "You?" she asked, her voice quiet.

He felt his stomach bottom out. It went against everything he'd been taught, everything he had been told to do if anyone ever asked him about his abilities. But there was no use lying. Hell, she'd seen Tai portal through a mirror. So he bobbed his head in answer.

A little noise escaped her before she managed to croak out, "Tai?"

He nodded again. It was easier this time.

Marissa cleared her throat. "I know this can be a lot, and I'll be happy to answer any questions, but please, it's not safe here," she stressed.

Trey chewed at his lower lip, worry for Ayesha eating at him a little, but Marissa was right. They had to make moves. "My dad'll be back any second."

"We've seen to your father. Don't worry, he's fine, just delayed. Right now, our main concern is you two and Tai. Where's your sister?"

"She got away," Trey lied.

Ayesha shifted beside him.

Marissa nodded slowly, and Trey wondered if she believed him. But then she caught a passing Black woman and told her to have someone stay behind and watch the house, in case the girl returned. Then she turned back to Trey, smiling. "Someone will keep an eye out for her, but the rest of us need to go." She aimed a disgusted but brief glare at the man. "I won't *make* you two come with us, but I highly encourage it."

Five minutes later, Trey sat in the back of one of the black SUVs parked in front of his house. Ayesha sat beside him. Marissa waited in the passenger seat while an Indian man sat behind the wheel. Most everyone waited in silence while Marissa's people set to work wiping the scene of their presence. She spoke quick orders into the phone, muttering every few seconds about sanitizing the scene.

There was a brief commotion while two Black dudes shoved the wriggling, duct-tape-bound white man into the back of a different vehicle.

Ayesha sat with her hands in her lap, picking at the polish on her nails. She hadn't said much of anything or looked at anyone since being ushered into the vehicle. She still had the backpack on, and hadn't let anyone touch it despite the questions posed.

Soon they were pulling off. Trey watched his house for as long as he could out the back window, then they turned the corner at the end of the block.

Up front, Marissa took a deep breath before turning to watch the two of them over her shoulder.

"Thank you for trusting us," she murmured.

"I believed you," Trey said. "Doesn't mean I trust you."

She pursed her lips and nodded once. "Fair. As I said, I hope we can earn that trust."

"By answering our questions," Ayesha said.

Marissa glanced at her and nodded.

"How did you know to come help us?" Trey asked.

"We try to monitor the activity of the Order of the Corvus and intervene when possible."

Trey arched an eyebrow. "The . . . what, now?"

"It's long and complicated. The short and sweet version is, there are people who think what we can do—magic—is somehow unnatural, despite the fact that we were born with these abilities. This belief leads those people to view magic users as a danger that needs to be dealt with, often with violence. We're here to prevent that."

"So you saw they were trying to start something and decided to step in?" Trey asked.

"Something like that." Marissa smiled. The corners of her eyes crinkled.

Trey felt something pull at this heavy feeling in his chest. Mom's eyes used to do that.

"How long has this been happening?" Ayesha asked. "People trying to purge magic, I mean, or whatever it was he said."

"*Purge* is a good word. As far as we know, Corvus has been trying to rid the world of magic since the early twentieth century. Maybe even longer. I've only been part of this group since the seventies."

"How do you 'get rid' of magic?" Trey asked.

Marissa's expression went carefully blank. A face she no doubt had practice using when discussing such things. "The truth is, you can't. Magic is energy, and energy is finite. It cannot be created or destroyed, merely channeled, shifted, repurposed. The Corvus believe that energy can be drained out of a person through mental and physical...They call them trials, but truly, it's torture."

Ayesha's shoulders hunched with each word Marissa spoke.

Trey understood why. His own stomach had begun to turn. "And...if that doesn't work?"

Marissa held his gaze. "I'm sure you can puzzle that out on your own."

21

ai stared at the quaint little scene that waited on the other side of the door. She found herself gazing into the small sitting room of a cottage. A fire crackled in the hearth. Two large chairs crowded the area in front of it, close enough to the flames to enjoy the heat but not be in any danger. Real cozy like. Occupying the chairs were two white women, and as Tai played her gaze over them, a weight settled in the center of her chest. These women wanted not only to be near the fire but also each other. They were dear friends.

While pondering over just how or why she somehow knew that, a faint, pained sound drew her attention and she turned.

Elva gazed at the display, her eyes wide and glassy. Her chest rose and fell with quickening breaths, and the way her expression twisted in equal parts distress and delight pinched at some delicate point on Tai's heart.

"Are ... you okay?" she asked.

The other girl clearly was not, but she wiped at tears as they sprang forth and nodded. "Yes, it's just I've never seen this one before."

Tai's head swiveled back and forth between Elva and the two women. "But you know them," she said softly.

A nod confirmed it. "My mother, and her ... our dear friend Mathilda."

Tai looked back to the door and what lay beyond. As her gaze moved over the women's faces, she could pick out pieces of Elva in the features belonging to the brown-haired woman on the right.

"This was so long ago," Elva continued. "I'd almost forgotten what their faces looked like."

Tension seeped into Tai, and she felt her shoulders lift with it.

People say time heals all wounds, but time was just a thief. It had stolen from Tai, and now she found it had stolen from Elva as well.

That pinch in Tai's heart tightened into a fist. Like someone had reached into her and closed their whole hand around her very being and started squeezing. It was a familiar ache. An empathetic burn prickled the backs of her own eyes.

She held out a hand.

For a moment, Elva didn't notice; she was still transfixed by the sight. When she finally noticed the offered invitation, she drew back a step.

"I—I don't know if I . . ."

Tai wiggled her fingers insistently. "If we are alike as much as you say, then I know you need this as much as I would. Do."

For a moment, Elva hesitated. She lifted her hand but didn't reach just yet. The emotional duology from before played out over her face again.

"It's okay," Tai murmured.

When the other girl finally took her hand, her touch not quite warm but not quite cool, Tai gave her fingers what she hoped was a reassuring squeeze. Then she led the way forward.

Stepping through the door was like diving headfirst into a pool of ice-cold water. It sent chills through her entire body, chased by tremors as her muscles rebelled against the sudden drop in temperature. Her limbs felt stuck, suspended and just enough outside of her control that trying to move anything was an exercise in testing her patience.

But as soon as the irritated thought crossed her mind, she felt the semi-weightlessness pressing in on her vanish. Just like that, they were standing at the edge of the room they'd been peering in on moments ago.

The first thing that hit Tai was the heat. The air was thick with it. That and the smell of something...floral? She knew this smell. It wasn't quite jasmine, wasn't quite lavender. Whatever the flower, the smell was cloying, and when Tai swallowed to try and relieve what felt like a blockage in her throat, she swore she could taste the petals.

On the other side of the room, Elva's mother lowered a teacup from where she'd taken a sip. "I don't mean to seem rude," she was saying, her voice soft. "It has been a long day, and I'm simply tired."

The woman across from her, Mathilda, frowned in clear concern. "I've not known fatigue to result in such trembling."

That's when Tai noticed the faint clatter of china.

Elva's mother set her cup aside. "Perhaps it is my nerves as well. I so want this to work. As does Oskar. It...*you* are our last hope."

Mathilda's frown melted away under a smile, and she reached out to press her hands to her friend's now free ones. "It will work, Agnes. I have promised you. And a promise—"

"Is like a contract," Elva's mother, Agnes, finished.

Mathilda nodded. "Yes. But between friends? A promise is a bond. It joins us together, like . . . like family, and I will not forsake such a tie."

Elva's hand tightened around Tai's, and she squeezed in return. Tears stained Elva's pale cheeks, her lips pressed between her teeth.

It's okay, Tai hoped her touch conveyed.

When she faced forward again, the scene had shifted. The fire was low, and as a result the room had gone cold.

Instead of two chairs near the dim hearth, there was only one. Mathilda occupied it. At least, Tai thought it was Mathilda. It was her same dark hair, but she couldn't see the woman's face. It was pressed to her hands where she bent forward, her body heaving in racking sobs.

"Wh-what," Tai started, wanting to ask what was wrong. She took a step forward. When she did, the room shifted, melting away into darkness, plunging her once more back into the cold, dark waters that had taken her when she first stepped through the door.

For the briefest, panic-stricken moment, she felt as if she was going to burst as something filled her, choked her, refusing to allow her to breathe. And in the next instant, she was on her hands and knees, her fingers clutching at the grass of the forest floor. Her chest heaved as she coughed, her body trying to expunge water that wasn't there.

"Tai!" Elva was at her side, helping her sit up. "Are you all right?"

She nodded, unable to stop coughing for a moment. When she could finally take a breath without feeling like she was choking on her own lungs, she lifted her gaze to search the area around them. There was nothing. The door was gone.

Elva guided her to sit back. "Take a moment to regain yourself."

"What...what was that?" Tai stammered around the last of the coughs.

Elva sighed. "I'm not entirely sure. Usually, I can see what happens on the other side of the doors, the ones I can open at least, but I've never been able to go *through* them." Her gaze trailed over Tai as she swiped at cheeks still flushed with tears. "You truly have an incredible gift."

"Thank you," Tai murmured, mostly because it was the response you were expected to give when someone complimented you. But her powers, incredible? They'd only ever been a problem, a situation that needed resolving. After a few moments, when breathing finally didn't feel like drowning, she pushed herself to stand. "So these are, like, memories?"

Elva watched her. "In a way."

"Whose memories?"

Elva frowned. "I believe they are our collective memories. Belonging to our family."

Tai nodded slowly as she began to pace. The anxious energy from before was back, and there was nowhere for her to channel it, so she just started walking. "What...what happened to Mathilda?" She could still hear the woman's gut-wrenching cries.

At first, Elva didn't answer. She adjusted her legs and settled into more of a seated position where she had been kneeling before. The white of her dress fanned out around her, and for a moment she looked like she was really a princess.

"My mother broke a promise to Mathilda," Elva finally said.

Tai stared, expecting there to be more of an explanation. When one didn't come, she snorted softly, and instantly regretted it. "Not to make light of Mathilda's feelings, but I break promises all the time. Not on purpose," she quickly added when Elva's head snapped up. "But, like, if I promise to do my homework, or promise to go to bed on time. Stuff like that."

Elva shook her head, vehemently, her golden hair billowing around her head. "No, this was a promised forged in magic. Mathilda agreed to help my mother, who longed for children. Mathilda understood, because she too was very lonely. So, she asked my mother to write to her, and sometimes join her for supper."

Tai turned the story over in her head a few times. "So...your mom promised to be Mathilda's friend? In exchange for babies?"

Again, Elva nodded, a faint smile gracing her lips. "A rather frank way to put it, but yes. And they were friends. At least, in the beginning. But then Mama stopped responding to the letters. Stopped going to the house. Because she and my father were afraid that if they were seen associating with Mathilda, they would be shunned by the townsfolk, who believed her to be a dangerous witch."

For a moment or two, Tai didn't say anything. Mostly because she didn't have anything *to* say. On the one hand, she could understand Mathilda's broken heart. It was hard to make friends, probably harder back then than it is now. And when you finally find one, to be betrayed like that?

On the other hand, demanding someone be your friend in exchange for a favor wasn't the best look either, but she kept that part to herself.

"So, they made a magic promise," Tai said. "And those kinds of promises are really like contracts?"

"Yes. They are binding in ways that I didn't fully understand, even when I myself met Mathilda later, then made and broke my own promise to her."

"Oh," Tai said quietly.

Elva's face went bright red again, and she swiped quickly at a few tears that managed to break free. "When I realized the magnitude of what I'd done, I tried to force a vision. To see a different future than the broken one I'd no doubt created. But I was still learning how to harness my abilities, and the backlash trapped me in the mirror, where I am forced to witness every promise our family has ever broken to one another, unwittingly strengthening the curse that was born the moment my mother decided to betray her friend. That I compounded with my own betrayal. A curse that has followed us for centuries."

It was like something out of a fairy tale really, except this was real. This had happened, *was* happening. Not just to Elva but to Tai, to her brother, to their mother, and everyone going back.

But in all of that, one detail stuck out to Tai the most. She waved her hands in the air, dismissing all of the noise around the single truth she'd honed in on. "Back up, *you* caused this?"

22

Trey sort of stared as his mind picked over what Marissa was saying without saying it. There were people in the world who hunted down others with magic, tortured them, and when that didn't work even killed them.

Marissa kept talking. "The Corvus take such monstrous measures because they fear magic. When *they* can't control it. If they can, then it's fine. Hypocrisy at its finest." She snorted and faced forward.

Trey's fingers tightened where he gripped his knees. Everything

Marissa said made a scary sort of sense, though a question had risen in the back of his mind while she spoke. A question he was terrified to ask, but knew he had to.

"My mom had—*has* powers. Mmm, magic. She disappeared. Ten years ago."

"I'm sorry to hear that," Marissa said. And she sounded like she was.

"Thanks. D-do you think she . . . ? Do you think those people . . . ?" Trey trailed off, gazing at the floor. The words lodged themselves in his throat, refusing to move down his tongue or past his teeth. He swallowed thickly and glanced up to find Marissa watching him in the rearview mirror, her gaze soft and sympathetic.

"I'm not going to lie to you," she said. "If your mother possessed a gift, then perhaps she was unlucky enough to cross paths with the Corvus. Or it could have been any number of reasons people go missing. Whatever the circumstances, once again, I am so sorry for your loss."

And there it was, the possible truth laid bare. He sank against the seat, pushed back by those words. It had been years since Mom disappeared, but confirmation was like losing her all over again. The faded-though-not-forgotten grief surged up full force, hollowing out his gut and simultaneously caving in his chest.

Memories of the last night Trey remembered spending with his mother rose unbidden. They were going to the grocery store. She had kissed his forehead, told him to be a big boy and help Dad keep an eye on Tai. Then she left the two of them upstairs to play, heading downstairs.

Tai was engrossed in their video game, but he had left to get something to drink. That's when he heard his parents arguing in soft, hushed, rushed words in the kitchen.

"Don't do this," Dad had begged. "Not right now. Not after what happened last time. What about the kids?"

"I'm doing it *for* the kids!" Mom snapped in return. "I don't want them to live like this! No answers, always glancing over their shoulders. I don't want this hanging over their heads."

As a tiny six-year-old, Trey hadn't fathomed that she was talking about then.

Dad pulled Mom in against himself and hugged her tight. For a good while they stood there, wrapped in each other's arms. Then they shared a kiss, and she walked out the door. That was the last time Trey saw her.

Trey had never told anyone what he'd witnessed that night. Mostly because he wasn't entirely sure, but also because remembering felt like holding his heart over an open flame. He'd spent years pushing the pain down, burying it deeper and deeper any time it tried to surface.

He thought he would be happy with answers. He tried to focus on anything but the hot emptiness filling him. He fought back the torrent of emotion that threatened to overtake him, like he'd done so many times for nearly a decade. He wouldn't break down, not here, not now.

A hand fell to his shoulder, and he glanced over into Ayesha's face. She looked briefly toward Marissa, then back at him. *What about the mirror?* she mouthed.

Trey sniffed, swiped at his eyes, and cleared his throat. "You said your group has been helping people with magic for decades?"

Marissa tilted her head to the side. "Yes."

"Do you know about magic items? Like, objects."

"What sorts of objects?" Marissa asked.

Again, Trey hesitated. Silently weighing the pros and cons of what he was about to say. If these people were legit, they could maybe help Tai *and* Elva escape the mirror. But he was used to keeping the family secret for so long, the truth felt like boulders in his throat. He swallowed around them. "Tai didn't get away. Not exactly. She wasn't captured, either. She sort of . . . went into a mirror."

Marissa straightened slightly. The leather of her seat creaked when she turned around fully. "Went into a mirror? How do you mean?"

"Well, I..." He glanced at Ayesha.

She stared at him, her eyes wide, clearly having not wanted to share that bit, but here they were.

Finally she faced Marissa. "She was holding a mirror. It started glowing, brighter and brighter. I had to look away. When the glow stopped, she was gone, and the mirror was on the floor where she stood."

Marissa ran a finger over her lips in contemplation. "This mirror, was there anything special about it?"

Again, Trey hesitated. "There was another girl trapped in it first."

"Do you know this girl?" Marissa asked. "Have you seen her?"

He shook his head. "Only Tai could see her. That was her power. Weird visions. And falling into mirrors, I guess."

Marissa nodded before pulling out a cell phone and punching in a number. She held it up to her ear for a moment before saying, "Rhoda, was there a mirror in any of the items that pinged for possible magical resonance? Have someone double-check the moment you can. Thanks."

She hung up, and Trey and Ayesha shared a look. The reason no one could find a mirror was because it was still in that backpack. And while he was happy to *talk* about the mirror, he wasn't quite ready yet to hand it over to anyone. Not until they got where they were going and he was certain it wasn't a trap. Certain as he could be, anyway.

"I had another question, about these Corvus people," Ayesha said in a smooth subject change. "How are they able to get away with everything?"

Marissa drew a slow breath and let it out heavy like. Clearly this was something that weighed on her. "Because they are everywhere. Various levels of authority as well. There have always been people that feared and demonized magic and those who use it. The witch trials happened, after all."

Trey blinked rapidly. "Wait, those were real? Er, is *witch* a good word?"

"*Witch* is just a word. Some of us use it, some of us don't. But to answer your question, most of those slain in Salem were non-magic users. All because of fear and bigotry. Ignorance. The real evils of the world."

"But you can't just burn people at the stake now," Trey said.

Marissa found his gaze in the rearview mirror again and arched an eyebrow. "Can't you? The Corvus have been around for as long as the witch trials, though over time their methods became much more . . . *subtle* isn't the right word. They're more deliberate with what they do, more focused. Outright murder is no longer an option, at least not on so grand a scale. And killing practitioners doesn't get rid of the magic, not when the gifts can be passed through families. Instead, the Corvus turned their attention to 'scrubbing' magic from the people blessed with it. That would be the torture I spoke of before.

"Some time ago, a member of the Corvus came up with the theory of scrubbing. He proposed that if magic could not be purged from a bloodline via death, maybe it could be shorn down to where it was too weak to manifest in future generations. Never mind that this scrubbing almost always leads to eventual death after years of torment. If the subject is lucky enough to survive, he doesn't just let them go. No. He still felt magic was dangerous in anyone else's hands but his, so he started indoctrinating a select few who survived his scrubbing. They would be his warriors, answerable to him and him alone. Now he uses magic to hunt magic. That man and his hunters have been a danger to everyone like us for nearly half a century."

"The people who came after us," Trey said. "They work for him. And they could use magic."

"The woman could," Marissa corrected. "The men were there to protect her. And to keep an eye on her. The Corvus doesn't give their magic users too much freedom. Can't risk them breaking the programming."

Well, that made a weird sort of sense, but only led to more questions, and a sudden prickle of anger in Trey's chest. "If you guys know all this and are supposed to protect us, why are you just now showing yourselves?" He met Marissa's gaze in the mirror. "Where the hell were you when these assholes popped up at our school yesterday? Twice!"

"I know this is a lot to take in and try and hold on to," Marissa said gently. "Believe me when I say you have my greatest sympathies, and my apologies that things went this far before we were able to step in. But you're safe now, and we're going to do everything in our power to make sure you stay that way."

That wasn't what he asked, but, "Whatever."

No one said anything for a while, merely listening to the rumble of the engine and the low rush of the wind whipping past. Brownstones swept by while the glass and steel skyscrapers of Manhattan loomed ahead.

Trey's eyes were drawn to the ridged profile of the city, the identical silhouettes of the Twin Towers. His mother loved this skyline and loved mapping the ways it changed over the years in sketches from various points in the boroughs. It was always in pursuit of trying to find the perfect way to depict the city, the life of it, the energy. Something inside him ached.

He closed his eyes and truly didn't know how long they'd ridden until Marissa's voice cut into the silence.

"We're here."

He blinked his eyes open. His lids were heavy, and his body slightly stiff with the beginnings of sleep. He hadn't realized he'd dozed off.

The buildings had dropped out of sight, giving way to a vast span of green. Patches of vibrant color rose here and there amid the lush grounds: reds, blues, violets, yellows.

Ayesha pressed her palm to the glass. "So many flowers."

The colors stretched out on both sides of the road, lined with thick brush and trees positioned like sentries guarding their gates. A cluster of buildings nestled in the center of the grounds, including a long garage where a few of the doors stood open, revealing a number of nondescript black cars. Some had their hoods popped, others were suspended on lifts with people in coveralls or T-shirts and dingy jeans leaning into or lying beneath them. A couple more structures stood off a ways. In the midst stood a house at least four stories tall and twice as wide.

It looked like someone had combined one of those old, classic homes with a modern mansion. The entire thing was hard lines, edges and angles, built with brick that burned bright red in the sun and large, sectioned windows reflecting the light. A huge porch wrapped around the entire ground floor. Balconies clung here and there to the sides. People sat in chairs or tilted against railings.

As the caravan pulled up, windows rolled down. The buzz of power tools and voices filled the air. A young white woman laughed and playfully slapped a brown guy's shoulder. A few kids played in the yard while an elderly dark-skinned couple watched. Nothing about this place or its inhabitants said "secret society honeycomb hideout."

The SUV came to a stop in front of a set of wide steps. The driver cut the engine.

Marissa turned to smile at them. "Everybody, out."

"Where are we?" Ayesha whispered, her voice somewhat awed.

Trey wondered the same thing as he racked his brain trying to figure out just where someone would manage to build a house this big on this much green in New York.

"Sanctuary." Marissa eased out of the car. "A hidden haven for magic users. For most of us, it's home."

"Hidden?" Trey asked.

Marissa nodded. "By powerful castings, we are concealed from prying eyes and wicked hearts. Only those who have been here can get back, and only if allowed. Otherwise, the instant you move beyond the woods, you forget you ever set foot here. Instead, you just went on a nice jog around the park."

"Park? *Central* Park?"

She chuckled and nodded, and Trey wondered how many times he'd wandered past this place and never even noticed.

"You live here?" Ayesha asked.

"Myself and several core members of this branch. There are houses like this in most major cities where we haven't been run out." Marissa waved to an old Latina woman in a rocking chair near the door, who simply nodded back. "A number of our elders who don't have any family to look after them are here as well. Think of it as a magical village north of the Village." She chuckled at her own joke.

Around them people were already unloading the SUVs, taking the tubs and bags of the Watson family's belongings up into the house.

"What are they gonna do with our stuff?" Trey asked as the group climbed the stairs.

Eyes followed their assent.

"Well, what we usually do is remove any magical essence present, if we can. Or we replace the item. That way it can't be tracked. Normally we would return the items to the owner, along with our information if they ever need help or somewhere to go."

Trey snorted. "Too late for that, in our case."

"Mmm. Maybe."

"Look," Ayesha said, and Trey glanced back to see she'd stopped at the top of the stairs while he'd followed Marissa toward the door. "What happens now? You brought us here, for our safety or whatever, and if I'm hearing you right, we have to *live* here?"

Marissa shook her head. "No, no. That is a choice some of us have made. Your situation is...progressing. Unfolding in the moment. I can't tell you what will happen. I can only assume based on what has happened in the past. The Corvus is after Trey and his sister—and possibly you, now that they've seen your face."

And the look that crossed her face was a mix of panic, fear, and something Trey couldn't name but felt in his gut. He looked to Marissa again. "They've seen my dad, too!"

The woman nodded, her brow furrowed but her expression open. There was understanding in her eyes as she bounced her hand in a placating gesture. "We've got eyes on him, like I said. He'll be guided away from anyone looking to harm him, eventually brought here to reunite with you. I promise, we'll do everything we can to keep him away from the Corvus."

As if on cue, a slew of shouted curses drew everyone's attention to where the duct-taped Gorilla guy was being unloaded. He hollered about purging their plague from the planet as he was hauled toward a large garage off to the side.

"What are they gonna do to him?" Ayesha asked as his screams quieted once they were inside.

"Most likely wipe his mind of the past few days. If they can, they'll pull serving Corvus from his memory completely. Then they'll drop him somewhere so he can make his way home."

"You can do that?" Trey blinked. "Wipe memories?"

"*I* can't, but there are some who can. It is a rare gift, even among the rarity that are we. Come. You should get some food. Rest. And we'll discuss how to help your sister."

Marissa slipped into the house, the screen door smacking closed behind her. She didn't pause to glance back at them, simply greeted those she saw inside.

Trey heaved a sigh, then glanced at Ayesha. "What you think?"

She smacked her lips. "I think we're in over our heads."

Trey snorted in agreement. His gaze shifted past Ayesha and out over the land one more time. This place was beautiful. Serene even. Hell, he couldn't remember the last time he used that word to describe anything about New York.

Movement in the distance caught his attention. He squinted, his sight lighting on a figure dressed in black, grasping some sort of assault rifle. The person walked the edge of the property, head slowly swiveling back and forth, and they weren't alone. Now that he was really looking, Trey picked out at least another half dozen guards. Guess this place wasn't completely sunshine and magic sparkles. He turned and followed Ayesha inside.

23

ai stared at Elva while trying to wrangle her raging emotions under control. Mostly the rage part. "So you're telling
me this whole promise thing, with your mom and Mathilda, and
you, is the reason *my* family is caught up in some mess?"

Elva looked ready to cry. She pursed her lips and screwed up
her face a little, but no tears fell. Instead, she tightened her jaw and
nodded.

Tai scoffed around a laugh and shook her head, glaring off into the mist. She could barely believe it. Trey's unpredictable abilities destroying stuff over the years, her troubled visions chasing her away from her own reflection, Mom missing, and now people following them to school and breaking into their house . . . was because a couple white women ghosted each other centuries ago?

"Jesus, this is the worst birthday bad luck," Tai muttered, then groaned when she realized this promise bullshit likely caused *that*, too.

"What is birthday bad luck?" Elva asked.

Her chest heaving, Tai had to close her eyes, disappear inside herself for a second, or she was going to scream. How unfair was it that her family was suffering through this nonsense because of some shit that had absolutely nothing to do with them! And yeah, Elva was her great-great-however-many-greats-aunt or whatever, but that didn't make things less messed up!

"It's . . . not important," Tai ground through clenched teeth before breathing deep through her nose. "I'm ready to try another door." Mostly she was ready to get the hell out of here.

Elva rose to her feet. "If you are certain."

"Oh, I'm certain." As if summoned by her words, the air where the last door had rested parted, and another pushed forward as if breaking the surface of water. It wasn't alone, however. An identical one popped up beside it, about five feet to the right. A third appeared after that. And then another. She counted six total. They formed a sort of carousel around the tree trunk. Hopefully one of them would take her back to her world.

But what then? Go back to hiding her powers? To not looking at anything with a remotely reflective surface? To not taking any more pictures for fear that some not-quite-dead relative might pop up in the viewfinder? To her and her brother spending the rest of their lives dealing with birthday bad luck, which only got worse with each passing year.

There had to be a way to counter it, right? A way to mend a broken promise. Maybe keeping it, even after all this time, was a start.

And maybe you don't know what the hell you're doing. True, but she'd never let that stop her before.

With another slow breath, she let the anger fizzle. Instead of a roaring fire in her chest, it was more smoldering embers. Agnes had broken a promise to Mathilda, abandoned her. And while it wasn't up to Tai to fix any of that, maybe she could do something to save her current family. She at least had to try.

And maybe . . . she could find a way to help Elva. Even if she didn't know how to get her out of here. It wasn't fair for her to be trapped, paying for her mother's mistakes. She deserved more as well, right?

"Tai?" Elva called softly.

She opened her eyes.

Elva stood staring at the door. It was the same as the other, only the tree at the center glowed softly, pulsing in a steady rhythm that mirrored the beating of a heart.

"I've never seen this before," Elva said, her voice betraying her wonder.

Without a word, Tai strode forward to open it. Like before, a scene bled into being before them. It was similar to the last in a lot of ways, a sitting room in what looked like an old cottage. It wasn't as homey as the other, no flowers and herbs hung on the walls, or blankets thrown over the chairs. The remnants of a fire glowed in a slightly smaller hearth.

"Where is this?" Tai asked.

"I . . . I don't know." Elva stepped forward to join her at the door's precipice. The two examined the scene a moment more, and just when it seemed like maybe they'd tuned in to the wrong channel or something, a muffled voice sounded from somewhere outside the house.

"Cay. Cay!" It was a man's voice, and despite his shouting he sounded amused. "Will you put those needles down and open the door?"

"All right! I'm coming!" A white man hurried into the frame. He looked to be somewhere in his late thirties, maybe early forties, with a shock of graying blond curls on top of his head. He opened the door in order to let in a second white man who was dressed in a cloak, covered in powdery snow, and carrying an armful of wood.

"Sorry, Ben!" the first man, Cay, said around a smile as he closed the door, then moved to take some of the load.

"It's cold as the dickens out there." Ben dropped what remained of his burden into a crate near the hearth and proceeded to blow into his hands. His gaze followed Cay as he deposited his wood as well, only to grab a couple of pieces and throw them onto the dying fire.

With a few aggressive stabs from the poker, the flames flickered to life again.

"And just what were you doing in here that you couldn't hear me hollering so?" Ben arched an eyebrow, but a smile pulled at his face.

"Baaah!" Cay waved a hand and set the poker down before moving to take the cloak from Ben's shoulders. He gave it a shake, then hung it on a hook near the fire. "I was working on your Christmas gift."

"*My* Christmas gift?"

"Aye."

"And what if I don't make it to Christmas because my beloved has left me to freeze to death in the snow!"

"You're being dramatic." Cay paused in fiddling with the fire again to aim a look at Ben, who hadn't stopped grinning yet.

"So what if I am. A theatrical truth is still the truth."

"You were no closer to freezing than I was to being strangled by a bear while you were gone."

"So you'd let a bear in from the cold, but not me?"

"Baaah!" Cay said again, his shoulders shaking with silent laughter.

As the two bickered, Tai felt her own smile stretch. This . . . was kinda cheesy, but still real sweet.

"Who are these two?" she asked, turning to find Elva quietly crying again, tears flowing over her cheeks.

Only this time, instead of her face being drawn up in pain, delight shone in her eyes.

"It—it's my brother," Elva sighed. "Oh, look at how big he's gotten."

"Your brother . . . The little boy I saw next to your casket?"

Elva nodded, the joy practically radiating from her face. "This . . . must be after Heidi and the kids. He looks so happy!"

Tai turned back to the scene just as Ben wrapped his arms around Cay from behind, burying his face in the side of his neck.

"Leave off!" Cay laughed, elbowing at Ben lightly as he wriggled in his arms. "Your hands are like ice!"

Ben wormed those icy hands up under Cay's shirt. "I told you. Freezing." But then he kissed his cheek and drew away.

The two went about preparing for a meal from the look of things, setting out stools near a small table and gathering bowls. There was a pot hung over the fire that Tai hadn't noticed before, and the two men scooped helpings of something that looked like stew—least she hoped it was stew—into the bowls. Then they sat down and ate together. They were quiet, though they kept casting glances at each other, smiling and such. Ben winked at Cay, who turned a hilarious shade of pink.

"What is this?" Elva asked. "How did you ... *What* did you ... ?"

"I really don't know," Tai said as her shoulders lifted in a shrug. "At first I just wanted to get out of here, but then I ... I thought about how you didn't deserve to be trapped here, either. That you deserved some happiness."

"And so you opened a door that would bring me joy," Elva murmured, awe once more coating her voice. "First you wanted to see the beginning, so you saw my mother and Mathilda. Now this. You can control this, far better than I'm able to."

Tai turned back to the scene, looking between it and where her hand gripped the knob. "So ... if I want, these doors will show me anything?"

"I cannot say for certain, but—"

Before Elva could finish her sentence, Tai shut the door. She twisted the knob to try and open it again, but it stuck in place. She pulled and yanked, but nothing happened. Staring for a moment, she drew back, stomped over to a separate door and took hold of that knob.

"Show me more!" As she pulled, a feeling like lightning jolted down her arm. She snatched away from the door with a yelp. The pain was brief but sharp, and it left the whole of her aching.

"Tai!" Elva was at her side in an instant. "What happened?"

"I—I don't know," Tai whimpered, clutching at the wrist of her throbbing hand. "First it wouldn't open, and then—"

Creeeeeeak.

The two of them glanced over as the door that had just shocked her slowly swung wide onto what was clearly an apartment of some sort. Paper lined the walls, vines wrapped around yellow roses against a cream backdrop. An electric light hung from the ceiling, over what looked to be a modern set of a couch and chairs.

Well, not modern. They looked old as hell, but more recent than the furniture that had been in the other houses. There was even a large radio set against the far wall. Crackly jazz music poured over the speaker, filling the air with the slow, swing rhythm.

Tai craned her neck this way and that, trying to catch sight of anything more. Just when she debated stepping through the door, the shrill ring of a phone made both her and Elva jump. It was immediately followed by the sound of a baby crying.

"Oooh, no, no, no," a woman cooed before shadows shifted at the end of a hall Tai could've sworn wasn't there before. "Hush now, or you're gonna wake your sister. You're all right. It's just the telephone."

The baby whimpered and whined but eventually quieted, and soon a figure came striding from the back room. It was a Black woman, a boxy dress hung on her thin frame in a style that screamed 1920s.

The woman cradled a bundle in the crook of one arm and reached for the ringing phone on the wall that led into the kitchen with her free hand.

"Hello?" she said into the receiver. Someone on the other end started talking just as the baby started fussing again. "Hold on one second." She adjusted the bundle, setting the baby to her shoulder while bouncing and rocking.

Tai played her eyes over her slowly. She'd seen this woman before, she realized. Which was impossible, and yet she knew better. Still, her brain was as fussy as that baby, just as unsettled.

"Zora," Elva murmured, as if she'd heard Tai's silent wondering.

That name stuck in her brain like a dart. She'd seen it in her mother's ledger. This was the woman from another one of Mom's pictures!

"No, I'm fine," Zora said. "The girls are fine, too. Delilah won't stay down for her nap, and if she don't stop fussing, she'll have Remi up. No, I haven't heard any news from Phillip's attorney, but I don't know what I'm gonna do if he's denied parole again. I'm almost out of the money I saved playing the clubs here in San Francisco while I could, before the girls, but I can't keep this up...."

With each new name revealed, Tai's heart went into overdrive. She might not know Zora's name personally, but Delilah and Remi? Those was her grandmother's and great-aunt's names. These doors were going down the family, line, and if that was the case...

Tai slammed the door closed and raced to the next one. She didn't bother to wait for Elva or even check to see if she followed. She gripped the handle, and braced for the pain she knew was coming.

Again, it slammed into her, this time with enough force to send her to her knees. But she held on, even as her vision waned and her body felt like it was being wrung out. She twisted the knob and pulled.

The scene didn't open onto any house but instead something that looked like an art classroom. People wearing bell-bottoms, go-go dresses, gauchos, and tight suits in any number of wild patterns were seated behind easels or on desks, chatting away about this or that. Tai searched the small crowd, feeling the hope that had swelled in her chest slowly deflate with each unfamiliar face.

Then the door swung open, and in *she* walked.

"Mom," Tai whimpered.

Blake swept into the room. Her long, strapless maxi dress billowed around her in folds of white and beige, making it look like she was drifting in on a cloud. Her hair was pinned atop her head in a bun. A pair of sunglasses perched near the end of her nose. She clutched a large bag thrown over a shoulder with one hand while the other held up a copy of some magazine. Tai couldn't tell which, because the cover was folded back.

The door was nearly shut behind her when it swung open again, and a young Black man slipped through.

Tai choked a little before she was able to croak out, "Dad?" Her throat tightened, her vision swimming for different reasons other than the throbbing steadily pushing in behind her eyes.

"Blake!" Dad called, shuffling around a couple people to get after her.

Mom didn't stop. She kept marching all the way to an empty desk, where she set her bag down and flipped the page of the magazine.

"Blake," Dad tried again as he caught up to her.

Mom finally glanced up, her face drawn tight in an expression Tai knew all too well. *This better be important*, that face said, and

Mom usually wore it whenever anyone was interrupting her stories or when she was reading.

Tai's entire being ached at seeing it again.

"Hey, foxy lady," Dad said, flashing some pearly whites and patting at his Afro.

He had an Afro. Tai had only known him to be bald!

"What do you want, Terrance? Before you answer"—Mom held up a single finger—"I don't have no Mary Jane on me, so don't ask."

Mary J—Tai did a whole double take. *Wait a—wait a minute. Mom!*

"Nah, nah, nah, next time 'sposed to be my treat anyway." Dad flashed a smile.

Mom rolled her eyes and looked back to her magazine.

"Aww, don't tell me you still mad at ya man?"

"*My* man wouldn't stand me up for the second time in a week." Mom plopped herself onto her desk.

"I told you, Moms asked me to pick up Geri from work. I can't just leave my lil sister hangin' like that!" Dad said, his hand gesturing sharply to the side. "And I didn't stand you up, I was late."

Mom wrinkled her nose and flipped a page. "Forty-five minutes."

"Thirty, max."

She glared at him over the top of those ridiculously large circular sunglasses, then pushed them up her nose and looked back to the magazine.

Dad reached to take her now free hand. "Look, I'm sorry. I am. But Geri's barely outta high school, working nights, trying to pay for college, she's making something of herself. I gotta support her."

Mom just arched an eyebrow, her eyes glued to the page.

"And we both know that if I'd've showed up on time, leaving her standing on some train stop after sundown, halfway across town, you'd've turned my ass into shoes." Dad reached to slide his hands against her bare shoulders.

They slumped.

Mom finally looked up again. She stared at Dad a moment before lowering the magazine. "You're so right. Damn, you know me."

Dad grinned and sang, "I know you, boo. Sugar?"

"Sugar," Mom said before the two shared a kiss.

Instead of being embarrassed or anything like that, Tai felt joy blossoming somewhere deep down. A balm against the sting of her anger that had hung with her this entire time.

Her mother and father, together, young and in love. How could she be mad while looking at that?

Her tears were flowing now, and she didn't want to stop them. Nor did she stop the sobs when they wrung themselves free. She pressed her hands over her face and wept, similar to how Elva had before. For how long, she didn't know, but when she finally blinked her eyes open, she felt Elva's arm around her shoulders and saw the scene had changed.

It was Mom and Dad again, sometime later. Mom's hair was shorter, and Dad wasn't quite bald yet but he was getting there. They stood with their arms wrapped around each other, him in a pair of jean shorts and a long tee, and her in a cute blazer with some high-waters and sneakers. They looked like something off *Family Matters*. They were at a party of some sort, Black folks holding drinks and beers, dressed in all manner of streetwear. Old folks, young folks, a couple kids even ran through. Then Tai saw her Grandma Richie push her way forward with a cake.

It was Dad's birthday, and everyone clapped when Grandma lit the thirty-four candles, then went around to kiss her son's cheek.

"Happy birthday, baby!" She brushed her thumb over a lipstick smudge she'd left behind.

"Thanks, Ma," Dad said, smiling.

Mom leaned in to kiss his temple, and Grandma smiled at her. There was warmth and love in that smile. Grandma Richie was always talking about how she found the daughter she never had in Mom.

Everyone gathered round the cake, Dad at the head of the table where it sat. "Now, before y'all start singing," he said, "I have an announcement to make."

Mom made a face that said she didn't have no idea what this was about. Meanwhile people murmured and Grandma mouthed, *Are you pregnant?*

Mom shook her head vehemently.

The whole time this was going on, Dad was digging into his pocket. "Actually, I just have a question to ask." Then he got down on one knee.

Grandma saw him first and actually screamed.

Confused, Mom spun around to see what was the matter only to find a room full of stunned friends and family, and her boyfriend on his knee. Her hands went to her mouth.

"Blake. I've loved you since the day I saw you. You walked past me at Georgie's party. You were with your girlfriends, looking fine in some jeans and that Prince sweatshirt you like so much. Your friends went into the house, but you stopped at the door, glanced my way, looked me up and down, and said hey. Then you went inside. I turned to my brother Bobby right then and told him, 'That's my wife right there.' And I mean to make good on that."

There wasn't a dry eye in the room. Grandma wiped furiously at her face while Mom wept into her hands.

Dad opened a case and took out the ring Tai had seen on her mother's hand, the dresser, different counters and tables all around the house.

"Blake Maria Estancia. Will you marry me?"

Mom could only nod. The room erupted in cheers.

Then Dad reached for Mom's hand. She offered it immediately, and he slid the ring on. As he stood, she wrapped her arms around his neck, and they kissed.

As Tai felt herself swept away on a tide of emotion, the scene changed right in front of her. It faded into a swirl of shadow and mist, the very same that filled the forest around her. Then it slowly revealed the living room in their old apartment. Tai remembered this place. They lived here before moving to the house. Mom sat on the couch. Dad lay stretched over it, his head in her lap. The two of them watched *Sanford and Son* while she patted his now-shaved head and he pressed his ear to her swollen belly.

Again the image shifted. This time, they stood in the kitchen of their current home. Mom tried to feed something to a uncooperative Trey while Dad was trying to discretely wipe away the whipped cream mustache he'd sprayed on little Tai because he thought it'd look funny.

Another skip. Mom and Dad were still in the kitchen but they were older, and arguing. The whole thing was a blur buffered against the tide of Tai's own reeling emotions, but she heard something about magic and hiding. Mom wanted to disappear. Dad couldn't break away from his family without a word.

"*This* is your family, Terrance. *We* are your family." She aimed a finger at the door. "Those babies, *our* babies, have our gifts. My abuela's, your great-grandma Subelle's. God, we didn't even *know* about that until your mom let it slip at the funeral! Two magic bloodlines mixing means they're already manifesting when usually it doesn't begin until adolescence. By that time they will be too powerful to ignore, he *will* come for them."

Dad made placating gestures before stepping forward to rub at her shoulders. "Baby, please, don't work yourself up. Look, I understand. I do. I'm not gonna do nothing that puts you in danger; I'm just gonna warn Momma that we're gonna be gone for a while but we'll be fine. That's all. I don't want her to worry."

Mom huffed. Her lips were tight, and she definitely didn't look like she wanted to agree, but she nodded anyway, and her shoulders dropped.

Dad drew her into a tight hug, promising that it would be okay. Then they kissed.

The scene blacked out, and just when Tai started to panic, it winked back in again. Mom was scurrying around the office at the gallery, pulling out notes, flipping through her ledger. She was dressed in overalls that were stained with various colors, her hair up in a messy bun. Just through the door to the side, Tai caught a glimpse of the concrete floor that was once Mom's studio.

Before she went missing, she did much of her work at the gallery itself. This was back when Dad still painted, too. The section that led into the office/employee lounge was walled in so they could work. Tai remembered days sitting on the floor messing over watercolors and finger paints with Trey while their parents honed their craft. She also remembered the day, three years after Mom went missing, Dad couldn't take walking through to reach the office anymore, so he had it renovated to add to display space. That's when he stopped painting.

In the vision, held by the magic doorway, Dad walked into the office from the studio space, staring at the mess of papers all over the floor. He had a cordless phone in one of his paint-smeared hands.

"Hey, babe. Mom agreed to take the twins tonight, we can finally have some alone time."

"I found them, Terrance!" Mom spun around. "Remi, Cole, they're alive!"

Dad stared, a bit dumbstruck. This sounded like it should be happy news, but he looked worried. "Was . . . was it those Corvus people?"

"Yes," Mom said. "But I found them. And I know someone who can help me get them."

"Help you? As in you're going?"

"Of course!"

"To the place that you said was deadly to people in your . . ." He gestured vaguely at her. "Situation."

"Yes, Terrance. They're the only family I have left, and they're *alive*."

Dad blinked, looking stricken a moment. "Ain't I ya family, B? Ain't the twins? Momma, Pops, Geri 'n' 'em, ain't *this* your family?"

It was Mom's turn to look struck. "Yes," she said. "Then you of all people should know what this means."

She turned to go, but Dad caught her arms. "Don't. Don't . . . I'm just worried. These people made your aunt and uncle *disappear*. You think I'm not worried that same thing won't happen to you?"

Mom stared at Dad, silently seething at him for being right, as he so often was when they were young. "I'm not like them. I know Ian. I know what he's capable of. Personally. I'll be ready."

"But I'm not ready, especially not to lose you," Dad said quietly as he stepped in and dropped his forehead against hers.

Mom melted. But she somehow managed to lift her hands to smooth over his. "You won't. I promise."

Then they kissed.

And instead of the scene changing, Mom just . . . faded. Thinner and thinner, until she wasn't nothing but a cloud, ready to be blown away. Then she was gone.

SPLINTERED MAGIC

Dad stared straight ahead as he lowered himself onto the couch in the living room. Six-year-old Trey and Tai were upstairs playing Nintendo. He could hear them thumping and arguing over whose turn it was to shoot the door.

They were making so much noise that Dad felt comfortable enough to grab one of the nearby throw pillows, wrap his arms around it tight, press his face into the fabric, and heave, great, sorrowful heaves. He sobbed for his lost love and how he should've but couldn't stop her. For his children who would have to wonder about their mother as she had worried about her family. And he sobbed for himself, for how he would have to face the future without his soulmate.

And then, like her mother had, the scene faded to nothing. Tai blinked.

"No. N-no! Why does it stop there? That's not where it ends." This time she closed the door fully, then yanked it open again. There wasn't even the swirling dark on the other side, just the rise of mist from the trees of the forest beyond. The window itself was gone now.

"No! This isn't fair! She was right there! She... she was..."

Tai slammed the door shut. Her heart raced. Her chest heaved. Sweat slicked her face and neck. She doubled over, her hands on her knees as her stomach churned and her lungs shuddered. Everything spun. She had to shut her eyes or she was going to be sick.

Hands gripped her shoulders.

"Tai?" Elva asked as she squeezed.

"I—I'm okay," Tai stuttered around deep gulps of air. She sniffed and swiped at her face, shaking her head. "I can't...see past this moment. Why?" Swallowing thickly she turned to peer up at Elva, whose eyes were once again shining with tears. Tai's own tears felt hot against her face. Then a rush of breath escaped her, and with it the whispered words "Why can't I see her? Now?"

Did that mean...?

Tai shoved that thought away violently. There was always this... ugly truth, a painful possibility waiting for her at the end of that train of thought, and she wanted no part of it. Not now, not ever.

"I don't know," Elva whispered. "I don't even understand how you've managed to do all of this." She glanced around the clearing, indicating the mirror. "But I know the fact that you *can* do it means something. I'm simply unsure of what. I was, am, still learning. Still trying to put all of the pieces together, but I cannot see everything. Even from here."

Then what good are you? Tai wanted to shout, though more at herself than at Elva. God, for once she's able to do something with her magic, something that let her see the fractured paths of her family's past, but there was still no way forward. What was it all for, why even bother?

That anger flared hot, burned through her body. She felt it in the palms of her hands and curled her fingers.

"You . . . will show me . . . what I want to see . . ." she whispered.

"Tai?" Elva asked quietly.

She drew a deep breath and straightened. She swayed but her legs held. "Show me what I want to see!" She turned and lifted her hand, concentrating.

The door flickered and started to shudder but didn't move, didn't change. Tai tried to focus on her desire, like she had when she wanted to help Elva or when she wanted to know more about why this was happening.

"Show me!" A wave of vertigo hit, nearly knocking her over, but she held on. "Where's my mother?"

"Stop!" Elva said. "I have no means of helping you here if you go too far. Breathe. You can't conjure something out of nothing. You must temper yourself."

Tai nodded, taking a slow and careful breath. Then she focused, her fingers waving slowly, flipping through the carousel of doors she'd already opened sending them spinning in a wide circle around the tree.

"So much of this is new to me," Elva murmured. "The forest has always shown me glimpses of our family, especially when they opened the door from their side."

"By...using the mirror, you mean," Tai said, sniffing as she wiped her face.

Elva nodded. "But this? You're opening doors that should be long closed, on lives long lived. You can peer into the past, the present, and the future." Elva shook her head, her expression and her voice awed as her eyes played over Tai.

It made her squirm a little, having someone stare at her like that. Like she was the most important person in the room. But, then again, there was only the two of them.

"So?"

"So?" Elva scoffed, but it was more laugh than scorn. "That is the entire picture, Tai. You can see it. And I want to help you, guide you through figuring this all out, but I can't follow the pattern."

"Pattern?" Tai glanced over her shoulder.

"Yes. Magic follows patterns. At least, the more potent spells. That's what I've learned from several lifetimes of observing various practitioners through our family. Occasionally I catch a glimpse of someone powerful outside our tree, but..."

"Patterns," Tai repeated before turning back to the doors.

She watched as they spun lazily along the newly formed

"carousel," twirling in and around one another. They all looked identical and yet, somehow, she was able to tell them apart.

"Like is drawn to like," Elva had said.

"Like is drawn to like," Tai repeated, her eyes widening slowly.

Planting her feet and steeling herself, she pushed at the carousel, willing it to spin faster.

As it did, her eyes fixed on the center of each door. The identical trees blurred together in the air, forming a single image like one of those old-timey projector things. It was out of focus, but it was there. She knew she wasn't tripping before, when she'd started to spin the door, but the flux of power had startled her and she'd backed off. Now she leaned into it.

"Wait," Elva said, in shock. "What are you doing? You'll hurt yourself!"

"I got this," Tai said through gritted teeth even as her head started to throb.

Elva seemed to relax at that, nodding as she withdrew her out-stretched hands.

The trees at the center of the door started to blend together. Their separate branches becoming one, the willow vines in gold relief began to glow, blossoming out into a familiar shape. The star flowers. The ones from her mother's picture and the box from the attic. They bloomed amid the vines of the tree, each petal illuminated with a single thread of magic that sung against her senses. Each time the line was splintered and re-forged into something new.

Mathilda.

Zora and Phillip.

Remi and Cole.

Mom and Dad.

Mom ...

Two families. Two bloodlines of magic, fragmented and reformed.

Mathilda and Elva were the beginning. She and Trey were the end. Her mother was somewhere in the middle, but she was missing. If they found her, if they completed the picture ...

"We ... we can fix it," she breathed as she watched the symbol crawl across what now looked to be a single door it was spinning so fast. A smile stretching her face. "We can fix it!"

All she had to do was reach out and grab the knob. But the last time she did that, she'd all but passed out.

And yet ... she knew she had to. If she was going to get out of here, going to get Elva out of here, going to somehow save her family from what was happening, she had to do this.

Swallowing thickly she took a slow breath. Then she looked at her fingers. They trembled. She could feel her knees threatening to give. Her whole body started to buckle. It was now or never.

"Show me my mother."

She took hold of the doorknob.

Fire raced up her arm. Light exploded across her vision. She felt her body lifted and dropped at the same time. Felt light as a feather, yet heavy as a bag of bricks. Her stomach threatened to empty itself. Her head felt like it might split up the middle. *She* felt like she might split up the middle.

Something at the center of her chest ... shattered.

She screamed.

24

rey wasn't sure what he expected when Marissa said that the council of elders might be able to help him rescue his sister, but it certainly wasn't a handful of old folks sitting around a scratched-up poker table arguing over dominoes.

They weren't too happy about having their game interrupted, but when Marissa explained Trey's plight—and what had happened leading up to it—five pairs of curious eyes looked in his and Ayesha's direction.

"Do you have the mirror?" an old Black man asked as he turned one of the dominoes over and over in his bony fingers.

"Unfortunately we haven't located it yet," Marissa said.

"Pity," said a woman with brown skin and a Spanish accent. She adjusted the shawl over her shoulders. "Without the mirror she used as a doorway, it will be almost impossible to track her."

"But if you did have it," Trey interjected, "you'd be able to help her?"

A Black woman picked at her dentures with a toothpick. "Maybe. Mirror magic is tricky, can't make no promises. But can make more sound guesses with access to the point of origin."

Trey glanced at Ayesha. The sour look on her face said everything he felt. He still wasn't fully into the idea of revealing the mirror. His mom had worked to hide it, and while he wasn't sure why, maybe it should stay hidden? At the same time, it was too late for that. Tai had found it and, somehow, jumped into it. He had to get her back. He nodded.

Ayesha huffed but swung the backpack off of her shoulder, unzipped it, and produced the mirror.

Trey's gaze flickered to Marissa, who simply smiled knowingly. While they hadn't exactly lied about the mirror, he still felt a little bad.

"Well, hand it over." The Black woman lifted her hand and wiggled her fingers.

Ayesha stepped forward to do just that.

Once the mirror was in hand, the woman turned it over in her grasp, examining it. She ran her fingers over the edge and lifted it to give it a long, slow sniff. Ayesha cut him a side look that said exactly what he was feeling.

Well, that's not weird at all.

"Old magic," the woman finally said. "Centuries old. Mmm, no wonder Ian's people were after you."

"Ian?" Trey asked.

"The man I spoke of earlier. He currently heads the Corvus," Marissa said.

"He's after the mirror?"

The woman shrugged before passing it to the man at her left, an older, round gentleman with deep beige skin and silver hair in two long braids down either side of his head. The man examined the mirror similarly, though didn't sniff it, before passing it on to the next elder.

"Maybe," the Black woman finally answered. "They like to collect magic items as well. Use them to help in their experiments and whatnot. Or just flat-out destroy them, sometimes."

Trey watched as the mirror made its way around the table before returning to the Black woman's hands. Marissa remained silent the whole time.

The Black woman knocked against the glass like it was a door. "Mmm. 'S locked."

"The mirror is ... locked?" Trey asked.

The Black woman angled around in her chair to stick him with a look. "You do anything else but repeat people? What, were you a parrot in another life?"

Ayesha tried, and failed, to hide a snicker.

"No, ma'am," he answered, taking a step back and folding his hands behind him, feeling a little silly.

The woman huffed and looked back to the mirror. "It's locked, but it's sloppy. Prolly an accident. We should be able to undo it. Then maybe she comes out. Or maybe you go in to get her. Or maybe we shatter the damn thing." She shrugged.

That brought a frown to his face. "Ahh ... don't want shattering, if it can be helped."

"Like I said, no promises." A smile stretched the Black woman's face. "But maybe a guarantee or two. Mari, hit the lights."

Marissa strode over to the door and flipped the switch.

The room was plunged into darkness that only lasted for a few seconds before a faint light started to radiate from the table. The mirror, Trey realized, and he took a step forward before he could help himself.

"Oh, well, you're in luck, young blood," said the old Black man. "Looks like someone is trying to get out."

"Lights," said the Latina woman.

Marissa flipped them back on, and Trey blinked to clear his vision.

The Black woman reached into a large leather handbag that was set on the chair beside her, rooting around inside before drawing out a faint blue crystal. Suspended inside the crystals were white petals from some sort of flower.

"Now, this door"—she patted the mirror—"is being primed to be opened from one side. We don't know who is doing it, but this should allow you to open it from this side and pull them through."

Trey hurried forward to take the offered crystal with thanks. "How will I know if—"

He didn't get to finish his question before the mirror started vibrating atop the table. The same light that had shone faintly in the dark began to brighten in intensity.

"This is what it did when she vanished!" Ayesha shouted.

"Out of the way, you fossils," the Black woman said as she gathered her things and pushed back in her chair.

The other four did the same, with the Black man doubling back to grab his dominoes before stepping away again. "Y'all be cheating," he said in a huff when the Indigenous man gave him a look.

"What do I do?" Trey asked as he shielded his eyes with one hand and held out the crystal with the other.

"Wait till you see the knob," the Black woman said. "Then set the stone on the glass!"

The light grew brighter and brighter. At this rate, he didn't think he was gonna be able to see anything! But then something etched itself against the light, and he . . . felt like it was being etched into the back of his eyes at the same time. It burned, searing hot, for a split second, and then what followed was a soothing cold as, before his very eyes, a willow tree of light sprouted against the glass.

"Use the stone!" someone shouted.

Trey reached out to set the crystal against the surface. The light filled the bright blue stone before it vanished entirely, leaving the petals that had been frozen within to fall against, then sink into, the surface of the mirror.

In an instant, the light faded, and the maelstrom of clouds and smoke that had filled the mirrors surface began to clear. The tree remained in place, the petals surrounding it, and before his very eyes, the image swung inward as if a door was indeed being opened.

Trey's eyes widened when he saw who stood on the other side. "Tai!"

His sister clung to the door, face ashen, barely holding herself up on her own two feet. But she gazed up at them, her chest heaving, and reached with a trembling hand.

Trey reached as well, without a second thought. His hand slid into the mirror like it was made of water and not glass. His fingers felt as if they were clawing through some sort of gelatin. A chill raced up his arm, the entire thing going numb with pins and needles.

He felt when Tai's hand brushed his. She latched on. He returned the squeeze, braced himself to pull, when something behind her flickered. A whisper touched Trey's ear. Apparently the same happened with Tai because she turned to glance over her shoulder. Then he blinked—that's really all it took—and she vanished. The swirling dark returned.

Before he could process what was happening, pain shot up Trey's arm sharp enough that he snatched it back with a cry.

"What happened?!" Ayesha shrieked, looking between him and the mirror.

"I—I don't . . ."

"Someone else looks to have opened a door as well," the Black woman said as she shuffled forward, her expression grim as she eyed the mirror, then raised her gaze to Trey. "Whoever it was got to your sister first."

25

Darkness went on forever. Whispers filled the void, along with a steady *beep-beep-beep*. Every now and then, fingers grasped random points along Tai's arms and legs. She tried to open her eyes, tried to pull away, but her body betrayed her.

The stillness became a prison.

At first there had been the impotent need to scream, but she couldn't. Eventually the attempts died into barely restrained fear.

She could only wait and listen.

The whispers grew clearer and louder; the words distinct as they filtered in. Voices talked about dosages and side effects, vital signs and chest rhythms. The fog lifted slowly, and with it the weight holding her captive.

Finally, Tai opened her eyes.

Darkness still danced at its edges of her vision. Nausea churned through her, and she swallowed the sourness rising in her throat. She blinked a few times and glanced around. Stained-glass windows poured in colored light but kept her from being able to identify anything outside. Marble columns helped stone walls hold the ceiling in place. Portraits stared at her from those walls, random scenes in forests and meadows, or angels watching over unwitting people. A massive candelabrum hung in the center of the room.

She tried to remember how or why she was here, but the result felt like an ice pick driven into her skull.

There was a knock at the door before it swung open.

In walked a small, elderly white woman with a wide smile plastered over her drooping face, her thinning hair pinned into a white nest atop her head.

"Glad to see you're finally awake." She set a tray she'd been carrying on a nearby table and uncovered a piping-hot bowl of soup.

The savory scent of chicken and vegetables made Tai's mouth water. Why did it feel like she was starving?

"I hope you're hungry." The woman poured a glass of some sort of juice.

"Who are you?" It hurt to talk. She swallowed to ease the burn. "Where am I?"

"You can call me Ethel." The old woman smiled. Her lips pulled back from teeth yellowed with age. "Best eat up, you need to recover your strength."

Tai lifted a hand to her throbbing head. Or she tried to, but the cold bite of metal on her wrist stopped her, and her attention snapped to the handcuff fastened around the railing on the side of the bed.

"What the hell?" Recollection bolted through Tai, flooding her mind and body. She'd opened the door, had seen her brother and Ayesha, but then it all changed. Shattered. She fell through, but it had *hurt*, and . . . now she was here. Had Elva come with her? Had she broken her promise to get her out of the mirror? After everything?

Tai's heart thundered. Her breath quickened. She yanked at the cuffs, resulting in futile clatters.

"Help!" she screamed. "Someone help me!"

No one answered. No one came.

There was only Ethel, who tilted her head. "Come now, you must be hungry."

Tai stared, a mixture of fear and fury bubbling in her chest.

Ethel hummed a cheerful tune as she held out a spoonful of broth. Her skeletal fingers curled like talons, and the spoon shook in her grasp. Somehow she managed not to spill a drop, even with the soup rippling like crazy.

"It's chicken noodle, made from scratch."

"I don't want any damn soup." Tai jerked against the pillow and yanked at the handcuffs again. "Let me go!"

"Oh dear, you've gone and worked yourself up." Ethel set the bowl aside and fished something out of the side table drawer.

When Tai saw the needle, her insides went cold. "St-stay away from me."

"Don't look so worried." Ethel drew close.

Tai recoiled but didn't get far, the metal around her wrists digging into her skin. She twisted and pulled, her eyes locked on the syringe.

"That won't be necessary, Ethel." A new voice spoke with a thick, British accent and made Tai jump so hard she banged her wrists in the cuffs. Pain shot up her arms.

A white man stood in the doorway, leaning against the jamb. Dressed in all white, he appeared a wraith against the wall's pale surface. Shaggy brown hair hung close to his pale face, and the sharp lines and angles of his features drew her attention to his stony eyes as they took her in. It was like trying to hold a statue's gaze, both in color and in essence. This man was cold. Rigid.

Ethel lowered the syringe and capped it.

"A moment, please." He stepped into the room, holding the door open for Ethel. Without a word, she doddered out. The man waited until the door clicked shut behind her.

"You have questions." His tone softened as he peered at Tai. "And I'll answer them. But first, I want you to know that no harm will come to you, here, so long as you cooperate."

"Where am I?" She was surprised how steady her voice sounded considering how shaky she felt. "Where's Elva?"

"Elva?" He approached the bed. He wasn't a large man, but he had a presence about him that filled the room and pushed Tai back against her pillows. "I'm afraid I don't know who you're talking about. You're the only one who came through. Which in and of itself should be impossible, unless ... Well, we'll get to that." He clasped his hands behind his back. "If there was someone with you, she's not here."

"Liar," she spat before she could stop herself.

"I have nothing to gain by lying to you." The man stared at her, scrutinizing her from head to toe. He settled into the nearby chair and pulled the tray of food over. "Ethel makes the best chicken noodle. Do you mind?" Spoon lifted, he looked at her in question. "Hate to let it go to waste."

"Knock yourself out." Tai shook at the cuff, twisting her wrist to try and pull it free.

"Thank you." He actually took a few bites before dabbing at his mouth with the napkin. "And apologies for the cuffs."

"Sure you are."

"Those are a precaution. Nothing more. If you are cooperative, they won't be necessary."

A precaution? What for? She bit down on the questions pouring through her mind, all except one. "Who are you?"

"Right, your inquiries. How about this, I answer one, then you answer one? Back and forth, seems fair, yes?"

Something about this guy set Tai's teeth on edge. He looked and sounded like a regular dude, but the longer she watched and listened to him, the more a part of her brain screamed danger, that she needed to get away. But she was handcuffed to a bed, and he seemed to be in charge, so she had to play this right. She nodded.

He smiled. "Good. You may call me Ian."

The sound of that name sent a sharp chill through Tai, like a needle-thin icicle driving into the top of her head and down her spine. She tried not to show it, hoping she'd fixed her face in time.

He wasn't looking at her anymore, gazing at his chest as he

smoothed his hand down the front of his shirt and crossed his legs. "I belong to an association. Not well known, but we have been around for a long time. The work we do is important, and you can aid us."

"Not inclined to help people who kidnap me."

His lips curled back far enough for her to see his molars, painting his expression with a borderline manic joy. It sent shudders trickling through her.

"We didn't kidnap you. In fact, you appeared here, on your own. Your methods were unorthodox, but results are results, mmm? Now, I've answered your questions, Ms. Watson. It's time you answered one of mine. That's the deal, after all." He reached to adjust a vase twice the size of his head where it sat atop a nearby pedestal, shifting it centimeters to the side. "Where is the mirror?"

Tai froze. "I do—"

"There's no point in telling me you don't know what I'm talking about." His gaze drifted to various parts of the room as if scrutinizing the decor, same as the vase. "You popped out of my mirror, or . . . what's left of it. The two are a pair. Sisters. Twins." He said that last word with emphasis. "This would not have been possible unless you had the other, so let's not waste each other's time or insult one another's intelligence."

Her scowl returned and she shook her cuffs pointedly. "Already insulted, thanks."

"If I remove those, will you be more cooperative?"

No. "I won't be as *un*cooperative."

Ian nodded and rose to his feet. He approached the bed, and Tai had to hold herself still to keep from recoiling at his presence.

Thankfully he didn't touch her as he produced a key and unlatched the cuff around her wrist with a series of clicks. The instant she was free, she threw herself to the other side of the bed and bolted toward the door.

Flinging it open, she raced into the hall. Instantly arms came down to trap her. At least she thought they were arms. They coiled around her like thick white pythons, crushing her against a massive wall of muscle. She struggled to break free, but all her twisting and kicking did was tire her out and rob her of air. The feeling flowed out of her limbs, leaving them hanging limp and useless.

Thump-thump. The steady beat of a heart. It couldn't be hers, which thrashed about as wildly as she had, trying to escape her chest. No, it belonged to the thing crushing her. *Thump-thump.* The sound filled her ears, along with the in and out of deep breaths. Her head lolled against a broad shoulder. The ceiling blurred as her vision grew fuzzy.

"Easy, James," Ian's voice echoed in her ears.

The pressure on her torso lifted, and the shadow creeping across her consciousness vanished. She drank in air with greedy gasps. Her eyes fluttered open, and the hall came into focus.

So did Ian. He was still smiling, completely unbothered by what just happened. "We don't want her damaged."

There was a grunt from somewhere over her shoulder. Hot breath brushed the back of her neck.

"You have your mother's fighting spirit," Ian said, his tone almost fond.

Something inside Tai cracked at the mention of her mom.

"I'd hoped you possessed a bit more insight than her. Pity." Asshole had the audacity to sound sad.

Her head still ringing, she managed to cobble together her best withering glare to throw at him. "The hell do you know about my mom?" she hissed.

"Much more than you do, I'd wager." Ian arched an eyebrow. "Especially since I know all about you and your brother, Tai, and I'm fairly certain—given your reaction—that this is the first you've ever heard of me. Would it surprise you to know your mother and I are old friends?"

"Liar!"

"That accusation again. And, again, false. Blake and I were

friends, for a time. I know what she's capable of. What all of you are capable of. The unnaturalness of it." His face scrunched, and this was the first time he'd looked less than pleased. "You think your abilities make you special, give you purpose? No, purpose comes from something ... more."

Tai wanted to tell him just what he could do with his more, but she was starting to feel light-headed again. James, or whatever the hell his name was, had gradually tightened his hold.

Ian seemed to notice this, his gaze flickering over her. He stepped aside and waved into the room. Tai jolted as she was carried back over the threshold. She tried to struggle, but the viselike grip made it impossible.

"Just drop her," Ian said as he shut the door. "There will be fine."

When the arms around her finally let go, the floor rushed up to meet her. She caught herself on her hands and knees, joints cracking against the stone and sending a jolt of pain through her limbs. The prickling sensation parading through her entire body told her that she wouldn't be able to get up for a minute or two.

James stood over her. It was hard to tell from this angle, but he appeared at least a foot taller than Ian and probably three times as wide. Time had etched James's face with deep lines, though a few of them looked to be the work of something sharp and jagged. His gray hair was shaved close, reminding her of a military buzz cut. His arms folded across his chest, the fabric of his white robe stretched to the breaking point over his frame. No wonder his bear hug nearly broke her in two. He stared down at her, a humanoid mass between her and the door.

"Please." Ian returned to his previous chair and took up the glass of juice from the tray now. "There's no need to drag this out. The sooner you give me what I want, the sooner you can go home to your family. I promise."

Tai pushed herself to stand. The whole of her shook in a mix of fury and fear. "You make that promise to my mom?"

Ian's condescending smile faltered. "I don't expect you to understand."

"This is what happened to her, isn't it?" Tai asked, ignoring the trembling in her gut, in her voice. "This exact thing. You took her, asked her for the mirror, and when she said no..."

There suddenly wasn't enough air in the room. Every possible outcome now lay before her, including so many horrible ones. At once the answer to the question that had been plaguing her for a decade was right in front of her, and she was too afraid to reach for it.

"I'm hoping you're smarter, Tai." Ian took another sip from his glass. "That you take a moment to think things through. The wrong reaction can result in consequences for not just you, but the ones you love most. You're already living with the results of your mother's choices. Maybe yours can save you *and* her."

Tai's head snapped up from where her gaze had fallen to the floor. "Wh-what?"

"That's right." Ian stood now, approaching her slowly. "I'm not an unreasonable man. You do for me, I do for you."

Tai swallowed the swelling lump in her throat. She shrunk in on herself as Ian came to stand over her.

26

T rey stared at the empty mirror clutched in his hands. He
searched the billows for any sign of his sister, but there was
nothing but the dark, depressing rolls of black-and-gray clouds.

Ayesha sat at his side, leaning in to try and look every now and
then as well, occasionally stealing glances up at him.

"I had her," he murmured. "I felt her hand. I could've pulled
her out, but..."

"That way lies madness," the old Latina woman said where she sat nearby.

After the first failed attempt at saving Tai, the elders had returned to the table and resumed their domino game, as if nothing had happened. Marissa had slipped from the room, intending to make a few calls to try and see if they could figure out what had happened.

"I already told you what happened," the Black woman had complained. "Someone else opened the door as well and pulled your sister through. Good news is, she's not in the mirror no more. Bad news, now we don't know *where* she is."

"I might have an idea," Marissa had said before departing.

Trey had no idea how long ago that was, only that every minute he sat here, staring into a mirror that wouldn't even look back at him, he felt himself slipping further and further into hopelessness.

He'd promised Mom he would take care of Tai. . . . For ten years he'd kept that promise, only for it, and her, to literally slip through his fingers in an instant.

"What am I gonna do?" he murmured.

"We'll figure this out," Ayesha said, nodding more to herself than anything. "I don't know how, but we will." She set her hand over the one that Trey had laid flat against the mirror.

Trey offered her a sad smile. It was all he had. "You know," he started, "I was mad jealous of you getting first chair."

Ayesha ducked her head a little and pulled her hand away from the mirror. "I'm not sorry I got it, but I am sorry you didn't, if that makes sense."

"It does. And I appreciate that." He took a slow breath and released it in a puff. "I also appreciate you being here."

"Not that I had a choice," she said. "But if I did, I'd choose this."

The Black man across the room smacked a domino on the table with a "Pow! Gimme my points!" The other elders groaned as he cackled.

Trey let his attention shift back to Ayesha. He considered her a moment. When the Corvus showed up at their school, she'd helped him and Tai get away, without question. Then she got caught up in all of this, and instead of running away as fast as she could, she was trying to help him save his sister.

"You're good people. I'm glad Tai found you. Like, I know she be lonely, sometimes. She got her friends, and we got family and everything, but she's been looking for some*one* for a minute now, and . . . well . . . I'm glad it's you."

Ayesha smiled, nudging Trey with her shoulder. "I'm glad she found me, too. And I'm glad she has a not-too-terribly-annoying brother."

He couldn't help chuckling, glad to have someone to take comfort in with this as well.

But then his smile started to fade. "How am I gonna tell my dad that I *lost* my sister?"

"I don't know," Ayesha murmured. "But you won't have to do it by yourself. I promise."

Trey smiled, then blinked when a flicker of light drew his attention back to the mirror. The fog was gone. "The door," he whispered. "I . . . think the door is back!"

Ayesha gasped, her eyes lighting up as she leaned forward to look as well.

At the poker table, chairs scooted as the council of elders all shifted to try and get a look at them.

The Black man pushed to his feet. "Is that—"

"Contact trace!" the Black woman gasped, looking caught somewhere between shock and fear. "Take your hand off that—"

Before the rest of that sentence could leave her mouth, Trey felt a sudden pull at his center, behind his navel. The emptiness of the mirror swept up to consume his senses, filling his insides. Time seemed to slow, leaving them hung in the air. It was incredible, terrifying, and over too quickly.

Gravity latched on, merciless, yanking him into a free fall.

Wind screamed in his ears. The sound resonated inside his

head, tearing its way out. Pain poured from his skull through the rest of his body, and everything went white. He doubled over, fighting a wave of dizziness threatening to overwhelm him.

Even when the noise faded, his ears continued to ring with distant echoes. But at least he was able to move without wanting to throw up. He slammed into something hard, pain radiating through his body. Groaning, he rolled onto his side.

"Aaaah, god," someone moaned.

He forced his eyes open, blinking the world into focus.

Ayesha lay beside him, coughing and whimpering as she shifted around, trying to get her hands and knees beneath her. He tried to do the same, though his body refused to cooperate. It was as if jolts of electricity were moving through him, robbing him of his ability to control his limbs.

"What . . . happened?" Ayesha whimpered.

"Don't know," he barely managed to croak out. "Someone said something about a 'contact trace'?" He had no idea what that meant.

"Mmmph, whatever it was, it hurt like hell."

Trey pushed himself up and glanced around. The table and the elders around it were gone. Instead, he and Ayesha were in what looked like some sort of weird-ass supply closet. Shelves lined the walls and formed aisles, oddly shaped items lining each one. He couldn't make out what any of that shit was; the light too low for him to be able to tell.

Actually there was no light at all, just the glow from beneath a nearby door. It was enough for him to make his way that direction,

"Trey?" Ayesha asked, her quiet, frightened voice following after him.

"Just looking for a light," he called back. He approached the door with his arms outstretched, and when they touched stone he started searching. Usually lights were near the— Aha.

He flipped the switch. Cold white light filled his vision, and he had to blink to clear it. As everything came into focus, he caught sight of what filled the surrounding shelves. Old-looking books, some crystals like that woman had given him. There were candles here and there, and something that looked like a freaking cauldron.

"Where are we?" Ayesha asked, finally getting her feet under her as well.

"If I didn't know better," Trey said as he managed to struggle to his feet as well, "I'd say the set of *Charmed*. Look at this stuff."

No joke, these shelves were lined with things that looked like they belonged in a museum or Dracula's basement. Was that a *Book of Shadows*?

As he turned, he noticed a flicker over Ayesha's shoulder where the light glinted off of shards of something. He gasped when he spotted bits of shattered glass and the familiar sight of a metal frame.

He glanced around, patting himself down as he turned. "Do you have the mirror?"

Ayesha paused where she had been examining a row of crystals. Her eyes widened, and she swung the back around to peer inside. "No," she murmured, shaking her head. "B-but I . . . I think that's because we went through it? I mean, the light was . . . the same as when Tai went in. And we're definitely not at Marissa's house right now." She glanced around, taking in more of the room.

"So we fell through, too?" Trey said, his gaze moving back to the mirror across the way. "Then what's this?"

Ayesha turned to follow him, he eyes widening. "A duplicate?"

"Should we take it? It might be the other door they were talking about."

"Yeah. Let's stick it in the bag."

Ayesha shuffled around before the sound of a zipper filled the silence. Then glass clinked against metal as the second mirror was lifted.

"It's broken," she whispered.

"You get all the pieces?"

"I think so."

"Good. The exit is this way."

Trey cracked the door just enough to peek through. It opened onto a hall that looked like something out of medieval times. Walls built from thick, old stone rose on either side of the corridor, windowless, cold and imposing, with pale light spilling from sconces that looked to have once been actual torches.

Seeing that the coast was clear, he led the way out and down the corridor.

"The fuck is this place?" Ayesha asked quietly, but beneath the faint tenor of her voice, Trey heard something else.

He lifted a finger to his lips, his brow furrowed.

Ayesha went quiet, cocking her head to listen.

The low hum of voices reached them from down the hall. The question was, which direction were they coming from? If Trey picked wrong, he and Ayesha might run into someone who definitely didn't want them here, wherever here was.

Ayesha grasped his arm and pointed to the left. Her left, at least. Trey tilted his head, straining to listen, before agreeing, and the two of them shuffled their way along the hall, away from the voices.

Only to round a corner and come face-to-face with three people wearing white robes like something out of *Final Fantasy*.

Ayesha and Trey froze, her breath catching, his chest tightening.

The people in robes also froze, staring. Then one of them pointed.

"Outsiders!"

Trey spat a curse. "Run," he said under his breath.

One of the robed figures rushed forward.

Trey spun on his heels and in the same motion shoved Ayesha in the opposite direction. "Run!"

27

"Tell me where to find the mirror, and I'll reunite you with your mother."

Those words hit Tai like a fist to the gut. A decade's worth of hurt and hope swept over her in an instant. But in the next, her mind closed in over the possibility with steely denial practiced for nearly just as long.

"Prove it," she said, the words low and loaded with the danger of . . . she wasn't sure what, but she would make this man pay if he was using this to try and mess with her.

Ian tilted his head to the side, either ignorant of or unbothered by her ire. "Is that a tacit agreement I hear?"

"It's a maybe," she snapped, the pain that had nearly taken her over quickly shifting to anger. "A very thin maybe."

Silence paced between them as Ian watched her. His gaze trailed over her, considering, before he finally waved a hand in an indication for her to continue.

Once again, that barest breath of hope caught in the back of Tai's throat. But she swallowed hard and lifted her chin. "I want to see her. If you have her, you show her to me, you let me talk to her, I want to see her!" Her voice, her entire being, shook. The last words escaped in a hoarse shout.

Ian nodded, his brow pinched. "I see this has weighed heavily on you." He didn't look exactly remorseful, his expression just the right side of sympathetic to make you think he might be. "You know I do what I do to help people. To save them. Well, most people. The majority."

"I don't care about whatever 'greater good' bullshit you have going on here," Tai snarled, her hands balling into fists. "Where's my mother?"

"I can appreciate the emotional intensity of this moment," Ian said as he picked at some imaginary lint on the sleeve of his shirt. "So, I will ignore your inability to keep a civil tongue. If I show you to your mother, and prove she is whole and of sound mind, let you speak to her, then will you tell me where the mirror is?"

Tai felt the line of her shoulders tense, but she nodded anyway. "And . . . you promise to leave me and my family alone."

Ian arched an eyebrow slightly. "Changing the agreement already?"

"We don't have an agreement yet. And I don't care about some dumb mirror, but you do, so." She let the threat hang unsaid between them.

He made a show of heaving a sigh before nodding. "Very well." He looked to James, who stood by silent and looming this entire time, his arms folded. "Accompany us."

With that, Ian moved toward the door.

James watched him a moment before looking at Tai and jerking his head toward the exit. "You next."

Tai hesitated only a second before heading that way, flipping him off as she went. Maybe she imagined it, but she thought she heard the low rumble of a chuckle as James fell into step behind her.

These people, she would not let them see her afraid. It didn't matter that the fear crawled through her like a living thing, spinning its web to wrap tightly around her heart. She'd spent so much of her life pretending to be fine, putting her armor on. She had fooled her family, her friends, for years. She could fool these two, and anyone else she needed to.

Ian led the way out of what had seemed a normal if not a little over-the-top room into an all-out castle hallway. Stone walls rose on either side, lined with what looked like old-timey gas lanterns converted for electric. Tapestries stretched over sections here and there, depicting great battles between knights and beasts, or maybe a group of people kneeling in what looked to be prayer. A few portraits of dour-looking white people watched the three of them as they strode past.

Every door they passed was closed. Every connecting hall identical to this one. So much for any hope of being able to figure out where they are. Tai half expected to run into a gargoyle or something. Seriously, the place looked like Xanatos's castle, but far less cool.

"You remind me of her, you know," Ian said, his voice low but still loud thanks to how quiet the rest of the building was.

Pulled from trying to mentally map their path, Tai glared at the back of his head. "I don't care."

"Same temperament. Same strong-willed determination. Same hardheaded stubbornness rooted in an inability to see past what's in front of her face...."

"Same healthy disdain for you, I bet."

He shot a look over his shoulder, and for the first time, his expression shifted into one of genuine annoyance. But it smoothed over shortly after. Ian seemed like a man who preferred to appear composed, even when he wasn't. Tai took what enjoyment she could in breaking that, even if only for a moment.

"A healthy disdain for the truth," Ian continued as he faced forward again. "I warned your mother, told her magic was dangerous in the wrong hands. When we met all those years ago, I thought she believed as I believed. That magic, while capable of great feats of power and ability, was also capable of great evil. We could have accomplished *so* much together, if only she'd just agreed to work with me instead of being a hindrance. Alas, her stubbornness won out." He made a show of shaking his head of disappointment. "I'm glad to see that, while stubborn, you can still be reasoned with to some degree—"

Ian stopped talking as something buzzed against his hip. He unclipped a phone from his belt, then lifted it to his ear. "Speak."

Whatever message came through on the other end was enough to make him stop in his tracks. "What did you say?" he asked, his tone disbelieving. "Where?"

James shifted behind Tai, pressing a little closer. "Problem, boss?"

Without warning, Ian spun to face them, his expression caught between disbelief and anger. His gaze, bright with fury, lifted to the man mountain. "You said she was alone."

James balked, which was fairly interesting to see someone his size do. "She was."

"Then why am I being told there are two intruders loose in my building?!"

Tai did everything she could to swallow her reaction. Intruders? Who could they be? . . . Were they here for her? Were they here for Ian? Did this mean she wouldn't be able to see her mother?

Ian stepped forward, a finger aimed at James's face. The big man recoiled as if he'd pointed a gun at him.

"The ability to do what we do depends heavily on the fact that we do it in secret. You are the head of security, meaning it's *your* job to keep things *secure*! Find out what the hell is happening and deal with it."

James fumbled for his own phone, dialing up someone as he stammered over an apology. "Of—of course, sir, I'll take care of it."

While Ian was preoccupied with jumping down James's throat, and the big man in turn fumbling to get a handle on things, Tai saw an opportunity and took it. She'd backed out of the way when Ian moved in to menace the other man, and now shuffled to the side, her shoes silent on the floor. Inch by inch, she put two feet between them. Then five feet. Then seven. She'd nearly gotten a good distance away before Ian turned. Shock flashed over his face as he glanced around, then directly at her.

Tai bolted. She just picked a direction and ran. She didn't know where she was going, and didn't care so long as it was away.

"Stop her!" Ian's bellow sounded through the hall, as did the heavy thud of steps in her wake.

James was big, but she was fast. If she could stay ahead of him and nothing got in her way, she might be able to lose him in this labyrinth. She rounded one corner and then immediately another ducking into an alcove and pressing her back to the cold stone of the wall. Her chest heaving, she did her best to quiet her panted breaths so she could listen.

As the sound of James's steps drew her near, she tensed, ready to run again. He stopped at the junction of the hall she'd just whipped through. His shoes clicked on the stone as he went partway up one hall, then the other. When it sounded like he was coming closer, fear nearly shook a whimper loose, but she pressed a hand over her mouth. Without the sound of her steps to guide him she hoped, prayed, he wouldn't be able to find her.

"James!" Ian's shout made her jump. The sound of his voice came from back the way they'd come. "Don't tell me you *lost* her!"

"Apologies, sir, I thought I heard her come this—"

"But you were wrong, of course, because you likely didn't hear a thing." Ian's voice was clearer, meaning he too was closer, and far angrier. "Now there are three brats running through my facility."

"I—I—" There was the sharp slap of flesh against flesh, and Tai's eyes went wide.

Did . . . he just *smack* him?

"There's no way out of the facility from this floor," Ian growled, his voice low and dangerous. "She's loose but trapped. Those two, on the other hand, could cause undue trouble. Get on top of this or so help me the cause will no longer have use for you."

"Y-yes, sir. Of course, sir."

The sound of their departing steps carried them swiftly away.

Tai felt like she might melt into a puddle right then and there, the tension seeping out of her. She was granted a momentary reprieve, but she couldn't stay here.

One minute, she silently decided. She'd wait one minute to make sure they were well and truly gone, then she'd try to find her mother, then find a way out.

Or maybe you get the hell outta Dodge and come back with help, because the bastard could be lying! Not to mention if she was somehow caught, she wouldn't be able to help her mom or herself.

But what if she's here . . . what if you leave and you never see her again?

The burn behind her eyes, the tightness in her throat, the twist in her stomach all warred against what her heart begged her to do. Go. Or stay.

Before she could bring herself to make a decision, a scream from somewhere nearby made her jump, her heart in her throat. The shout trailed off into a garbled sob before silencing entirely.

For a moment Tai stood frozen. Questions filled her mind, bumping into and tumbling over one another. Who was that? What was being done to them to make them scream like that? Was that same thing happening to her mother? If she was caught, would it happen to her?

Trying not to think about any of the possible answers, Tai hurried toward the other end of the hall. She peeked around the corner and, seeing no one, slipped down that hall. She strained her senses, trying to hear anyone that might be coming her way.

Silence pressed in around her. She couldn't hear another soul, which is why sudden movement at her right nearly made her black out from fear. Thank god she recognized her own reflection before she screamed, that would've been a dead giveaway.

Jesus. She tried to breathe through the waning terror. Her heart felt like it was going to ooze out of her nose, she'd been so scared. She paused to take a few slow, calming breaths, and her eyes were drawn to her own face and the way it rippled like water. In that instant, she realized what was happening and that she was too late to stop it.

The vision had hold of her, its grip pulling her down like lead in her limbs. Before, if she caught it soon enough, she could look away or at least close her eyes. But now? Now her entire body seized up as the world around her faded to shades of gray, the image in the mirror brightening in contrast. A scene unfolded before her, two people running down a series of halls, chased by a small group wearing white robes.

These halls, she realized with a clarity that startled her. A clarity that quickly revealed the ones running were Trey and Ayesha! They had to be the two Ian had jumped down James's throat about.

As she watched, Trey flung himself around a corner and right into a pedestal holding some sort of statue. It and him went tumbling. Ayesha hurried back to help him up, the two of them taking off again, but the group in pursuit of them had gained ground.

"I have to help," she whispered to herself. She didn't know how, she didn't even know where they were just that they were in this building, but she needed to do something, she needed...

The thought barely coalesced before Tai felt herself yanked off her feet and pulled, bodily, toward the mirror. It all happened in an instant, and she couldn't do much more than wrap her arms over her head and brace for impact.

28

Trey felt like his heart was going to burst right out of his chest. His ears were ringing, his vision blurred, and a pressure under his skin made his arms and legs feel too tight, as if all his joints were attached at the wrong angles. But he breathed through it, ran his fingers over the stone wall, and pulled.

This wasn't like pulling with his hands or arms. This was like reaching out with something inside him, with the very idea of wanting to grab hold of an object and draw it in. He truly had no idea what he was doing, but this had worked so far. And it worked again as the stone beneath his fingers cracked, crumbled, then came tumbling down to block the hallway behind him and Ayesha.

Shouts of alarm and orders to "Get back!" rang from the other side as the assholes in white hoodies came up just in time to nearly have the ceiling collapse in on them.

Similarly, Trey collapsed to his knees as the thrumming inside him felt like it was going to shake him apart.

Hands gripped his shoulders, and Ayesha's voice filled his ears. "Get up!"

She pulled at him, and he tried to rise, but the world tilted on its axis and he dropped all over again.

"We can't stay here, you have to get up!"

I'm trying! he wanted to scream, but he could barely manage to stay upright, and he was lucky breathing was involuntary.

Ten minutes ago he had no idea he could wield his magic like this, until—in a panicked scramble to get away from their pursuers— he flung himself into a locked door and blew it clean off the hinges. Then he pulled a pillar down to buy them some time. Now he just blew out a wall. With each purposeful use of his magic, he felt more and more like his body was going to unravel.

At first he thought he was tired from running, then he realized using his powers was draining him. If he kept it up, he wouldn't have any steam left for escape attempts. But the more his fatigue slowed him, the more they needed obstacles to buy them time, meaning he had to use his magic, which added to his fatigue, which slowed him. It was a downward spiral outside of his control, and it *hurt*.

Ayesha was still pulling at him, trying to run at the same time and sort of half dragging him along. "We gotta go!"

His legs felt like linguine, his knees unable to lock.

Ayesha did most of the work, pressing in at his side to help keep him upright. "Come on, we— What the hell?"

At her shout, Trey lifted his head from where it'd started to roll a bit. He wasn't sure just what he was looking for, glancing around before finally thinking to follow her shocked expression.

A mirror hung on the wall across from them. At least, he thought it was a mirror. He could see his reflection, but the image was distorted by a warbling light at the center. A pulsing that could be any number of things. It should've scared him, especially in this place. Sent him scrambling, crawling even, if his legs refused to carry him more than a few steps. Instead, he was rooted to the spot. And it wasn't fear he felt but a sense of . . . familiarity.

Then he felt pain when the light flashed like lightning and something came shooting out of the glass, slamming into him and Ayesha, taking the both of them down in a tangle of limbs. They hit the floor, and pain ricocheted through his already-taxed body. He groaned, attempting to roll off of his pinned arm.

"Tai!" Ayesha's shocked but ecstatic shout snatched at his clouded thoughts.

Sure enough, when he managed to draw back and twist himself around, there was his sister, flat on her ass, looking like . . . well, like she'd just been shot out of a mirror.

She stared at them with wide eyes before panting a soft "Holy shit."

Ayesha threw her arms around her, half tripping over Trey's legs to do it. "What happened to you? Where were you? Are you okay?"

Tai nodded and returned the hug, still looking like she'd seen a ghost. "F-fine, I'm fine. You two?"

"Trey's hurt or something," Ayesha said, and finally pulled away, moving over to his side. "Help me get him up; those assholes are after us."

He wasn't hurt exactly, but he was definitely *hurting*. And having a hard time getting to his feet again. He managed to get on his knees before two sets of hands took hold and pulled.

With Tai under one arm and Ayesha under the other, the three of them hobbled down the hall. The shouts of the people in robes faded behind them, and while it meant they were safe for the moment, they couldn't bet on it staying that way.

They passed a few doors, pausing long enough for one of the girls to try the knobs. Locked, all of them, until they came across one that didn't look half as fancy as the others. The CUSTODIAN sign explained why. Tai flung the door open, and they slipped inside.

The room was dark and stank like bleach and something mildewy.

"Find a spot toward the back," Tai ordered before she turned to close the door.

Darkness fell over them like a curtain, making it harder for Trey to pick his way around buckets and what he assumed was a mop cart, even with help. Ayesha didn't sound to be having much luck herself, cursing after kicking something made of metal.

Behind them, there was a low scraping sound as something heavy was hauled across the floor. Tai likewise pulled something in front of the door.

"Here," Ayesha murmured, her hands guiding Trey around. "You can sit on this box."

"Thanks." With her help he lowered himself onto it just as a light clicked on.

Shelves packed with cleaning supplies nearly hit the ceiling. He could see Tai between the stacks as she made her way toward him and Ayesha.

Trey went to push himself up, wanting to hug his sister, but she beat him to it. She squeezed him hard enough it hurt, but he didn't care. He held tight, too, the shaking in his limbs gradually subsiding. She sniffed a couple times, and he had to blink to clear his vision.

"You jumping outta mirrors now?" he asked, sure to keep his voice quiet.

Tai laughed and sniffed again. "I—I guess. I don't know how, I . . . One minute I'm watching you and Ayesha being chased through this place, and I knew I needed to help! The next I'm falling on top of you."

Trey snorted through his own laugh, though it kinda hurt. "That what happened when you disappeared into Mom's mirror?"

Tai nodded but still didn't let go. "Sorta."

"You see the white girl?"

"Elva," Tai corrected. "She was there, and there was . . . so much more." Her voice hitched on a fresh set of tears, and for a second Trey was worried.

But when she pulled back to wipe at her face, he could see she was smiling. "I'll tell you later. Are y'all okay? You look like hell." She said the last while staring at him.

"I'm just tired," Trey said, hoping to reassure her. "Used my powers too much, I think. Takes a lot out of me."

"Do you know where we are?" Ayesha asked. "What is this place?"

Tai shook her head. "I don't know, but the guy running the show is some dickhead named Ian. He wants to get rid of magic, I think."

"Shit," Trey muttered as he put two and two together. "We must be in some Corvus compound." He shared a look with Ayesha.

Tai glanced back and forth between them. "What's Corvus?"

The thought of explaining everything made Trey's head hurt. "No time, but the short of it is it's a dangerous secret society that wants to get rid of magic, and magic users. Like us. We heard about them from..." He trailed off, not really sure what to call Marissa and her people. What was the word she had used? Practitioners.

"From *who*?" Tai demanded.

"Some friends. I think." Trey felt a headache coming on and pushed the thoughts aside. "We can compare notes later. Point is he's a bad dude and we need to get the hell outta here."

"Maybe you can take us back!" Ayesha offered, hurriedly shrugging off the straps of her bag and pulling it around.

Tai aimed a finger at the pack. "Is that my backpack?"

Ayesha's shoulders rounded and she'd probably be blushing if she could. "We don't have your mirror. It stays behind when someone goes inside, which makes sense when I think about it, but we have pieces of one that looks just like it."

"Where'd you find that?" Tai asked.

"It was in some room," Ayesha explained, gesturing around to indicate the building. "Saw it matched yours, so we grabbed it."

Tai reached into the bag, drawing free one of the shards of glass. "The twin."

Trey asked, "Me?"

"No! It—" Tai waved her hands before heaving a breath. "Ian has a mirror identical to Elva's, but he wants both! Apparently he's been after it for years; it's why he took Mom!"

Those words shot through Trey like an arrow through his heart. He felt the immediate sting of it near the center of his chest, followed by the hollow ache that rapidly spread outward. If he hadn't been sitting, he would've fallen over.

"Mom's here?" he asked, his voice quivering.

Tai lifted her shoulders, shaking her head, then nodding. "Yes? Maybe, I don't know! He was asking me for the mirror, saying he would take me to her if I told him where it was, but he could be lying. He probably is, but I— Trey?"

He blinked, jolting out of staring at nothing really. His brain had shoved every other thought aside save for one: his mother was alive. Maybe in this very building.

"How do we find out?" he asked, his voice shaking.

Tai eyed him, looking worried. "Whachu mean?"

"If she's here! How do we find out?" Trey felt his throat work hard as he tried to swallow the hope rising in his chest. "We gotta find her. Right? We—we gotta look, we can't just..." In truth, he didn't know what he was saying. The words were just there, falling out of his mouth.

This was the first real lead anyone had had on their mother in years. An actual connection that made sense on the surface, and probably more if they did digging they didn't have time for, but if there was any chance, they couldn't just ignore it...could they?

"Trey, listen." Tai reached to take his hands, and that brought his focus up to her face. "You're feeling and thinking everything I did. It's a lot, I know, and I know you wanna tear this place apart looking for her. But you're hurt! We need to get out of here."

He started to protest, but she squeezed his fingers hard enough so he flinched.

"If we get caught, it's over. We're stuck here, too, or worse. We can't help Mom, *and* Dad loses all of us." She took a slow breath, her gaze unwavering. "We have to leave so we can come back with the police or anyone who will listen to us."

Trey held his sister's steady gaze, wondering just when she'd grown to be so strong. *She always has been*, some small part of him whispered. And while most of him bucked against the idea of maybe leaving their mom behind, a sliver of his mind said to trust Tai. So he swallowed and nodded.

"Okay," he breathed. "But I don't know how to do that, neither. We ain't pass nothing that looked like a way out."

"Neither did I," Tai said.

Silence rose between them again, and for a few moments Trey didn't know what to do. He didn't know what to say; he didn't . . . He didn't know how to fix this. And he hadn't felt so helpless in a very long time. Not since the night years ago, when the last of the concerned visitors that had been trickling in less and less in the months following their mother's disappearance finally departed and no one came the next day. Except for the detective who asked to speak to their father in private. The twins had been sent upstairs to play, and Trey—as always during those fraught days—had left his sister, claiming to want to use the bathroom, only to go listen from the top of the stairs.

"I'm sorry," he could hear the cop saying. "There's just nothing more to be done, at the moment. We'll keep following on anything that might come in, but all our leads have dried up."

"Does . . . does this mean, uhm . . . ?" Dad's voice had sounded gruff and thick.

"It only means what it means, which is we don't have anything else to go on," the cop had said. "But that could change, Mr. Watson. It could change tomorrow . . . or ten years from now. I'll leave you with your family."

There had been a grunt of acknowledgment and then the sound of steps as the officer came out of the kitchen. It was another Black man, tall, skinny, with a surprisingly wide face. He paused when he spotted Trey, pursed his lips, and hurried for the door.

As it closed behind the man, the sound of Dad's broken sobs filled the silence. They were quiet, muffled, like he was crying into a pillow or something. The way it used to sound when Tai would cry after getting one of her visions.

Trey had wanted to go to his father then, but something kept him frozen to the spot. Minutes later, that same something turned him around and sent him onto the bathroom, where he pretended to have an upset stomach while he cried himself.

"I have an idea," Ayesha said quietly, pulling him from the memory. Her voice managed to sound like an explosion in the silence. "You can see things in mirrors, right? You saw that girl and then went in. Met her?"

Tai nodded slowly. She was staring at Ayesha with a weird look on her face, a mix of fear, confusion, and wary acceptance.

"Then you saw us and did the same. What if you tried to see someone else? Like your dad. Then maybe you can take us through with you."

Trey straightened where he'd started to fold into a slump. He glanced over to his sister, who didn't look too sure about this potential plan. She pursed her lips, her eyes darting around, like she was trying to think.

"I—I . . . I don't know," Tai murmured. "I've never . . . I mean, I didn't . . . I wasn't trying to do it. Either time."

Ayesha reached for Tai's hand. "It's okay. You can try now."

"Wh-what if . . . what if it doesn't work?" Tai said, her eyes dropping to the broken shards, a sort of haunted look crossing her face. "Or worse, what if I'm able to get you in, but can't get you out! You'll be trapped!"

When she put it that way . . .

A *thunk* made all of them jump and whip around toward the door. The knob jiggled, trying to twist against being locked. Then came another thump, and a hard knock before someone on the other side shouted, "This one's locked!"

"Shit!" Ayesha hissed. She started to zip up the bag, but Trey reached forward to stop her.

"Tai," he said.

She whipped around from where she'd been staring at the door to look at him, her eyes wide with fear.

"You can do this, okay?"

She opened her mouth, looking ready to protest, when another set of fingers wrapped around their joined hands.

Ayesha gazed at Tai, her eyes soft but her face set in determination.

"We don't have time for you not to believe in yourself, boo. I believe in you, so does Trey. Come on."

Tai nodded, though her shoulders hiked up to around her ears when another series of bangs and shouts came from the door. "I just need a reflective surface, preferably not in pieces." She jumped to her feet. "Find me something!"

Trey struggled to stand, only there wasn't much struggle to it this time. Surprisingly, most of the pain had subsided, leaving a dull ache along his entire body, but he could move easier. He wasn't about to look a gift horse in the mouth, though, and he split off from the group to start searching.

The pounding and shouting at the door grew steadily louder. The room seemed to shake with it all, like they were caught in an earthquake and not some shabby ass closet. He kept throwing glances over his shoulder, peeking through the gaps between the shelves to try and keep an eye on the girls.

Bang! Something metal hit the floor. That sounded like . . .

There it was. The top hinge fell off the door. Now Trey could make out the whir of a drill amid the angered voices. They were gonna take the door out of the frame.

"Over here!" Ayesha called from somewhere near the back.

He and Tai found her at the same time. She was on her knees, brushing something off. An old bathroom mirror, the kind that swung out from a medicine cabin. There were three of them, though two of them didn't have any glass, while this one was cracked.

"Can you use a cracked mirror?" Trey asked, glancing at his increasingly nervous twin.

"I—I...I don't know, I..."

Bang! The last hinge. The door was being worked out of the frame. They'd be in any second now.

"You can do it," Ayesha said, reaching for Tai's hand. "You got this. We got you."

Trey took Tai's other hand, squeezing her fingers.

Tai glanced to him, then Ayesha, back and forth, tears in her eyes. She nodded, took a breath, then looked to the mirror.

And stared.

And stared...

Her lips pursed, her brow furrowed.

He wanted to ask if it was working, but he didn't want to break her concentration.

Behind them, there was a loud scrape, a low creak, then a *CRACK!*

The Corvus were inside.

29

Tai tried to focus on the image slowly crystallizing before her. Usually she did everything she could to ignore the visions. So of course the one time she leaned into it, it wasn't working right! It didn't help that this mirror was cracked in about four places.

"Taaaaaai," Trey said anxiously as he pitched glances toward the door where Ian's people sounded like they'd finally busted in.

But she couldn't worry about that. She was caught up in the

storm, the twisting gray that flooded her senses as the image finally solidified. At least, mostly. She could see a female figure pacing in a small room, wearing something that looked like hospital scrubs and slippers. The woman was talking to someone else, other people in similar outfits, all of them looking various degrees of anxious and worn-out.

Then there was a crash behind her.

"Tai!" Ayesha screamed.

Tai felt the familiar tug at her center and squeezed their hands. "Jump!"

The three of them leapt at the same time, and the pull of gravity both released and latched on to her. She shut her eyes and braced herself for what she knew would come next.

Trey and Ayesha shouted in shock or fear, maybe both.

Then the icy-rush washed over her. Once again, the chill permeated every inch of her body, freezing her from the inside out. She felt the shudders move along her limbs and felt her fingers start to slacken and fought to hold tight.

Almost there, she wanted to say, but the feel of something not quite liquid pressed around them made her too scared to open her mouth.

Then, just like that, they were let loose. Flung even, into the open air. She could feel the instant they were through, could tell by the touch of air on her skin and the sudden pull that replaced the slightly weightless feeling from before.

She hit the floor, pain radiating through her. Somewhere, Trey did the same, yelping as he did. Ayesha grunted, then groaned.

Around them, people gasped and murmured in shock. They shuffled away from the kids who had likely popped out of the nearest reflective surface.

Tai's arms trembled as she pushed herself up onto all fours. Her stomach attempted to heave, but there was nothing inside. Every inch of her vibrated, felt like it wanted to pull away from the frame of her skeleton. But at the same time, fatigue fell over her heavy and shackling. It was a chore to blink the world back into clarity as she tried to glance around.

"Tai..." someone breathed, and then arms locked around her and she was crushed against a body.

Despite her exhaustion, she started to recoil instinctively, but then fingers found the back of her head, and words were whispered brokenly in her ear.

"Mi vida."

It had been more than a decade since she heard that voice, but she knew it instantly. Every ounce of fight left Tai's body. She sunk forward into the embrace, and those arms mercifully tightened. More words were spoken, but she could barely hear them over the sound of her wildly beating heart, or the sobs that broke free without warning.

"¡Trey, mi amor!" There was jostling, and then Tai felt another body press at her side.

She recognized her brother's voice even as it cracked and shattered the same way hers did. "M-Mami? What...? How is...?"

"Shhhhh, shh, shh, shh," that voice whispered, followed by sniffles and quiet thanks. "It's okay, baby, it's okay."

"Mom," Tai managed to croak, and that was about it. Her throat wouldn't open for anything more.

The arm around her tightened, and she felt kisses dropped to her hair, her face, everywhere that could be reached. And in that instant, Tai was six again, sitting in her mother's lap, turning her face this way and that until every inch had been covered in love and affection. Only then did she deem herself ready for the day. That was the routine. After her mother did her hair, it was multiple kisses and then she was scooted off to finish the rest of her morning.

She hadn't felt that, felt this, since then. And the joy, the longing that had been buried beneath it, could've blown a mile-wide hole in her chest.

Trey was whimpering something that Tai couldn't hear. Mom answered with her own quaking but gentle tone and again that arm tightened. Mom was here. She was okay.

"Blake!" someone nearby said, their voice low with alarm. "He's coming!"

"He can't find them," Mom said, fear clear in her voice.

"Over here!" someone else said.

Before Tai could make sense of what was happening, she was being pulled away from her mother.

"No!" She wanted to kick, to scream, but it came out as a whine. She twisted and fought to keep hold of her mother, desperation renewing the strength in her tired limbs.

"Shh, it's okay, baby!" Mom whispered quickly, twisting to pull away. "You have to hide, okay? All of you."

This time when the hands pulled, Tai let them. She was able to take in her surroundings properly. At least a half dozen people, young and old, stared at her, her brother, and Ayesha, the unfamiliar faces watching as the three were ushered across what looked like a sparse but still nice enough waiting room. There were chairs here and there, a couple plants, a clock and a mirror on the wall.

That's probably where they came through, Tai realized. She didn't have time to dwell on it before she was steered into a standing wardrobe. Trey and Ayesha were pressed in beside her. And Mom . . .

Mom stood in the door, her face drawn, her eyes red from crying. Her hair was so long and bunched around her face and shoulders. "Stay in here and don't make a sound, okay?"

She didn't wait for a response before closing the doors.

A sliver of light poured into the dark space. It was just enough for Tai to be able to make out Trey's and Ayesha's confused expressions as they gazed at her from either side, the three of them squeezed in there like the Scooby gang or something.

"What's happening?" Ayesha said, sounding somewhat dazed.

"That . . . that's really . . ." Trey looked to still be trying to come to grips with what was going on.

Tai nodded and stayed silent, like Mom had said. She craned her neck forward just so in order to peer through the small slat between the double doors.

She couldn't see much, but she could make out everyone positioning themselves on the furniture or floor. Silence fell over the room, but it lasted maybe thirty seconds before there was the click of a lock at the door. It swung open and in stepped Ian, with James at his back.

Immediately a handful of folks were in his face, demanding to know what was going on, asking why they were in here, what was going to be done to them. James less-than-gently moved them aside so Ian could make his way to the center of the room. A handful of people in white robes spilled in to block the door behind him.

Tai couldn't remember ever seeing an angrier white man trying to *not* look pissed. His nostrils flared, and his lips were pursed. His eyes flashed as they flickered over everyone.

"Where is she?" His voice was a low hum of fury.

"What now?" Mom's almost casually annoyed tone rang out to counter his from somewhere to the left.

Ian spun in that direction. For a moment it looked like he wasn't certain he believed what he was looking at. His gaze moved up and down, then narrowed, almost like he was trying to make sure his eyes weren't being deceived.

Once satisfied with whatever he was looking for, he gave a single nod, then turned to head for the door. "Bring her," he said over his shoulder.

The room erupted into chaos. James tromped over to Mom's direction, all but flinging anyone unfortunate enough to be in his way out of it.

"Don't you *touch* me!" Mom shouted just as James stepped out of sight.

Fear lodged itself in Tai's throat. She twisted to try and see what was happening, but the slit between the doors only allowed for so much.

"What's going on!?" Trey demanded.

"I—I don't know!" Tai said.

Mom had told them to stay in there, no matter what happened.

But then Tai saw James with his arms around Mom, hauling her kicking toward the door.

"What is this?" Mom shouted. "Ian! Ian, what are you doing!?"

"He's taking her," Tai whispered, her voice softened by shock. "He's taking her!" Louder this time, her eyes moving to her brother. "Block the door!"

"What?" Trey asked, shifting to try and look out the crack as well.

"Block the door! Rip it down, cave it in, they can't leave!"

For a half second, Trey looked uncertain, but then he nodded. Tai took a breath and threw the doors open. "Ian!"

Everyone turned toward them, and for a split second the room froze. Everything crawled to a stop.

Then Ian, eyes wide, lifted a hand, his mouth open to bark orders.

Tai saw the fear on her mother's face. The same fear she felt somewhere deep inside her. But that fear was nothing compared to the anger she felt for this man who had clearly kept their mother from them all this time. An anger she knew her brother shared.

The growl that escaped Trey was animalistic as he lifted his hands into the air. He curled his fingers, as if taking hold of something, and pulled.

The room bucked and shuddered, before a loud crack filled the air. Then the archway over the door fractured and collapsed in on itself. The people who had been standing there, the ones in white robes, scrambled out of the way just as stones tumbled inward, the wall and the ceiling above caving in.

The lights flickered as cracks worked their way across the walls, the floor, the ceiling. It looked like the whole room was coming apart, sounded like it too. Along with the crackling stones, there was a low groan of metal before a bang sounded above them. Within seconds, at least an inch of water covered the entire floor, spraying everyone down in the process.

Mom wriggled free of James's hold, by way of slamming her elbow into his face. The big man reeled, groaning low like some great beast in pain.

"Tai! Trey!" Mom hurried toward them, only to draw up short when Ian grabbed her from behind. She screamed, her hands going to her hair where he had hold of it.

"No!" Tai shouted when she saw a glint of silver.

The man had a knife to his mother's throat.

"Stop," Ian said, then louder. "Stop! Everyone, stop where you are, or Blake will have drawn her last breath."

Tai froze.

The other people in scrubs pulled back from where they'd

rushed James in his moment of weakness. The big dude shook himself free, lumbering over to his boss.

"That's quite enough of that," Ian muttered before his eyes moved to Tai. "This wasn't part of the bargain, my dear."

"Shit," Trey groaned before dropping to his knees.

Tai reached for her brother, her hands at his shoulders. He shook like a leaf, panting like he'd just run a marathon.

"Trey baby, breathe," Mom called. "Just bre— Ah!" she shouted when Ian yanked her hair.

His furious gaze pinged to Tai, then roamed the room. "Let's all take a moment and assess the severity of the situation, yes?" The calm in his voice was such a contradiction to the fury etched into his face. "Now I don't know what you believed was going to happen here, but it's obvious you weren't thinking clearly."

He was saying something else, but Tai wasn't paying attention. No, her focus was drawn to the floor and the rising water at their feet. It rippled and churned, like a gentle storm.

A storm that drew her eye along the roll of the soft waves, the hypnotic quality to a rhythm that seemed almost impossible yet there it was. And she could still make out everyone's reflection. The angles of their bodies, their faces, tilted slightly.

All of it flickered and shivered with an odd sort of movement. One she recognized. The doors from Elva's tree, the way they formed a carousel that had spun so fast they all melded into a single image. That was happening here. On a semi-reflective surface.

Maybe . . .

A ripple of power moved through Tai. She felt it, like a frigid shock against the inside of her skin. It started at the top of her head, then moved down through her and flowed outward. The ripples in the water answered in kind.

"Tai?" Ian's voice cut into the slight haze that had started to fall over her mind.

A familiar haze at that.

She glanced up.

He still had that fucking knife to her mother's throat. "I held up my end of the bargain. Here's your mother. Where's my mirror?"

Tai lifted her chin and sunk her hands into the water. "Here," she murmured as she shoved at the door beneath her feet.

It flew open and dropped them through.

30

rey felt like he was drowning. Granted, the longest he'd ever held his head underwater was twenty-four seconds for the record at his cousin's birthday party when they were nine, but the burning lungs? The feeling of fire being poured down his throat? The weightless loss of control in his limbs? He figured this was very much what drowning felt like.

And just he when he thought his chest might burst with his

struggles to breathe, he coughed. Air filled his body, and the pain subsided. It was as if he'd broken the surface of water, but he hadn't. He ... couldn't really tell what the hell was going on.

Darkness went on in every direction, but at the same time he could see everything. Well, everyone. Ayesha floated beside him, clutching at her throat with one hand while her other limbs flailed around in some failed attempt at swimming.

"It's not water!" he shouted, before jolting at the echo of his own voice.

Ayesha's head snapped around. Her eyes widened as she took him in. And in her shock she coughed, then gasped, then panted.

"What the hell?" Her voice held a similar resonance to his own, like someone had recorded what she was going to say, and played the sound over her actual words, with a hint of reverb. The dissonance would have been beautiful, if he wasn't freaking the hell out.

"I—I don't know...." He took a look around at all of the nothing surrounding them.

Except it wasn't actually nothing. They were floating, swimming? In some sort of mist. He could make out the silvery swirl of it now, wafting in around them, gathering at their feet, pooling near the ... ground?

The instant his gaze perceived the notion of a surface, and of gravity holding the mist near that surface, he felt the weight of his own body before it dropped a short distance and landed on something solid. Pain radiated through him, sharp but brief.

Beside him, Ayesha had jolted in surprise. He could tell when she "noticed" the gravity as well, before she dropped similarly with a shout.

Trey pushed himself to stand, crossing the short distance to offer her a hand up.

"Where are we?" she asked as she rose with his help. "What . . . happened?"

He wasn't sure. They'd all been standing in that room with that Ian guy. He'd said something about a mirror, and then Tai . . .

"I think Tai pulled us into a 'mirror,'" Trey murmured as he glanced around. The mist shifted and rolled, parting here and there to reveal odd shapes in the not-quite-dark.

Trees, he realized. And the instant he did, a forest seemed to materialize out of nowhere. With the trees came dirt, grass, bushes. An entire ecosystem simply materializing around them.

Ayesha squeaked, "This is wild."

Trey snorted as his gaze roamed the newly formed canopy. "You telling me." He turned full circle, coming around to face Ayesha and drawing back in surprise. She was glowing. Literally. Soft blue light emanated from her, outlining her entire body.

"You're glowing. . . ."

She spun from where she'd been examining their surroundings, blinked once in confusion at him before looking at her hands. Her breath caught.

"Whoa. What's . . . ?"

"Magic." The word left his lips before he even realized he'd thought to speak it.

Ayesha's head snapped up, her eyes wide. "What?"

Trey nodded slowly, certain now. "Magic. What it's for or what it can do, I don't know, but if I've learned anything the past couple days, if you have an aura, you have magic." His eyes widened slightly as Marissa's words came back to him. Words he spoke. "Like attracts like."

Ayesha stared for a second before waving her arms in the air. "I ain't never had no magic!"

"Well, you certainly do now," Trey murmured before glancing around again.

"And what the hell am I supposed to do with it?"

As soon as the words left her lips, her glow pulsed, then swept outward in a small tendril that reached toward a cluster of trees, forming a trail.

Trey stared a moment—they both did—before he looked in her direction. "I think your magic wants us to go this way."

She made some annoyed sound at the back of her throat but didn't protest.

Trey took the lead, stepping into the thick of the brush. As he did, he tried to discern as much as he could about wherever the hell they were. A forest, yeah, but where was the forest? There was no sky, no sun or clouds. No birds or animals, just trees. Trees that were . . . talking? At least, he thought he heard voices.

He gestured for Ayesha to stop, and she did, her gaze questioning.

Setting a finger to his lips, he strained to try and hear what was being said.

"How do we get out of here?"

"Where even is here?"

"We are going to die. After all this time, we are going to die!"

"Everyone, please, calm down."

A jolt of recognition moved through Trey. "Mom." He pushed forward without a second thought, ignoring Ayesha's hiss for him to wait for her. She could keep up, he had no doubt of that, but he couldn't stop.

His mother, here, after all this time. She'd been there, in the room, but so much happened so fast, he wasn't really able to . . .

He broke through the brush line and into a clearing. At least half a dozen heads swiveled around to take him in. It was the people from the room, the ones wearing the same scrubs as his mother, who was now charging through the small crowd toward him.

"Trey!"

He met her at a run, pressing instantly into open arms like he was six instead of sixteen. She dropped kisses all over his face, and the burn from before returned. He tried to breathe through it. She was really here.

"Thank god you're all right." She squeezed him before drawing back, her hands going to his face, turning it this way and that. "Have you seen your sister?"

Trey shook his head. "N-no, it's just me and Ayesha."

Who had stepped up behind him the way his mother's gaze shifted over his shoulder, then widened. "Miércoles..."

Ayesha shuffled forward, her shoulders hunched slightly as her gaze played over their surroundings. Her glow had brightened as well, and instead of a single blue tendril there were now two. One heading off to the left, the other two the right.

Mom breathed a disbelieving laugh "A contact trace. I haven't seen detection magic this strong in a long time."

"Contact trace?" Ayesha asked.

"Someone back at the center said something like that," Trey recalled. The old Black woman said it, he thought. Then he and

Ayesha woke up in a closet full of magic artifacts. They were being thrown around together a lot here.

Mom beckoned Ayesha forward. "A contact trace is a type of magic that is only active when in proximity to other powers, particularly spells or rituals that have been completed. The trace can reactivate them in order to follow their magic signature, sort of like a trail. Do you know what spell you're tracing?"

Ayesha slowly shook her head. "I didn't know I was *tracing* anything."

A frown crinkled Mom's brow, and she gave a thoughtful hum. "Latent, then." She opened her mouth, looking ready to say something more, when a shout boomed through the air.

"Let GO of me!"

The words rippled like thunder overhead setting off a chain reaction through the mist, a maelstrom of shimmering that resembled lightning. As quickly as it began, it faded, trailing off in the same direction of Ayesha's tendril of light.

Trey bolted in that direction. That was Tai's voice. She was in trouble.

31

Tai felt like she'd been falling forever. Her stomach roiled against gravity's pull. Her limbs windmilled outside of her control. Her body pitched and rolled in fits as the rush of air snatched at her mercilessly. She had to fight just to keep her senses from collapsing inward into panic whenever she caught sight of the nothingness beneath her. Nothingness that seemed to go on forever.

Every inch of her ached with exhaustion. She'd used too much.

She was already hurting after carrying Trey and Ayesha through that first time, and now? Having pulled so many? God, how she could be so foolish.

She lost them. . . . All of them.

Mom, Trey, Ayesha—they drifted away from her the moment they dropped through the door, and now . . .

Now she was left with fucking Ian, who spun and twirled not too far away. James had been with them when they first fell through into the watery darkness. He'd kicked and flailed, same as they had, but where Ian had managed to reach her, latching on to her like some kinda leech, James had tumbled off a short distance.

That then became a bit farther. Then a bit farther. There was nothing out here, but the big guy was definitely drifting away, and when he realized that, he'd tried to swim their direction, scream- ing as he did.

They could only watch as the darkness swallowed him. She and Ian were left alone together, tumbling through more nothing ever since.

She'd tried to put distance between herself and Ian, tried to get *away* from him, but somehow he was always right there! His eyes wide and furious where they fixed on her, unblinking. He said noth- ing, merely glared as they fell through the abyss, snatching at her whenever she drew within arm's reach.

Twice he'd almost gotten hold of her. She'd felt his nails scrape her arm a couple of times he made a grab for her. But somehow she managed to stay just outside of reach.

At least she had, until fingers clamped around her wrist hard enough to hurt.

"At last," Ian snarled, his voice still somehow low, and he pulled.

Fear bubbled up inside her and she fought to get free. "No!"

"You will undo this." Ian's grip tightened. She tried to twist out of it, but then he had a fistful of her shirt and was shaking her. "Take me back, do you hear? Take me back!"

Tai threw an elbow at him. "Let GO of me!" It connected with his chin.

Ian grunted in pain and swung wild.

His hand connected with the side of Tai's face, and she saw stars. The taste of blood coated her tongue.

"Take me back!" he roared.

She curled her legs in against her stomach and kicked out in a move she vaguely remembered from a one-time self-defense class they made a lot of the girls take at school last year. He grunted but didn't let go.

"Tai!"

Despite the ringing in her ears, she heard, at least she thought she heard . . . Was that Trey?

"Tai!"

Mom!!! Tai twisted, trying to follow the sound of those voices all while fighting against Ian's crushing grip.

On a cliff below that certainly wasn't there before, Tai could pick out her brother, her mother, Ayesha—why was she glowing?!— And those people from the compound. Relief swept through her, nearly robbing her of her strength as she fought to get away from Ian. They were all right. They were okay!

And now she had to make sure she would be.

She twisted again, trying to pull free. His hand came loose from her wrist, his nails digging into her skin, but his hold on her shirt remained. Then he had hold of her other arm.

Suddenly her stomach lurched as she was yanked downward. Ian shouted as he was pulled as well.

"No!" He tightened his grip.

Another pull. This time they both shouted.

"What are you doing?" Ian growled, though there was a twinge of fear in his voice. "Stop, or we'll both go spinning into the abyss."

"It's not me!" She felt *another* pull. This one spun her around, bringing the cliff and her family into sight again.

Standing there at the edge, his hands outstretched toward her, Trey made a tugging motion. At the same time, Tai felt herself yanked in his direction. Pressure around her waist flexed, like fingers were adjusting where they had hold of her. Trey was the one doing this, using his magic to reel her in. Reeling Ian in as well.

"I got you!" Trey called, his voice tremulous. "I got you, I swear!" She could hear the fatigue of his words. He was throwing everything he had into this, and he'd already given so much back at the compound. If he gave out before they reached the edge...

Tai felt her hands grow hot with the telltale start of the burn. The one that had allowed her to control the doors. She'd tried to summon it while falling earlier, but only the cold emptiness had answered. Now she felt her brother's magic tighten around her and felt her own nearly exhausted energy rise to meet it. One more try, one last shot, together. But first, she had to get rid of Ian.

Bone weary as she was, aching as she did, Tai drew a deep breath and started wriggling and twisting with all of her might. "Get him AWAY from me!"

The feeling of fire blazed in her palms. She pressed them to Ian's hands.

He howled in pain, smoke rising from where she'd touched him, the smell of burning skin hitting her noise. Ian yanked away so hard that he wound up throwing himself backward. By the time he realized what he'd done, it was too late, he was already spinning off into the mist. His wild screams and curses gradually faded, but she could still make out the words.

"I will find you! I will find you and I will end you, for this. All of you! Mark me!"

And then he was gone.

The fire faded from Tai's hands. She felt it wither from the rest of her as well. A tingling and prickling replaced the burning in her palms, then spread to cover her from head to toe. She was done. That was the last of her strength. And it looked to be the last of Trey's as well because she felt gravity latch on to her. Not the floaty sort of feeling she'd experienced this entire time, but the heavy drag. And she knew without looking that she hadn't reached the edge of the cliff, yet.

She dropped past it.

Her mother screamed.

Tai shut her eyes.

Something slammed into her, hard and unyielding with a hollow *thunk*. Something . . . wooden? It hurt, god it hurt, but then she wasn't falling anymore. She opened her eyes to find herself cradled in the branches of a great willow tree. *The* willow tree. *Their* willow tree.

The cliff was gone. So was Trey, Mom, Ayesha, and the others. But Elva gazed up at her from the safety of the meadow, her eyes wide with worry.

"Tai! Oh, thank goodness, I thought it was too late." Elva reached to take hold of Tai as the tree offered her up.

"Wh-what...?" Tai tried to get her feet planted when they touched the ground, but her legs buckled. She would've fallen over if Elva wasn't there to help gently lower her to the ground. "What happened?"

Elva shook her head. "I'm not...sure. After you disappeared through one of the doors, I kept opening them to try and find you, but I couldn't. At least, not until the tree answered your call."

"My call?"

"I don't know what you did, but a new door appeared." She pointed up.

Tai followed her finger to where, sure enough, a door hung horizontal in the air above the top of the tree.

"It opened and you fell through. Are you all right?"

"I...think so." Tai winced as she shifted to tilt back against the trunk. Damn it but she felt like crap. Extra crap, with a side of crap, just for fun. "Everything hurts."

"You've used up all of your magic—oh...Oh no..." Elva murmured, her hands going to her mouth. "Did you try to change something? Are you trapped here?"

Tai wasn't sure what Elva was talking about until she

remembered her story of how *she* wound up here. She shook her head. "N-no, I came through another mirror. Sorta..."

Elva heaved a relieved sigh. "Rest. I don't know how long it will take for you to recover your strength, but—"

Boom. Boom. Boom.

The sound echoed around them.

Tai blinked, her brow furrowing as she glanced around. "What?"

"I don't know," Elva murmured as the carousel of doors shifted, turning until one faintly outlined in blue light came to rest in front of them.

Boom. Boom. Boom!

More insistent this time, and clearly from the other side. Someone was knocking.

Tai's chest tightened. "Can we open it?"

Elva spared her a brief, curious glance before rising, biding her to wait there. She crossed to the door, took hold of the knob, and pulled. It swung wide, the blue light brightening then fading to reveal the last face Tai expected to see.

"Ayesha?"

The same blue light that had outlined the door poured off of her, filling the immediate area with radiance.

"Come on!" Ayesha said, waving her forward frantically. "I can't hold the trace for long!"

"Trace?" Tai said as she struggled to try and get to her feet.

Ayesha huffed, frustrated, then held out her hands. "I'll explain everything, but you need to hurry!"

With Elva's help, Tai stumbled over to the door, her hand out. The cool tingle from before passed over her skin as her arm slipped through. Ayesha's warm grip latched on to it.

"I got you! Come on!"

Tai started to step forward but paused, looking to Elva. "Wh . . . at about you? I promised I would get you out of here."

"And you still have time to keep that promise," Elva said. "But not if you're trapped in here. Go." She gave an insistent push.

Between the three of them, they managed to get Tai through the door. She crumpled against Ayesha, who did her best to stay upright. She didn't have to work at it long, because soon arms were around her, holding her tight. Her mother's arms, she knew without opening her eyes.

"Give them some room," a woman called over shuffling sounds of steps.

"Oh my god" came Trey's voice before he was pressed in at Tai's other side. "When you fell I—I thought . . ."

"'S'what you get for thinking," Tai managed, a small smile pulling at her face. Man, she was tired. Her whole body sagged with it. She felt like she could sleep for a week.

Pressure at her hand made her open her eyes. She was wrapped up in her mother's and brother's arms, but Ayesha had hold of her hand, swiping her thumb back and forth across it. She smiled when their gazes met.

"Hey."

"Hey," Tai returned.

"I think you owe me more than a funnel cake for this one."

Tai's smile widened, and she started to close her eyes again, when a loud *BANG* sounded from across the room. Everyone jumped and turned to find Terrance Watson standing in the doorway, his bald head shiny with sweat, his red eyes wide and glassy, the door still shivering from the force with which he'd flung it open.

He stared. And stared. And stared. And then took one halting step forward.

"Blake . . ." He breathed the word, a fragile thing that flaked away in the air. Tears spilled over his cheeks.

Tai felt her mother's arms loosen and had to swallow the protest.

"You still have time." She remembered Elva's words, heard them as if the other girl was standing right there. While Elva hadn't been talking about this, it eased the anxiety that had risen at the sight of her mother walking away.

What banished that anxiety completely was the sight of Mom crumpling forward against Dad with a quiet sob, and his arms immediately folding in around her. He held her tight, his face pressed to the top of her head. His shoulders shook, his whole body heaved as he wailed.

Tai had never heard her father cry like that, and to know it was from joy and not pain left tears spilling over her cheeks as well.

Beside her, Trey tried to discreetly wipe at his face with the hand that wasn't currently helping hold Tai up. Ayesha hiccupped as she cried, too, while scooting in close. Both of them looked as beat down as Tai felt. But they were there. With her. Safe.

They were all safe. Together again. That's what mattered.

"You forgive me for dropping you over a cliff?" Trey asked quietly.

Tai snorted, then winced. "Ow. Don't make me laugh. And yes, so long as you forgive me for . . . I don't even know."

"I forgive you both for dragging me into your shenanigans," Ayesha said softly as she squeezed Tai's hand.

Tai returned it, marveling briefly at the faint blue light that still enveloped Ayesha's body. She was definitely going to ask about that later, but first . . .

Steeling herself, she pushed to sit up fully instead of leaning on her brother. He aimed a curious look at her, but she waved it off, instead angling her weight to press against Ayesha, who took it on easily enough, though her eyebrow arched.

"I'm sorry for dragging you into my shenanigans," Tai murmured.

The smile that spread across Ayesha's face was stunning. "Like I said, forgiven. Unless you *do* wanna throw in another funnel cake."

Tai sighed and hung her head as if defeated. "No funnel cake, but . . . will you take a little sugar instead?"

Trey groaned, but she ignored it as Ayesha's expression softened. "Sugar sounds nice."

That was all Tai needed before she leaned forward and caught Ayesha's lips with her own.

32

Trey watched his father rub at his bald head with one hand, the other firmly clasping Mom's fingers where she sat beside her husband. He wore the same *I'm too old for this shit* look that hadn't left his face for the better part of an hour.

"And this Ian guy, he's gone." Dad glanced among the three of them, Trey, Tai and Mom, his gaze settling on the latter. "For good this time?"

All three of them nodded.

"He threatened vengeance," Tai said. "But it's unlikely."

"Because you dropped him in some alternate dimension that only you can reach," Dad continued. "Through mirrors."

"Through any reflective surface," Tai corrected him from where she was curled up in a blanket in the other corner of the couch she and Trey shared. "But yeah."

Dad nodded this time. "And we're really... This is really over, all this... Corvus stuff?"

There was a soft cough from Trey's left and Marissa leaned forward in her own chair. "Corvus was bigger than Ian, but he was the head. Without him, they won't be as much of an immediate threat. We may even be able to dismantle them completely, before they recover."

Dad let loose a slow breath, sinking into his chair. He had a haunted look about him, the kinda look that made old folks go, "He done seen some thangs." And really he had. All his life, up to three hours ago when his son, daughter, his daughter's girlfriend, half a dozen strangers, and his long-lost wife came spilling out of the bathroom mirror of a magical safe house he'd been brought to when said children went missing earlier in the day.

What Tai had managed, to take that many people through the mirror, was a miracle, Marissa had said. And a lucky one at that.

"Or a testament to how powerful the girl is," the old Black woman that had helped him and Ayesha had offered in passing. "You may want to keep an eye on that one."

Everything had been a whirlwind since, and things were explained the best they could be. From Corvus to Mom going missing—having tracked down her missing aunt and uncle only to be captured as well. To Elva and the mirror, Ayesha's own magic surfacing in an ability to trace or follow someone else's magic, which is why she and Trey wound up following Tai to Corvus to begin with.

Damn, his head hurt just thinking about it. He considered writing everything down but decided against it. At least for the moment. Maybe later...

There was a faint knock at the door.

They all turned, including Marissa, to find the elderly Black woman standing there.

"Mama B?" Marissa asked, moving toward the elderly woman, her hands lifted to offer aid should the old woman need it.

Mama B waved her off. "She's ready." The southern twang in Mama B's voice was ripe. She held the mirror, Elva's mirror, in her hands.

"I'll give you all a moment," Marissa said before turning to leave the room. The door closed and Mama B shuffled forward.

Trey leaned in a bit, scooting to the front of the cushion. As the old lady approached, he could see a face in the glass. Elva's. Her eyes roamed around, taking all of them in, a smile pulling her cheeks high toward her eyes. She wiped at tears he couldn't quite make out. This was wild. There was actually a girl in that mirror. Not that he hadn't believed Tai, he just . . . it was something else to see it himself.

"Now, then," Mama B said. "I'm acting as a conduit for Elva here. Meaning you should be able to see her, even without the gift. And you're gonna hear my voice, but they're her words."

"We understand," Mom said.

Mama B nodded, then shut her eyes. She took a deep breath, and when she opened them again, they were milky white.

For a second, no one said anything, then Mama B sighed.

"I can feel it," she said, her voice suddenly lighter. As her mouth moved, so did Elva's. It was kinda trippy to watch.

"Feel what?" Tai asked, scooting in beside him.

"I can feel the magic fading," Mama B, or rather Elva, answered. "I don't have much time."

"So that's it, then? You're just gone?" Tai asked, her voice crackling faintly with emotion. She'd really formed an attachment, it seemed.

"No. Not really," Elva said. "But I will be free and able to rest. Thanks to you."

Trey glanced at his family, then back to the mirror. "We didn't exactly do anything?"

"But you did," Elva insisted. "By fulfilling the promises you made to one another, to be there for one another, to never give up on one another, to take care of one another. Long ago, one family promised another to be there. That promise was broken. And in that broken promise, the two families were bound, but not reconciled. Cursed to strife and brokenness until the original contract could be fulfilled."

"What's going to happen to you?" Mom asked.

Elva looked thoughtful. "I imagine the same thing that happens to any spirit laid to rest. Do not be troubled, for me. I am glad! I got to see my family grow and was able to glimpse more of their happiness through you."

Trey thought he saw her look at Tai then, but soon her gaze drifted over everyone else.

Elva's smile widened. "Take care of one another. And tell Morpheus goodbye for me? What a strange name for a cat."

As it did, she began to fade, like the fog on a mirror wiped away.

Tai's fingers gripped the couch cushions, and Trey set his hand over hers.

Soon, Elva was gone, and their own reflections faded into view, gazing back at them.

Mama B's eyes fluttered open, and she huffed a faint breath. "She moved on. Oh, don't worry, chérie." She moved to set a hand atop Tai's head.

Tai sniffed and wiped at her face.

"This is good. That poor girl's soul should be able to rest now, with the people that love her." Mama B's gaze moved over the rest of them. "Especially seeing how things turned out." She smiled in that way old folks do when they know a thing or two extra about something, but don't seem too keen on telling.

"Thank you," Tai said quietly.

"Of course. Dinner will be ready soon. Marissa said y'all are welcome to stay as long as you like. That was quite the ordeal you all been through."

Mama B turned to go, but Tai leapt to her feet.

"Wait," she called, stepping over to the old woman. "Can I keep it? The mirror?"

Mama B glanced down at it, then huffed as if surprised she was still holding it. "Well, it is yours, isn't it?" She held it out, and Tai took it gingerly, folding it in against her chest.

With a quiet thank-you, she made her way back over to the couch.

Mama B nodded, then shuffled out the door.

As she went, Ayesha came in, likely having been waiting out

in the hall this entire time. She hurried over to settle at Tai's other side, taking up her hand, weaving their fingers together similar to how Mom's and Dad's were.

Dad shifted Mom's hand to his other one so he could wrap an arm around her shoulder.

Trey glanced back and forth between the two couples. "Well, I feel left out," he grumbled.

There was a pause before laughter filled the room, long, loud, and loving. He could pick out each voice in the harmony of it. His father's tenor tones, his sister's high-pitched partial wail, even Ayesha's staccato snicker. And there, amid it all, his mother's steady tempo.

It was like music to his ears.

EPILOGUE

The scream isn't what woke Tai, but it's definitely what pulled her out of bed. She looked up from where she was nearly finished reading her fanfic—the writer got Kikyo's temperament wrong, but there was lots of Sesshomaru, so Tai didn't care—then thew back the covers. "What the hell?"

"You better quit!" Mom's voice, bright and jovial, reached Tai's ears just as she yanked the door open and stepped into the hall.

Any and all worry evaporated when Tai caught sight of her parents standing just outside their room. Dad had his arms around Mom, who wriggled to try and get away from him as he in turn tried to rub his chin against the side of her neck.

"I better what, now?" he said, smiling wide.

"Terrance, that *tickles*!" Mom howled, palming his face and shoving at him, but he only laughed and redoubled his efforts, earning another scream. "You need to shave!"

"I will! Later!"

Something inside Tai warmed at the sight of them. Dad in his sweatpants and tank top, Mom in a set of mismatched pajamas and a robe.

Trey's door opened, and he stepped into the hall, rubbing at his eyes. "What is—" He paused when he caught sight of their parents as well, stared a second, then made a face and turned to slip back into his room, muttering something that sounded like "Gross" as he went.

"Boy, quit it!" Mom laughed out the words. "I gotta go make breakfast."

Dad stopped tickling Mom in order to wrap her in a hug in earnest. "Let's make it together, yeah? Just like old times."

Mom stopped trying to get away, and hugged him in turn. "I'd like that."

Tai felt something in her chest melt at the adorableness of it all. She slipped into her room, slowly closing the door. Then she sunk back against it, suddenly overwhelmed with a wave of emotion that just swept in out of nowhere. The sound of her mother's voice, her laughter, filling these halls again? She was finally home. After all this time, their family was whole again.

It took a few moments for Tai to compose herself, but she swiped at her eyes and moved back over to her bed, where Morpheus had already curled up on her laptop.

"Really?" she asked, her tone low and annoyed before she reached to gently shoo the cat away.

He padded to the end of the bed and curled up, licking at his paws.

Offering a few apologetic scritches, Tai went to get dressed. It didn't take long before she was standing in front of the mirror, admiring her outfit. "Now the finishing touch," she said as she fetched the red Converse from her closet. Magic shoes, the ultimate accessory.

After getting ready, she headed downstairs to find the rest of her family already in the kitchen, still wearing their pajamas.

Mom stood in front of the stove, frying some bacon in one pan and eggs in another, which smelled heavenly. Dad dug around in the fridge for something. He bounced to and sang along with Aaliyah playing on the radio on the counter. Trey sat on a stool at the island, eating a bowl of cereal despite the fact that food was being cooked. He'd probably still eat that, too.

"Morning," Tai called as she entered.

Trey jumped. "Where did you—" His eyes fell to her feet and he snorted. "You shouldn't be allowed to wear those in the house."

Mom looked over her shoulder briefly before turning back to the stove. "Morning, baby. You look cute."

Dad shut the fridge, jug of orange juice in one hand and coffee creamer in the other. "Breakfast will be done in a few minutes, if you can stand to wait that long." He shot a look at Trey, who held up his arms as if to say *What I do?*

"I'm still gonna eat it!"

"Boy act like he ain't ever been fed in his life," Dad murmured.

Tai chuckled. "I'm meeting Ayesha and her parents for brunch, remember? Sorry."

Mom flashed a smile. "Oh, that's right. Don't be sorry, we're so happy for you."

"Brunch?" Trey scrunched his face and wobbled his head from side to side. "Ain't we fancy. Must be nice, having a loaded girlfriend."

"As a matter of fact, it is," Tai said as she moved to give Trey a side hug, wrapping one arm around his shoulders and then reaching out to snatch up his glass of apple juice with her free hand.

He stiffened, blinked at her in confusion, before realizing what was up. He tried to swipe at her, but she had already danced away, glass lifted to her lips. She drained it in a few swallows.

"You just said you was going to breakfast!" he lamented, eyes on the now-empty cup as she set it back down.

"I am."

"Punk."

"Crybaby."

Mom sat a plate piled with foodstuffs on the counter, and Trey instantly snagged a piece of bacon, his pilfered drink forgotten.

"Hope you have fun," Mom said before pulling Tai into a hug.

She sunk forward into it, shutting her eyes and just . . . taking in the moment. Even after three weeks, it was still surreal to have her mother here, like this, doing everyday Mom things.

Tears sprung to Tai's eyes, but she took a quick breath to keep them at bay. It seemed like she was always crying these days. From joy, but still. She'd done her makeup and didn't want her liner to run.

Mom pressed a kiss to Tai's forehead, smoothing her hands over her back. "Let them know we're still excited to have them over for dinner tomorrow."

Tai nodded, not able to trust her voice just yet. She wasn't exactly bursting into sobs—which had been her response for the first week any time her mother stepped into the room let alone hugged or kissed her—but she still needed a second.

"I'm cooking my world-famous ribs," Dad said as he started making himself a plate.

"World famous?" Trey asked with a snort. "They not even famous on this block."

Dad paused in the middle of buttering a piece of toast and flicked a look at Trey like he'd just insulted his honor or something. "Don't make me put you out."

Mom chuckled and squeezed Tai one more time before letting go and moving to start on her own plate. "Bring me back something sweet if they have any baked goods."

"Sure thing," Tai said before a buzzing in her back pocket drew her attention.

Three short blasts from a horn sounded from outside.

"That'll be Pete," Tai said. "I'll see y'all later."

"Be careful," Dad said.

"Have fun!" Mom said.

"Bye," Trey said, waving her off with a shooing motion.

Tai smacked him in the back of the head, then hurried out the kitchen when he turned to retaliate. She headed for the door, pausing just long enough to check her reflection in the mirror hung just before the entryway. Elva's mirror, only . . . Elva wasn't in it anymore.

After the curse had been broken, and the mirror had reverted to just that, it was decided that it would stay in the family, even without its magic properties. A reminder of what they had been through, and what they were capable of weathering, as long as they were together.

Tai studied her reflection for a moment before reaching out to carefully trail fingers along the frame. No visions rose to press in against her senses, no wavering images or ghostly hauntings. Practice with Marissa and the others was paying off, she'd learned more control in this short time than she had her entire life. Things really had taken a turn for the better.

"What?" Trey's high-pitched shout pulled Tai from her musings.

"You heard me," Dad said. "You insult my cooking, you don't get no ribs."

"I didn't insult it, I—I just said *world famous* was exaggerating!"

"The disrespect."

"Don't disrespect your daddy," Mom said.

"Augh!"

Tai smiled just as something nudged her leg. She glanced down to find Morpheus winding between her feet. She bent to offer more scritches. "Look after them until I get back."

Morpheus mewled softly, then trotted toward the kitchen.

Tai stared after him for a second, her brow furrowed. Was she tripping or did it seem like the cat understood her?

"Nah." Shaking it off, she turned and slipped out the door.

The End